TAKEN

FRANKLIN WEST UNIVERSITY

ADDISON ARROWDELL

Heated Heart Publishing

BEFORE YOU READ . . .

FRANKLIN WEST UNIVERSITY

The Wolf Den αΨΔ

Swimming Pool & Gymnasium

The Hive βεΔ

Franklin West Hall

Ezekiel West Halls

Rosalind Hall

Lacrosse Field & Stadium

Halston Hall

Grump & Grind Coffee Shop

Dining Hall

Emmett Franklin Lecture Halls

Francis Rainer Library

Invenire. Crescere. Consequi.

BE

Thirty-eight million. That's how many search results appear when you google me. Even after twenty-one years of staying out of the limelight, or more specifically, my father's shadow. You'd think a name as generic as Smith would make it easier, but I can guarantee that the majority of those thirty-eight million articles are about me and my family. It's a big-ass shadow, and things don't grow in the shade.

Keeping my back straight, a slight smile on my face, it takes a lot of effort not to tap my foot against the polished floor of the waiting area. My newly manicured mauve fingernails dig into the portfolio on my lap, and I admire for the tenth time since I sat down how the color compliments the golden brown of my skin.

Of the four local news stations I applied for internships at over the summer, I've only heard back from this one. Drawing in a subtle breath, my heart speeds beneath my navy blazer. I don't just want this internship, I *need* it.

Ever since freshman year, I've been top of my media and communications class at Franklin West. I've worked my ass off every goddamn day for this opportunity—something

I've earned entirely by myself—and I'll be damned if I'm going to mess it up. This is for me. This is a future I'm choosing for myself.

Everyone's moving back to campus this week, and as much as I'm excited for what comes after college, I can't quite believe it's the last time I'll be coming back to FWU.

This year, as vice president of the Beta Epsilon Deltas, I get one of the two rooms at the top of the house. Not only the biggest, but the only ones with ensuite. Sasha, one of my two best friends, and this year's president, had already moved into hers when I arrived yesterday. I haven't seen Abi, our other bestie, yet, but she messaged our group chat to say she'll be back tomorrow. I'm looking forward to having my girls together again. Summer is always weird without them. Although, I suppose I'm going to have to get used to that.

Trying not to stare at the oversized clock above the secretary's desk, I mentally run through everything I've researched about the station. It's the smallest of the four offering internships, having only been established fifteen years ago, but it has an excellent reputation and a steadily growing viewership.

The general manager, Kendall Marks, is one of the youngest women in the country to hold the position and is total goals. It's one of the reasons I wanted a position here above the other stations. Not only is the general manager a woman, but so is the news director, and both anchors, too.

"Ms. Marks will see you now, Miss Smith."

My head snaps toward where the secretary is tapping away at a keyboard, her head down, and I wonder whether I imagined it.

"Miss Smith?"

I stand, at the very definite sound of my name, to find

Kendall Marks herself standing at the door to her office peering over the top of her glasses at me. She's shorter than me, with a blunt black bob, and a slash of red lipstick, which compliments her dark tailored suit perfectly. Not to mention her shiny scarlet pumps, which I recognize from Louboutin's fall collection.

"Sorry," I bluster, already hating how worked up I am as I cross the small waiting area toward her.

Reaching out, I shake her hand, surprised when my firm handshake meets her barely-there limp grip. Determined not to let it throw me, I hold my head high and walk confidently behind her into the office.

"Please, take a seat, Miss Smith."

My heart hammers in time to the click of my heels as I cross to one of the gray leather chairs opposite a sleek black vinyl desk. Sitting down, my back straight and my eyes forward, I try not to get distracted by the large prints and framed awards behind her. All my attention is on her—the woman with the power to hand me the keys to my future.

"So, Miss Smith." Kendall sits down behind her desk, leaning back and crossing her legs. "Tell me why you want to slum it here at KPDU."

My mouth opens to reply before her words fully sink in, and I falter for the second time in as many minutes. Maybe I misheard.

"I'm not sure what you mean," I answer carefully. "I'd be honored to gain the internship position here at KPDU. I've been following the station's growth and successes over the last couple of years and would love nothing more than to be a part of that journey."

Kendall continues to stare at me over the top of her glasses, so after a few awkward seconds, I continue.

"I brought my portfolio with me if you'd like to take a

look. I've worked on several projects which showcase what I'm capable of, and—"

"Do I really have to sit through this pretense?" She uncrosses her legs and leans forward on the desk. "I googled you, Miss Smith. Just as I would any candidate. So, can we just skip to the part where you give me the check from your father?"

I blink. "Excuse me?"

"Oh, come on." She sighs and tilts her head, looking me up and down. "We both know you'll never have to work a day in your life. If I hire you, all you're going to do is trot around the station distracting people and probably making my life more difficult than it's worth. So, I'm going to cut to the chase and assume there's a check in that pretty little Marc Jacobs purse."

My face burns, and I'm not sure how much is embarrassment and how much is the anger churning my blood into froth beneath my skin.

"There is no check," I grit out, trying not to let the full force of my annoyance show. "I want this internship and I'll work harder than anyone else who applies. I can assure you; I might come from money but I'm not afraid of hard work. If anything, I'll work harder than anyone else you interview because I have more to prove. Let me prove myself, Ms. Marks."

Kendall does all but laugh in my face as she leans back and crosses her legs again. "Why? Daddy doesn't have enough money for you?"

"Because this is what I want. I want to be you, Ms. Marks, and I'm willing to work my way from the ground up." It's only part of the truth. Becoming general manager is only a stepping stone on the way to my dream of owning an entire network.

"Can't Daddy just buy you a news station to play with?"

My fingers grip the portfolio on my lap so hard it bends. Trying to calm my frantic heart, I remind myself that I deserve this just as much as anyone else. My dad didn't buy my 4.15 GPA or grades at FWU. Everything on my application I achieved all by myself. Forcing myself to meet her stare, I lift my chin. I will not break.

"I would appreciate it if you took the chance to judge me on my merits and not whatever Google has to say about me," I say through gritted teeth. "At least do me the courtesy of reviewing my credentials before you dismiss me."

Kendall has the fucking audacity to roll her eyes as she holds out her hand. "Fine. Let me see your sad little portfolio."

I hand it over, watching her eyes skim over the carefully curated collection of research projects, papers and assignments, proving I have what it takes to nail this job.

It's almost laughable. People assume that when you're rich, you don't have to worry about doors being slammed in your face. What they don't realize is you have to pay for some doors to be opened. And even though I could—I mean, I'm fairly certain my family could buy this station and everyone in it if they wanted to—I don't want to. I want this internship on my own merit.

Maybe I should have applied under a fake name.

"This is all very impressive," Kendall says, her voice flat as she slides the folder back across her desk. "I'll be in touch."

My heart sinks. She won't be in touch.

Forcing a smile, I stand and follow her to the door. "Thank you for the opportunity, Ms. Marks. I look forward to hearing from you."

Her tight smile tells me everything I need to know.

My head remains high all the way to my car—my baby. The white Bentley Continental GT Convertible was my eighteenth birthday present and is, without doubt, the love of my life. So much so that, when I climb inside, I refrain from smashing my fists against the steering wheel, no matter how much I want to.

Even though I want to scream until my throat hurts at how unfair it is, I swallow it all down. I'm acutely aware how lucky I am to never have to worry about money, but it doesn't mean it's not frustrating as hell to be judged for it. I purposely didn't tell my parents about the internship. Honestly, I'm not even sure they know what my major is. In hindsight, perhaps that should worry me more than it does. But Dad has never suggested that he wants me to take over his business in the future. No. He decided a long time ago what role I'll fulfill.

Slumping my head back against the soft Italian leather headrest, I exhale heavily. Even when I purposely try to leave them out, my family still manages to keep a fist wrapped tightly around the throat of my future. It doesn't mean I won't stop trying to find a way to escape their grip.

ZAK

Even before I leave my room, the wrongness aches deep in my bones. But I can't let the fact that it doesn't feel right get in the way. It's the whole damn reason I'm doing this. Tugging at the neck of my white button down, I glance in the mirror a final time before grabbing my keys and phone from my desk.

"You look like you're going to face a firing squad."

I turn to where Sol's squinting up at me from my bed and flip him off with both hands. "Helpful as a fucking headache, man."

"Just telling you the truth." He shrugs. "You're going out to get laid, you should look a bit happier."

"I'm not getting laid. It's a first date, you fucking heathen." Turning back to the mirror, I prod the inch and a half of afro I've grown above the shaved sides of my hair over the summer. Every day, I think about cutting it back to the half inch I've had since high school. And every day I put it off. New school year, new me. Or something like that.

"Where are you taking her?" Sol asks.

"Sushi place in Portland." My friend looks surprised,

and I laugh. "What? Did you think I was taking her to Grinds?"

Sol chuckles, sheepishly pulling a hand through his dark blond hair. "I mean, there's not exactly a lot of options around here."

Ain't that the fucking truth? Franklin West is in the middle of a forest in the ass crack of Oregon. Even ordering a pizza is a nightmare.

"Yeah, well, I wouldn't take a first date to Grinds," I mutter. "Are you staying in my room or going back to your palace on the top floor?"

Sol rolls his eyes and stands as I usher him out and lock the door behind me.

"Good luck!" he calls as I jog down the stairs.

I don't reply. We both know I'm going to need it.

If you'd asked me when I arrived at FWU three years ago, as a bright-eyed eighteen-year-old lacrosse star with the world at my feet, whether I believed in soul mates, I'd have laughed in your face. I might even have gone as far as to make some crass joke about too much pussy, not enough time. Honestly, I'd still probably make that joke. But then, *she* happened.

Standing as a freshman pledge to the Alpha Psi Deltas, I'd watched the most beautiful, confident girl I'd ever laid eyes on, stare me down with a sneer that told me she thought I wasn't worthy. And something just . . . clicked. The next couple of months were spent wearing her down, until I finally got my reward.

A single kiss.

Less than five perfect minutes in a dark corner during the Thanksgiving Blow Out three years ago, and all it did was confirm that my stupid heart was right. Jaime Smith is mine.

Which is why going on this date is a mistake.

A fact I'm reminded of forty minutes later when Tara enters the small Japanese restaurant I suggested, tugging off her white woolen hat and running her fingers through her sleek black bob as she reaches me.

"Hey, Zak." Her cheeks are flushed pink from the cold, and her smile is shy as I bend to kiss her on the cheek. "How was your summer?"

I shrug, taking my seat again as she sits opposite. "Same old. Catching up with friends and family. A fuck ton of babysitting."

Tara shrugs off her coat, the shoulder of her soft blue sweater falling low enough to show the black lace of her bra. "Babysitting? Really?"

"Yeah. My two sisters have three daughters each."

"Wow." Tara's dark eyes widen, stark against her pale skin. "That's . . ."

"A lot," I finish with a laugh. "Yeah. They're way more than a handful, but I adore them."

It's the truth. Holidays are messy and loud, but I wouldn't have it any other way. Plus, six grandchildren definitely help to take the spotlight off me and my murky future post-graduation.

"What about you?" I ask. "How was your summer?"

I settle back, nodding along as Tara tells me about spending most of the break on her family's yacht in the Med, and wonder for the millionth time why I'm here. Then push the reason right out again. I won't think about that. About *her*.

"I can't believe it's your last year," Tara says, causing my stomach to somersault. "Do you know what you're going to do after graduation?"

"I'm not sure yet." I poke at the menu, wishing I'd

suggested the campus coffee shop, Grinds, after all. "My folks are pretty chill, so . . ."

"Are you ready to order?"

I could kiss the waiter as he interrupts. It's not that I'm dreading next year, but I kind of am. Everyone else has plans. Jobs to go to, whether they want to or not, careers to chase and build. My mom has said she's got positions open at her company, but she's not pushing me.

They've never really pushed me.

I've always appreciated the fact that my parents are easygoing. They've always been firm with my sisters and me, but whatever path we want to take, they're fine with it if it makes us happy. So, when I graduated high school with little more than a solid GPA and a love of lacrosse, they suggested economics as a major. I had no feelings about it either way, so I figured what the hell.

For three years, I've been waiting for something to click. Driving down the highway of life, waiting for an exit sign to call out to me. But it hasn't. And now graduation is looming in the very near future. Suddenly, coasting through life without a destination feels a lot like I'm about to run out of road.

"And what about you, sir?"

Dragging myself back to the present, I give my order and return my focus to my date with a smile. Tara's on the swim team and I've run into her at the gym a few times. She's always made her interest clear, and I finally caved and gave her my number right before the summer. I'm not sure what I was thinking.

I open my mouth to ask her about her course when my phone buzzes loudly in my pocket.

"Sorry." I wince and pull it out, but then pause. "Shit. It's my coach. Do you mind?"

She holds up her hands and shakes her head. "Not at all."

Apologizing again, I stand and head outside, swiping to accept the call the second I'm away from the table. "Hey, Coach."

"Coach?" Sol's laughter echoes down the line. "Sex coach?"

As the door shuts behind me with a tinkle, I let out my own laugh. "You fucking wish. I couldn't exactly tell her my bestie was calling to give me an exit strategy, could I?"

"Do you need one?" he asks. "How's it going?"

Leaning against the wall of the restaurant, I exhale, watching my breath plume in front of me. "She's nice. She's pretty. It's not awful."

A familiar voice groans dramatically in the background. "You don't have to marry her, Zak. Just fuck her. I swear, it's like you don't understand college at all."

"Am I on speakerphone, Sol? You traitorous asshole."

"Sorry," Sol says, not sounding it at all. "Alex wanted an update, too."

"I can't believe you thought you could leave me out," he grumbles. "If anyone's a fucking sex coach, it's me."

Tipping my head back with a groan, I stare up at the icy blue sky. "You weren't even on campus when I left for this date, Rainer."

"Whatever. She knows you're a senior, so she's clearly just in it for your dick. Just give the poor girl what she wants."

"I watched videos in high school warning me about people like you," I say, shaking my head.

"Me too." Sol chuckles. "The ones about peer pressure, right?"

I grin. "No. Perverts."

"Fuck you, Aldridge."

"You wish, Rainer."

"Okay, enough," Sol breaks in. "Zak? Are you going back to your date, or are you needed back on campus for a lacrosse emergency?"

Blowing out a slow breath, I consider my options. Tara's nice. She's pretty. We have stuff in common. There's just one huge, glaring problem. She's not Jaime.

I close my eyes and thud my head against the stone wall. That's exactly the reason I'm on this date in the first place. Yet another attempt to flush Jaime Smith from my system.

"He's going to bail," Alex mutters. "I called it."

"I'm right here," I snap. "And I'm not going to bail."

"Seriously?" Sol asks. "You're going to go through with it?"

"Go through with it?" I echo. "It's not like I'm donating a fucking kidney. I'm perfectly capable of eating sushi and talking to a pretty girl."

"Yeah, well," Alex grunts. "Just don't be so . . . you."

I bark a laugh. "Why the hell are we friends again?"

"You know what I mean. Try to be a little serious or you'll never see her tits, let alone—"

"She asked for my number after watching me pretend to lift weights with my dick," I interrupt. "I think we're good."

Sol laughs and I grin at the thought of the disgust that's almost certainly on Alex's face right now.

"I'm heading back in. Later, fuckers." I hang up and turn my phone to silent before walking back into the restaurant, grateful to be back in the warmth.

"Everything okay?" Tara asks as I sit back down.

"Yeah. Coach Pearson has scheduled a couple of preseason games and couldn't get hold of Sol, so he was checking in with me."

Tara nods, and I feel a twinge of guilt for lying to her, but she buys it without hesitation.

"You're so lucky lacrosse season doesn't start until spring," Tara says, sipping the green tea that arrived while I was outside. "The best part of summer was not having to wake up at five."

I shudder. "Yeah. There's only one way you should be getting wet at five in the morning, and that's not it."

Tara almost spits out her green tea and I chuckle, handing her a napkin. I honestly can't help it and imagining Alex's frustrated face makes the joke even sweeter.

"Your hair's longer." She smiles, nudging my leg under the table with her foot. "It suits you."

Immediately, I reach up and scrunch my fingers through it. "Thanks. I'll probably cut it come spring. No one wants helmet hair."

She laughs, and I realize it's a little too much considering what I said wasn't even that funny. A rarity in itself. Perhaps she's as uncomfortable as I am. I watch as she licks her lips, watching me over the rim of her cup, and Alex Rainer's voice fills my head. *She's clearly just in it for your dick.*

Fuck.

It would be easy, I guess. There's no way there's going to be a second date, so maybe I *should* just give her what she wants. There's just one problem with that, though. I've tried it before. And it doesn't fucking work.

I know exactly what would happen. We'd go back to campus. We'd kiss. It would get hot and heavy and then when I'm balls deep, I'll look down and see *her*. Not Tara, but the flawless brown skin and bright brown eyes belonging to a woman who rarely gives me the time of day.

It's always her.

I have no desire to go through that again, and as Tara 'accidentally' nudges my leg for the second time, a new resolve settles in my gut.

Instead of going on dates to try and get over Jaime, I need to try harder. I need to up my game. This year, senior year, is my last chance. I might not know where I'm headed after graduation, but I know one thing with absolute certainty. Jaime Smith is the only thing that's called out to me my whole life.

Alex and Sol may think I'm obsessed. But I'm not. I'm convinced. Convinced that she's the one.

And this year, I'm finally going to convince her, too.

JAIME

BE

"We look good enough to eat, ladies." I smack my freshly painted lips together, completing a last-minute inspection of my makeup in the mirror by the front door. "Let's start our senior year with a bang!"

Sasha snorts and raises her eyebrows, tucking a strand of long auburn hair behind her ear. "Two doses of sexual innuendo in one breath? Are you planning on getting laid tonight, Jaime?"

I shoot her a look that says I won't be dignifying that response with an answer. Abi whoops beside me, snapping a group selfie before opening the front door of the Hive, our sorority house, and leading us out into the cold night air.

Our senior year. The last year of college. Excitement bubbles in my stomach, but I squash it down. While everyone else is going to be emerging from their college chrysalis, ready to start the next chapter of their lives, mine is already DOA. Not that you'd know. Not that anyone knows. I've learned to live with it. There's no other choice.

And that's without factoring in that the news station hasn't gotten back to me. Even though I walked out of there convinced I'd never hear from them, it turns out an inkling of hope had hidden somewhere deep in my chest.

Not anymore.

Pushing the smile back on my face, I smooth down the skin-tight silver of my vintage Hervé Léger, inspecting the shimmer coating my arms and legs, the golden flecks offsetting the rich brown of my skin perfectly. Tossing my hair over my shoulder, I thank the hair gods for the way the new caramel ombre through my relaxed and blow-dried waves turned out. I feel like a million dollars. I mean, I'm worth a hell of a lot more, but you get what I mean. No matter what happens after graduation, I plan on enjoying this year to the max.

I lift my chin, a little extra spring in my stride as we lead the way down the winding path, the rest of our sorority sisters laughing and chatting behind us. Reaching out, I take Sasha's hand and squeeze. I can tell she's nervous. Not just because she has an important role to play tonight, but because of who she's going to have to face off with.

It's the fraternity's turn to host the first welcome back party—a Franklin West tradition—and although this is the fourth one I'm attending, it's the first where I'll be wielding my power as vice president of the Beta Epsilon Deltas, or 'Bees', as we rebranded ourselves back in sophomore year.

The old white dudes who founded the university were either as misogynistic as you'd expect, or completely clueless when they gave the sorority a name that spelled out 'bed'. After a year of being called sluts and bedbugs, Sasha, Abigail, and I decided to try and put an end to it. If nothing else, the Bees and the Hive will be our legacy after we graduate.

Of course, the teasing hasn't stopped, because most boys are stupid and immature, but it's a hell of a lot better. It doesn't help that the Alpha Psi Deltas, or Psi-chos as we call them, are so much more than your typical bunch of frat boys. Almost everyone at Franklin West is rich, but they're a different brand of entitled assholes. And the worst of the bunch is Alex Rainer, their president this year. They call themselves the Wolves, and for some, like him, it couldn't be more appropriate.

My stomach tightens at the thought of one Wolf in particular. Of broad shoulders and kind brown eyes. Of a quiet moment in the dark that lit a spark inside me I've been trying to extinguish ever since. Taking a deep breath, I squeeze Sasha's hand and she gives me a small smile.

"What up, bed bugs?" Someone shouts from where they're loitering outside the Wolf Den, having a smoke.

Some other Wolves howl and laugh, but I toss my hair over my shoulder and lift my chin. "Idiots."

"That's for sure," Sasha mutters.

Abi makes a sort of growling sound as we climb the steps to the large wooden door that matches ours. "I hate them."

A laugh bursts from me, loud against the evening air. "You've had sex with at least four of them since freshman year, so you can't hate them that much."

She scowls at me, her blue eyes crinkling, and I stick out my tongue, righting my dress one final time as Sasha pushes open the heavy door.

"Come on, ladies," she says, her nervousness disappearing behind a bright red smile. "No point prolonging the inevitable."

It's always a little trippy going into the Den. It matches the sorority house identically in layout, from the circular entrance hall to the bedroom layout on the three floors above. Thankfully, they're decorated completely differently.

Where ours is calm pastels and metallic accents, the leather and mahogany of the Den reeks of toxic masculinity strong enough to make my nose wrinkle.

I expected the Wolves to be waiting, although now I'm not sure why. They're such preening assholes. Of course, they want to make an entrance.

I roll my eyes before clapping my hands loudly, the sound echoing in the empty foyer. "Come on, boys! Let's do this thing!"

Sasha elbows me but I just prop a hand on my hip and grin as the doors open and the Wolves file in looking like they're trying to film some sort of TikTok. I'm half tempted to look around for a phone set up somewhere. Either way, I'm sure they think it looks way better than it does.

As much as I try not to look, my gaze gravitates to him. Even when they're all wearing nearly identical designer black suits and white shirts, he stands out. He always does.

He looks great in his suit. The shirt unbuttoned just enough to show the smooth brown skin of his broad, muscled chest, toned from years of lacrosse. Taller than all of them at around six four, when I finally reach his eyes, I'm not surprised to find his attention already on me. His hair is a little longer than it was at the end of last year, more than a solid inch of tight curls on top of his head. I preferred it shorter. Not that I have any say in matters when it comes to Zak Aldridge.

"Welcome to the Wolf Den," Alex Rainer booms, dramatically sweeping his arms out to the side. "It is my honor as president of Alpha Psi Delta, to receive you at our inaugural event of the year."

It takes everything I have not to roll my eyes again. These aren't his words, though. It's all part of the tradition that started back when Franklin West was founded in the eighteen hundreds. His bright blue eyes roam over Sasha, a little too much like an actual wolf, and I sway a little closer to her.

"Thank you," she says, sounding more confident than I know she's feeling. "We are humbled and blessed to be in your presence and look forward to reciprocating your hospitality next week at the Hive."

"That's it," Alex says, turning to his Wolves. "Let's get this party started!"

Predictably, they all start howling, and I shake my head. Somewhere, music starts up, and the atmosphere shifts, kicking everyone into gear.

Even though I try to look anywhere else, my gaze finds Zak and I press my lips together to suppress my smile. Three years ago, we stood on opposite sides of the Hive entrance hall as freshmen pledges, excited and awed by the formality of the opening parties. I remember it like it was yesterday, the way his soft brown eyes met mine, his wide grin just on the charming side of goofy. Those dimples . . . He looked like trouble then, and he still does.

I look away.

Zak was a moment of weakness a lifetime ago, and one I can never let myself repeat.

"Let's go get a drink," Abi declares as everyone starts filtering into the living room and toward the bar they have set up.

Alex saunters over, giving Sasha a salacious grin and ignoring me and Abi completely. "Enjoy the party, ladies."

"Oh, we will," I say, looping arms with Abi and heading into the party. It's only as the crowd swallows us, I realize Sasha isn't following us. "Shit! Sasha."

"She'll be okay," Abi says, tugging me toward the counter covered with drinks. "She can handle Alex Rainer."

I huff in response. Sasha's tough, but Alex is a slimy fucker who hangs the underwear of women he's slept with out of his bedroom window. Grimacing, I pour a couple of shots and hand one to Abi before knocking my own back. I've perfected the balance of knowing how much alcohol is required for Dutch courage to survive a party knowing that Zak is here, and not so much that I give in to temptation.

I'm pouring a round of vanilla vodka and Coke when Sasha finally appears beside us looking more than a little shaken.

"That went well," I say, pressing a glass into her hand.

She gulps it down and shudders. "Douchebag."

"Yep," Abi and I agree.

"You'll get wrinkles if you frown that hard," Abi says, leaning into Sasha. "What's up? You're supposed to be having fun."

I raise my eyebrows, staring into my drink so I don't say something I can't take back. Sasha doesn't really do fun. I love her to pieces, but she works way harder than she plays.

"I am having fun."

I snort. "You need to tell your face that."

"Come on." Abi takes our glasses and places them back on the counter. "Let's dance."

Grabbing our hands, she tugs us to where people have already filled the makeshift dance floor. I make a beeline to Trey, the DJ, requesting one of our favorites, and the squeals Abi and Sasha make as they recognize the song lift my heart. For the first time since I started getting ready for tonight, I relax.

Closing my eyes, I inhale and throw my hands in the air, letting the music envelop me. Despite the ominous feeling that's been growing in the pit of my stomach since the end of the summer, I still have high hopes for this year. There's still a chance I might hear back from the other stations I applied to, and if not, I'll just have to investigate other avenues.

It's strange. Sometimes, I can see my future so clearly. Owning my own network, the world at my feet. Other times, it's dark and uncertain, hidden in shadows just outside my grasp. I'm trying to carve out my own future—one that I've chosen—but so much has already been decided for me. I can't think like that, though. I can't let the sinking feeling drag me down or it'll consume me.

When I open my eyes, they meet his.

Leaning against the wall at the edge of the dance floor, Zak lifts his bottle of beer in a salute and smiles. It's a smile I feel in my core. A smile I've spent three years shielding myself from. As I watch him lift the beer to his lips, his eyes never leaving mine, all long muscled limbs and dimples, it takes me a hot minute to remember why.

But when I do, my smile becomes a little more forced. Zak Aldridge is gorgeous, funny, and sweet, but he can never be mine. I walked away from our kiss three years ago with plans to never look back. But he won't let me. Every year he tries to get closer to me, and every year it gets harder to say no. I can pretend that our kiss meant nothing—did nothing—to me, but we both know I'm lying to myself. There was no denying the spark. The way we fit together like two pieces of a puzzle. Every time we're in the same room, those feelings stir in my belly, rising and filling me until I might burst. It's why I can't let that happen. If I let Zak close, if I open the door just a little, I know I won't be able to hold back.

And that's exactly what he's waiting for.

ZAK

Jaime Smith is perfection. From the very first time I laid eyes on her, I knew no one else could ever compare. Even as an eighteen-year-old, I was aware how ridiculous that thought was, attempting to convince myself it was just a crush. But it's a crush that's still going strong three years later.

Sipping my beer, I watch her dancing with Sasha and Abi, her head thrown back and a smile on her lips. With every sway of her curvy hips, her silver bandage dress shifts up her thighs, and I sip my drink as my throat runs dry.

Sol and Alex have teased me relentlessly over the years about my unrequited crush. But that's just it. It's not unrequited. I know she feels whatever this thing is between us. I can see it in the way her breath hitches whenever I'm too close—in the heated way her eyes meet mine from across the room.

What I don't know is why she refuses to give us a shot. We'd be great together. The stuff of dreams. I'm sure of it. I might be an economics major, but my science has always been pretty strong, and Jaime Smith and I match on a molecular level.

Taking another sip of my beer, I let my attention linger on the way her long, sleek hair slides over her shoulders, her huge brown eyes shining at something Abi's said, her perfect full lips parted in laughter. Her hair's lighter than before the summer. I like it. Clutching the bottle tighter, a new wave of determination settles in my chest. *Mine.*

Forcing myself to turn away, I push off the wall and head back to the other side of the Den where I left the guys. Sol is nowhere to be seen, but Alex is leaning against the wall, looking like he's on some sort of photo shoot. He always does. Shaking my head, I grab two beers from one of the shiny metal coolers on the scattered tables.

He doesn't see me approaching, his expression far-off and glazed, so I stoop a little and shoulder check him. "Where'd you go?"

He looks up, his eyebrows raised. "What do you mean? You're the one who went AWOL."

I take his empty bottle and hand him the fresh one. "You zoned out. Completely different planet."

"Just thinking."

I frown at him and shake my head. "This is the first party of our last year of college. No thinking. Just drinking."

Lifting my beer in a salute, I let out a holler and chug half of it while he laughs.

"Don't you and Sol have lacrosse practice in the morning?"

I roll my eyes, wiping my mouth with the back of my hand. Lacrosse season doesn't start until February, but every year Coach Pearson likes to set up friendlies with the local colleges. He says it gives us an opportunity to see their strengths and weaknesses before the season starts.

"Don't be such a fucking killjoy," I say, finishing off my beer and placing it down on the table.

Alex holds his hands up in front of him. "Just saying. You might want to take it easy."

I wrinkle my nose and shake my head. "When did you become so boring?"

"I'm not boring." He scowls at me. "Get drunk out of your fucking skull if you want to. All I did was remind you that you've got practice."

"Who's got practice?"

I chuckle as Sol appears with three beers grasped in his hands. Alex's face is a fucking picture.

"I'm joking," Sol says, handing out the beers. "This is my last one."

Alex folds his arms.

"Okay, fine. Maybe my penultimate one."

Alex snorts. "Taking your new role as captain seriously, then?"

My eyebrows shoot up at his scathing tone. He's not joking. Alex can be a dick sometimes, but we're never usually on the receiving end of it. I glance at Sol, who's staring at him with the same confusion I'm sure is mirrored on my own face. Perhaps it's the pressure of hosting the opening party.

Ever since freshman year, everyone knew Alex would end up being president of the Wolves. He's a natural leader. That doesn't mean he's finding it easy, I guess. When Sol gives a small shake of his head, I know he's reached the same conclusion.

"I'm going to get Jaime tonight." The words fall from my lips before I can think better of it, but they have the intended effect as Alex's expression shifts.

"Seriously?" he asks. "She turned you down four times last year. Learn when to quit."

His eyes narrow at something on the other side of the room, and I follow his gaze to find that Jaime and the others have stopped dancing and are making their way over to the bar.

"This year, it's different," I say, my lips curling into a small smile as Jaime pours them all shots. "I can feel it. Plus, if I get in with Jaime, I can put in a good word for you with Sasha."

Alex laughs. "Why the fuck would I want her to put a word in with Sasha?"

"Because," I say, leaning smugly against the bookshelf and shooting a look at Sol. "You haven't stopped staring at her since she arrived."

"Not true," he mutters.

"So true."

"Whatever."

Sol snorts, drawing Alex's glare, but he's no longer paying attention, instead shrugging out of his suit jacket, and throwing it on a chair. The movement attracts the attention of a few girls, but Sol doesn't notice. One of the many things I love about the guy. He's an incredible sports-man, and academically clever as hell, but he's fucking clueless.

Meanwhile, Alex is surveying the party like a shark, and I watch as his attention falls on a group of Bees.

"You going for Courtney?" I ask, watching as the pretty, blonde sophomore bats her eyelashes at him.

He glances at me before looking back at her. "Courtney?"

"The girl who's so hot for you, she's squirming in her

seat," I explain. "The one you're eye fucking. Like, right now."

"Oh?" He grins, wiggling his eyebrows. "*That* Courtney."

He pushes off the wall and I shake my head. When it comes to sex, Alex has issues for days. I've got nothing against a casual fuck, but he goes through women faster than I can keep track. Although, you could always just count the panties hanging from the line out his window.

"You okay?" Sol asks, nudging me with his elbow.

My eyebrows shoot up at the concern in his voice. "Of course. Why wouldn't I be?"

He shakes his head, glancing over at where Alex has Courtney practically eating out of his hand. "I don't know, man. There's something off about you tonight."

"Off?" I echo. "Thanks."

"Fuck off." He nudges me with his elbow. "Did you mean what you said about Jaime?"

My gaze meets hers across the room and I feel it in my bones. It's now or never. This year is my last chance. "Yes. I did."

Sol sighs. "I don't get it, Zak. You could have your pick of women. Why her?"

I press my lips together, watching as she looks away, talking with her friends. How do you begin to explain something you don't understand yourself?

"Do you think that, maybe . . ." Sol trails off and I turn to him.

"What?"

He grimaces and shakes his head. "Nothing."

Unease swims in my beer-filled stomach. "Don't do that, man. Spill."

Sol frowns, his blue eyes creasing before he exhales.

"Do you think you might be so obsessed because she keeps saying no?"

I blink. "What?"

"I mean, if she'd said yes to you in freshman year, do you think you'd still be together?" He shifts from foot to foot as I stare at him. "Like, maybe it's the chase you're infatuated with."

My jaw clenches, my grip tightening on my beer. "No."

I never told either of them that Jaime and I kissed at the Thanksgiving party. At the time, it was because I was waiting until I got my second chance. But it never came, and my crush just didn't fade. And now, it almost feels like it didn't happen. Until I see her. Then the memory steals my breath all over again.

Sol pushes a hand through his Captain America hair, messing it up in the process. "You know I love you, Zak. I just don't want to see you hurt. What if this thing between you and Jaime is just something you've built up in your head?"

I swear my teeth begin to crack. He doesn't understand. I've tried a couple of times to explain it, but he just looks at me with big blue eyes filled with pity. But he knows. He knows how serious I am about her, and to talk about her so dismissively . . .

I can count on one hand the number of times I've been pissed at my best friend, and until now, they've all been about lacrosse.

"I'm taking a lap," I say. "I'll catch you in a bit."

Sol reaches for me, but I shrug him off, pushing through the crowd. I'm mad at him now, but it won't last. Even after a few paces, I know he's coming from a good place. He's looking out for me. I just need a breather.

Moving through the crowd, almost everyone I pass says

hey or offers a smile. It's one of the things I like about Franklin West. It's small. A community. Although, I know that's not everyone's jam.

I'm so lost in thought, I don't realize where I'm headed until I find myself in the huge open kitchen, a few feet away from Jaime.

I freeze, allowing myself to drink her in. From her long legs to her incredible rack, lingering on the curves encased within her tight dress as she sways in time to the music. The urge to close the distance between us and slide my arms around her, is almost all consuming.

She looks up from where she's finished pouring a shot and I swallow. "Hey."

"Hey, yourself," she says. "Want one?"

I open my mouth to say yes, then shake my head. "I have lacrosse in the morning, so I really shouldn't."

Offering a shrug, she picks hers up and knocks it back. I chuckle to myself and close the remaining distance between us, leaning against the counter.

"Having a good night, VP?" I ask.

She licks her lips and I tighten my grip on my drink. "It's okay. Next week will be better."

My grin widens. It's the Bee's turn to host their opening party next week at the Hive. "I'm sure it will if you've got anything to do with it."

Her smile softens, her gaze dropping from mine, and it takes a lot of effort not to flex as I watch her unabashedly check me out.

"Excited for senior year?" she asks, propping a hand on her hip as she drags her eyes up to meet mine once more.

"It's going to be tough," I admit. "The reading list for my course is ridiculous."

She hums, her gaze flitting to where the top three

buttons of my shirt are unfastened. "You heading back to Chicago after graduation?"

My eyebrows shoot up. We've chatted several times over the years, but it's always been surface stuff. How does she know I'm from Chicago? My chest swells at the knowledge she's been paying as much attention to me as I have to her.

"I don't know," I say carefully. "I'm open to suggestions. I hear Florida's nice."

She rolls her eyes at the mention of her home state, and I smile. I know everything there is to know about Jaime Smith. Her family is hella famous in the business world. Mason Smith is old money, and huge in the import export trade. People would sell a kidney to get in with him. He's like the Simon Cowell of business. If you get a 'yes' from Mason Smith, you're a guaranteed millionaire.

"So, we're doing this again, this year?" Jaime asks.

I shrug. "Doing what?"

"The whole cat and mouse thing." She gestures between us.

A deep laugh rumbles from me. "That's a really crappy analogy because I'm doing the chasing, and you're definitely not a mouse. If anything, I'm the mouse, presenting myself to you on a silver platter."

Her brown eyes narrow. "Maybe you need to get off that platter before you find yourself skewered by a claw."

I swear I try, but the idea of her clawing at me does nothing but send tingles down my spine, my dick thickening in my pants. I just know she's a hellcat in the sack. She's not afraid to ask for what she wants, and I've jerked off more times than I'd like to admit to the thought of her riding me into oblivion, her long nails piercing my chest. *Fuck.*

"You're a masochist," she says, dragging me from my thoughts.

I grin. "Only when it comes to you, Kitty Cat."

She glowers at me, and I lean closer, reaching out and pulling a strand of her long hair between my fingers.

Her eyes widen a fraction, flitting to my mouth, but then she steps back, her hair falling from my fingertips. "This needs to stop, Zak. It's not fair."

"What's not fair?".

"This," she says, shaking her head as she takes another step back. "Pursuing me. We're not going to happen. Why won't you accept that?"

I press my lips together because I don't know. Maybe it's because she can never give me an answer—no real reason why we can't happen. If she didn't find me attractive, or thought I was a dick, I'd get it. But neither of those things are true. That kiss didn't lie and the way she looks at me like I'm her last meal certainly doesn't either.

"I'm sorry," I say, even though it's not true. "How about a fresh start for our last year?"

"Fresh start?" she echoes, her expression dubious.

I shrug. "Yeah. Let's start over. Be friends. I promise not to cross any lines."

Her eyes narrow. "Friends?"

"Yeah, friends." I grin. "You know, people who talk and spend time together but don't have sex? If you refuse to date me, then at least let me be your friend."

Her lips press together, and my gaze almost drops to them, but I keep focused on her eyes. If this is the only way to get close to her, then fine.

"I have enough friends," she says, although I can tell she's faltering.

Before I can chicken out, I pull my phone from my pocket and hand it to her. "Put your number in, Kitty Cat, and I swear I won't ask you out again. This mouse will take himself off the platter and find some cheese instead."

Jaime is a smart cookie. I have no doubt she sees this for what it is and is trying to figure out a loophole. But she's also not saying no.

When she reaches out and takes my phone, I mentally punch the air, trying to keep my expression neutral. The second she hands it back, I send her a text, because I wouldn't put it past her to give me a fake number. Her phone buzzes in her purse and she sighs as she pulls it out and checks it.

"Hi, Bestie," she reads. "Cute."

I grin. "Speaking of which, I should get back to the guys. See you later, Kitty Cat."

Her scathing expression makes me chuckle as I walk away. I've promised I won't ask her out, but that doesn't mean I've given up. Not by a long shot. I have Jaime Smith's number. I'm just getting started.

BE

Tugging down my burgundy pencil skirt and straightening my jacket, I take a deep breath before approaching the large, glass-fronted building. Three weeks into the semester, I'd all but given up on hearing back from any of my other applications, so when I got the call from KBCX, I couldn't believe it. The universe has granted me a second chance, and I'm trying not to think about how much is riding on it.

There are videos my mom has of me in kindergarten, standing in front of the TV wearing a pair of her heels, using my hairbrush as a microphone. Back then, I thought the shiny lady on the screen was the boss. Because that's what I want to be. The boss.

My family's legacy in the trade world is one I'm proud of, but it's not a mantle I'm interested in taking. I want to forge an empire of my own, and media and communications is where my heart is.

As I catch my reflection in the shiny glass, I realize that my smile is somewhere between too bright and too fake, but when I try to dial it down, it feels like a grimace.

"Good morning." The young brunette woman at the

reception desk smiles up at me as I approach. "How can I help you?"

"I'm here for an interview with Brad Longstead," I say. "Jaime Smith."

She taps at her computer for a second before handing me a visitor's badge. "Fourteenth floor. Check in with the secretary there and they'll let him know you're here."

I give her a grateful smile and step into the elevator, hoping she didn't notice the way my hands are trembling where they clutch my portfolio. As soon as the doors close, I exhale, trying to calm my nerves.

It's a different type of nerves this time around. When I went to the first interview, I felt invincible, like my nerves were merely a part of the process. Now, I know what it feels like to fail, and I have no plans of letting it happen again. Even if the circumstances were out of my control.

My phone vibrates in my purse, and I pull it out, frowning at the screen. We're barely into senior year and already the drama has hit new heights. This morning, someone posted an entry from Sasha's diary online. We were supposed to rule the school this year and scandal was never part of the plan.

Tossing my hair over my shoulder, I tap out a response to Abi's frantic texts in our group chat before switching to flight mode and dropping my phone back into my purse just as the doors open.

The fourteenth floor isn't what I was expecting. Unlike the foyer, with its tall glass windows, up here it's dark and moody, with picture blocks on the walls and blue neon accents along the ceiling.

I'm still taking it in when a cool voice pulls me back to Earth. "Good morning. How may I help you?"

I snap my mouth shut and stride over to the high desk,

offering the slender man behind it a smile. "Hi. I'm Jaime Smith. I'm here to meet with Brad Longstead."

His smile is nowhere near as warm as the woman downstairs and I swear he looks me up and down before turning to his computer, his eyebrows slightly raised beneath his perfectly coiffed pompadour hairstyle.

"Take a seat, Miss Smith," he says, cool blue eyes flitting up to me briefly before returning to his screen. "He'll be right with you."

I try to keep my smile warm and friendly as I thank him and do as he says. The seats are not as comfortable as they look, the teal leather tight and hard, forcing me to sit tall, my portfolio balanced on my lap.

Right now, the rest of my classmates will be sitting through a lecture. I'm not worried about missing it, though. Professor Brierley okayed me to miss class today and Wes has said he'll email me his notes. Things are already in place for if I get the internship, and my heart flutters in my chest at the thought.

Once again, I'm so close to getting everything I've ever wanted.

And just like that, my heart drops like a lead weight. No. Not everything I've ever wanted. There are some things that can never be mine.

"Miss Smith!"

A deep and booming voice has my head snapping up, and I try to stand as gracefully as I can to greet the man striding toward me with a blinding million-dollar smile.

I've researched the hell out of Brad Longstead. I swear I could tell you what brand of underwear he prefers. But despite seeing a thousand pictures of the man, it's nothing compared with seeing him in the flesh.

A legend in the industry at only thirty-six, he's tall and

muscular with a square jaw and perfect hair. He's like Clark Kent without the glasses and nervous energy. Superman in a three-piece suit.

Coming to a stop before me, he holds out his hand and I grip it firmly. A good handshake is the ultimate first impression, and I'm relieved when his is firm and sure, unlike Kendall's limp grasp. What I'm not expecting is the way he holds onto my hand a little longer than necessary, his bright blue eyes trailing down my body in a way that makes my skin crawl, despite how attractive he is.

"A pleasure to meet you," he drawls, finally dropping my hand. "I was very impressed by your application. Won't you come into my office?"

"Thank you," I say, following as he turns and leads me to one of the many black doors along the corridor.

He pushes it open and holds it for me to enter first. The door opens inwards, which means I have to almost brush past him to step inside, his expensive cologne hazing my senses.

"Please, take a seat."

I do, glancing around his office, decorated in dark wood and touches of teal, as I try not to think about the nerves fluttering in my stomach.

"So, you're a senior at Franklin West," he says, sitting behind his desk and leaning back on his chair. "How are you planning on juggling your coursework with an internship?"

Wow. Cutting right to the chase. I shift in my chair, mildly more comfortable than the ones in the waiting area.

"I spoke with my professor before accepting the interview," I explain. "He's agreed to give me course credit for completing the internship as long as I still complete my written assignments and thesis."

Brad nods and steeples his fingers together. "And you can manage that?"

"I can."

He stares at me a few seconds longer and I take a breath, ready to ask whether he'd like to take a look at my portfolio, but he pushes back from the desk and stands.

"One thing you need to know about me," he says, scratching his sharp jaw. "Is that I don't sugarcoat things. So, trust me when I say, this isn't going to be easy."

I sit up a little straighter. "I can take it."

"You say that now, Miss Smith." He moves around the desk and leans against it, crossing his ankles. "But interns are the lowest of the low. You'll get great insight into how the station works and, of course, it's a foot in the door, but you'll be grabbing coffee, talked to like trash by some of our divas, and you won't be getting paid for it."

He waits, his eyebrows slightly raised, as though that information is going to have me scrambling for the door.

"I'm prepared for that," I say. "There's nothing you can tell me that will change how much I want this."

He lets his gaze roam over me again, lingering on my legs, and it takes all my self-control not to tug my skirt further down. "I just mean, it might be a little tougher than you're used to."

My eyes widen as I realize what he's getting at. I thought I'd imagined his tone when he mentioned Franklin West, but perhaps I didn't.

A sinking feeling builds in my stomach. Once again, I'm blocked by preconceptions. He thinks I'm some spoiled trust fund brat who's never done a day of hard work in their life. My heart speeds as Kendall Marks' face flashes in my mind. Her unabashed sneer over her glasses. I won't let that happen again. I can't.

Willing my face not to fall into a scathing scowl, I smile, readjusting my grip on my portfolio. "I assure you, Mr. Longstead, if you give me this internship, you won't regret it. I can take whatever you throw at me and then some."

His lips curve into a smile and he shakes his head. "We'll see, Miss Smith."

Usually, I'm good at reading people, but other than the fact this guy gives me the creeps, I can't figure him out. I'm not sure whether to go quiet or unleash the sass. My gut tells me he prefers women to be seen and not heard—perhaps the reason I'm not liking him at all—so I keep my mouth shut and my smile plastered on my face.

He gestures to the door, and I realize this 'interview' is over. Panic flares in my chest. I didn't get to sell myself—to give him one of the hundred and eighteen reasons I'm the perfect woman for this job.

"It was a pleasure to meet you, Miss Smith," he says as I'm left with no choice but to stand. "We'll be in touch before the end of the week."

Fuck.

His hand lands on the small of my back as he guides me out of his office, and I try not to cringe at the over familiar touch.

"Thank you for your time, Mr. Longstead," I say. "I look forward to hearing from you."

He maneuvers us to the bank of elevators, pressing the down button. "Take care, Miss Smith."

As soon as the doors close behind me, I exhale, my body trembling. I have no idea how that went. Not a clue. Longstead is sleazy as hell, but if I get the job, I probably won't have to deal with him directly. Besides, I meant what I said. I'll do whatever it takes. I'm not afraid of hard work and I'm more than willing to start at the bottom and work my way up.

A shudder runs through me at the way Brad looked at me. Maybe he thought I meant I'd do *anything*. Well, he's going to have a very big wakeup call and a fucking lawsuit if he thinks that's happening. Even if the only reason he gives me the internship is because he thinks he has a chance at some head, I don't care. Once I'm in those doors, I'll prove myself invaluable. I'll be the best damn intern they've ever had.

I don't want my success handed to me. I want to earn it. I want to sweat for it. Dig it up from nothing and shape it with my bare hands.

The cool autumn air hits me as I step outside, and I take a second to calm my racing heart before heading down the block to where I parked my car. I smile as she comes into view, clicking the fob to unlock the doors.

Settling back against the soft leather, I close my eyes and draw in a breath. I should have said more. I should have made myself impossible to say no to.

My phone buzzes in my purse and I pull it free, my eyes narrowing as I swipe to answer. "Hey, Mom. What's up?"

"Jaime. I have some good news."

I lean back against the headrest and close my eyes. My mom's idea of good news is rarely the same as mine. "Oh?"

"The Chevaliers are coming next week."

Bile rises in my throat, and I swallow hard. "What?"

"Pardon," my mother corrects. "Manners, Jaime. They're arriving on Tuesday. I'll be in touch once we have more details. Be ready."

Ready. Sure.

"Okay, Mom."

"Take care, honey. Love you, bye!"

I keep the phone pressed to my ear for a few seconds after she hangs up. This wasn't supposed to happen so soon. I was supposed to have more time.

Exhaling, I drop my phone onto the passenger seat and wipe my damp palms on my skirt before turning the ignition. I was planning on going back to Franklin West, but I don't want to see anyone. I don't have the energy to fake it right now.

Smashing my hands against the wheel, I turn off the engine and climb out of the car, slamming the door behind me.

ZAK

ΑΨΔ

My steps come to an abrupt halt as Jaime gets out of her car just a few feet away from me and slams the door. Eyes wide, I watch her touch her fingers to the roof of the Bentley, almost in apology, even as her entire body trembles. With her back to me, I'm not sure whether it's with anger or sadness, but I'm pulled toward her regardless.

Even as I step closer, my lips parting to speak, I realize I have no idea what to say. She has no clue I'm even standing behind her, and I don't want to startle her.

"Coffee?" The single word tumbles from my lips like one of my nieces spitting the vegetables out of their pasta, and I wince as she whirls round to face me.

She stares at me, her lips parted, and I realize I didn't even say 'hi'. There's no point, though. Why falter through formalities when we can just get straight to the point?

Shifting my bag higher on my shoulder, I note the way her eyes are narrowed, her mouth tight. There are no tears in sight, so she's not sad, but whoever made her this angry, I want to kick their ass.

"Want to go for a coffee?" I try again, offering a smile.

"What are you doing here?" she asks, eyeing me as though perhaps this isn't a coincidence and I've upgraded my pursuit to full on stalking.

I show her the store bag I have slung over my shoulder. "I needed some new gear for lacrosse."

Jaime continues to stare at me, and I hold my ground. I want to tell her that it's just coffee, but I know the best plan is to stay silent. We might have known each other for years, but this tentative fledgling friendship is fragile, and I don't want to break it before we've even had a chance to let it grow. Everything about her is tense, and I half expect her to get back in her car and drive off. Whatever just happened has her wound tighter than I've ever seen her.

She huffs out a short breath. "Now's not a good time, Zak."

"It's just a coffee," I say, taking a step closer. "You shouldn't drive when you're this upset."

"I'm not upset," she snaps, tossing her hair over her shoulder.

It's then, I take in her outfit. A dark red suit. Something I've never once seen her wear. She looks fine as fuck, the skirt showing off her incredible legs, accentuated by the shiny black Louboutin heels. And the fact that her silk blouse is buttoned to the top only makes the whole ensemble more tempting. There's only one reason she'd be wearing a suit, and I'm guessing it didn't go well.

"What was the interview for?"

Jaime's eyes widen. "How . . .?"

"The suit." I grin, dusting off a shoulder. "Just call me Sherlock."

"You're such a loser."

She rolls her eyes, but I notice the tension bleed from her shoulders. "A loser who wants to buy you coffee. And if you play your cards right, Kitty Cat, I might even stretch to a muffin."

"I'd rather have a brownie."

My smile stretches wide. "Is that a yes?"

"Whatever." She steps away from the car and looks up and down the street. "It just better not be someplace shitty."

I clutch my chest in mock horror. "It's like you don't even know me."

She opens her mouth to retort, but when I smile and start walking, she sighs and follows. I haven't sent her another text since she gave me her number, even though it's been so fucking tempting. But I don't want to push things.

At the Bee's party last weekend, we chatted again, but only briefly. She was busy as VP making sure that everything was running smoothly. Which it did. It was a great party. Better than ours, although I'd never tell Alex that.

"Here we go," I say as we reach Joe For Joe, my favorite coffee spot in the city.

Pushing open the large glass doors, I step to the side to let her pass, and I definitely don't breathe her in as she does.

Jaime stops just inside, staring at the sprawling warehouse style space. "I've never been in here before."

"Hidden gem," I say, leading the way between the green velvet sofas and chunky dark wood tables to the counter. "What do you want?"

She doesn't even glance at the chalkboard menu above the long brass-covered counter, instead continuing to look around, taking it all in. "Oat milk vanilla latte, please."

I watch her for a second—the way the pale sunlight catches her hair and the gentle slope of her nose—then she turns, and I snap my gaze away, focusing on the specials board instead.

"Are you going to tell me about the interview?" I ask.

"Maybe." She hums, glancing up at me before tilting her head to peer at the open second floor above us. "I'm going to go get us a seat."

She doesn't wait for my response, but I don't care because I get to watch her walk away. When the barista calls out for my attention, it's a struggle to pull my gaze away from her perfect ass and calves.

I order, grabbing myself a sandwich, Jaime a brownie, and then a couple of other options in case she's hungry for proper food. Because it's quiet, the barista says they'll bring the coffees over when they're ready.

Jaime's settled on one of two plush sofas on the ground floor, right by a huge arched window. The sunlight spills in, casting her in hues of gold, and my pulse skips. It always does.

She looks up as I approach, slipping her phone back into her purse, and even though I really want to sit next to her I take the seat opposite.

"I bought us some food," I say, placing the brownie down in front of her and arranging the rest of the sandwiches and salads on the table. "I wasn't sure what you liked, so I got a selection."

"Thanks," she says, not making a move to take anything, her attention settling to the sidewalk outside.

It's fine. I'll eat whatever she doesn't. My metabolism needs five meals a day plus snacks. Tearing into a sandwich, I sit back and give her space. It's hard, but I'm already playing the long game. I've been biding my time for three years.

Chewing thoughtfully on my ham and cheese sandwich, I partake in my favorite pastime. Trying to pinpoint what exactly it is about Jaime Smith that has me tied up in knots. Sure, she's gorgeous and confident and clever. But it's more than that. Sol asked me to try to explain it once on the way to a game in Seattle. I tried, but I couldn't. The best I could come up with was: everything.

"So, you were right. I had an interview."

I swallow, putting my sandwich down so I can give her my full attention. "Yeah? What for?"

"An internship at KBCX." She looks away from the window and meets my gaze with a sigh. "I don't think it went very well."

As much as I want to assure her that it did, I bite my tongue. "What makes you think that?"

Before she can answer, the barista arrives with our coffee order, and we wait in awkward silence while she unloads the tray. When she's gone, Jaime picks up her latte and takes a sip, her attention falling to the window once more.

"I barely got to say anything," she says after a pause. "He didn't ask me any questions. It was strange."

I frown. "Maybe he didn't need to because of your application. Perhaps he just needed to meet you in person to gauge your vibe."

"My vibe?" she echoes with a small smile. "And what is my 'vibe'?"

I smirk, picking up my own coffee. "Confident. Strong. Capable. Reliable." *Sexy as hell.*

"Yeah, well, I get the feeling he was thinking more along the lines of entitled bitch."

My spine straightens and I lean forward, immediately wanting to find this douche canoe and kick his ass. "What do you mean?"

"He mentioned Franklin West and that the job might be 'tougher than I'm used to'." She shakes her head, her long, golden-brown hair falling over her shoulder. "I assured him I'm not afraid of hard work, but I just don't know."

I blow out a long breath, sitting back in my seat. "Well, it'll be his loss."

"No. It'll be my loss." She puts her coffee down and presses her fingers to her temples. "I really want this, Zak. It's all I've ever wanted."

My pulse kicks up. As much as I know everything I can about Jaime Smith, it's based on observation, Google, and scraps. The fact that I'm being given the opportunity to finally see beneath the surface sends a shiver of anticipation down my spine. "What's the end goal? I know you're majoring in media and communications, but what's the dream?"

She blinks at me, then laughs softly. "I forgot."

"Forgot what?"

"That we don't really know each other."

Her words prick at my chest, but I force a smile and wink. "Well, whose fault is that?"

"Zak . . ."

"I'm just saying, Kitty Cat. You've had unlimited access to this for three years. It's not my fault you never used your membership."

She rolls her eyes and picks up her latte. "Anyway. In answer to your question, I want to run my own network."

I sit back and smile. "I can totally see that."

"Yeah, well, you might never get to."

I quirk an eyebrow, but bite back the first response that jumps to my mouth—that her family is so freaking rich, she could start her own network. But it's not what she wants, or needs, to hear.

She might be a lot richer than my own wealthy family, but it's a world I understand. You could probably draw a line down the middle of Franklin West, dividing the students into those who want nothing more than to step out from their parents' shadow, and those who want to step into their shoes and take the reins. Jaime is definitely the former. I have no doubt about it. The fact that she's taking media and communications instead of business or economics speaks volumes for a start.

I try not to think too deeply about the fact that, in my own analogy, I have no idea which side of the line I'd be on. It's more likely I'd be watching from Grinds, hiding behind a bagel.

"Don't write it off just yet," I say. "When did he say they'd let you know?"

"By the end of the week."

"There you go, then." I give her a small smile. "Wait until Friday to spiral. And if you do, give me a call and I'll come spiral with you. Hell, we can even plot this jerk's demise. I think I have a dartboard somewhere under my bed."

She chuckles softly and my soul soars. Shaking her head, she puts down her coffee and picks up one of the sandwiches I bought. Some repressed caveman shit preens that she's taken one of my offerings, and I try not to sit and watch her eat like a creep.

"How's your year going so far?" she asks.

I shrug. "Same old shit, different day. Only it keeps hitting me that this is it. This time next year, there'll be no more Den, no more lacrosse, no more Franklin West. It puts a lot of pressure on everything. You know?"

"Yeah." She nods. "Like everything's on a countdown timer. Guess we need to make the most of it."

An amicable silence settles between us as we eat, and I

just enjoy the fact that I'm spending time with her alone. It's different than at parties, or when our circles occasionally overlap at events. There are so many things I want to ask, but I don't want to risk pushing her away. She seems a lot more settled than when I ran into her by her car, and I hope that it has something to do with me. I want to be that person for her—someone she can turn to when it all gets too much.

"What are you doing after graduation?"

Jaime's question pulls me from my thoughts, and I smile. "I've got a few options, but I'm not stressing."

Her eyebrows shoot up. "A few options? What about your parents?"

"What about them?"

"Surely they've got ideas." She blinks, staring at me as though I've just revealed a third eye. "They must have opinions about your lack of direction."

"Lack of direction?" I lean back with a chuckle. "My folks just want me to be happy. If that means I take a year to figure shit out, they're fine with that."

Jaime just continues to stare at me, and a lightbulb flicks on somewhere in my brain.

"Shit." I lean forward, my voice softening. "Are your folks pushing you to make choices?"

Her gaze falls and I swear I don't breathe as I watch her, waiting for her answer.

"Thank you for the coffee, Zak." She brushes off her skirt and stands, sliding the strap of her purse over her shoulder. "Enjoy the rest of your shopping."

It all happens so fast, it takes my brain a second to catch up, and I leap to my feet. "Wait a second. Where are you going?"

She shakes her head, avoiding my eyes. "I need to get

back to campus. I have lots of reading to catch up on ready for class tomorrow."

My mouth hangs open, a thousand reasons for her to stay on my lips, but I swallow and nod. "Okay. Let me grab the food and I'll walk you to your car."

"You really don't need to do that," she says, trying to escape again.

I raise my eyebrows, pinning her with a look. "I'm asking for ten seconds, Kitty Cat. Please let me walk you to your car."

Her mouth opens and closes as though she's going to fight me, but then sags a little and nods. Relieved, I give her a smile and scoop up the unopened sandwiches and salads and toss them in my bag along with my new gum shield and shoes. My gaze falls on her untouched brownie and my heart sinks. This was so much more than I expected, but still nowhere near enough.

When I straighten, I find Jaime looking much as she had when I first saw her slam her car door. Tense. Haunted.

"Ready?" I ask, forcing a smile a lot lighter than I'm feeling.

She nods and we head toward the exit in silence. I don't like this one bit. Quiet, sad, Jaime doesn't sit well with me. Whatever pressure her parents are putting on her is enough to flip a switch that dulls her sparkle, and that will never be okay with me.

The walk to her car is agonizing. I try to get her talking, but she's completely shut down. Shoving my hands in my pockets, I admit defeat.

"Enjoy your reading," I offer as we reach her car. "I guess I'll see you round campus."

She turns, a smile on her lips that doesn't reach her eyes. "Thanks, Zak. I'm happy I have a friend like you."

My own smile tightens in response, and I watch as she buckles up and drives away without a backwards glance.

Friend.

I huff and turn, heading to where my own car is parked a couple of blocks away. The friend zone might be where I am right now, but if Jaime can count on anything, it's that I'm not staying there a moment longer than I have to.

JAIME

BE

Dim sunlight filters in through the gauze layer over my window, and I snuggle deeper into the mass of pillows I'm nested in. I really should get up. It's almost nine on a Wednesday morning, and I have shit to do. Well, kind of. I have around sixty-pages to read for my Rhetoric, Language and Political Communication module, and I need to meet up with Ellen, who I've been partnered with, to discuss our Communication Theory project.

Groaning, I stretch and try to muster enough enthusiasm to propel myself out of bed.

And I fail.

Instead, I allow my thoughts to wander. It had been such a shock to find Zak standing there on the sidewalk after my interview, almost as if the universe had conjured him for me. He'd looked gorgeous in black jeans, a thin mustard yellow sweater and a well-worn leather jacket. The look of concern on his handsome face when he saw me so close to losing my shit was almost enough to send me into his arms, consequences be damned. But not quite.

A loud buzzing fills the quiet morning air, and my heart

leaps into my throat. Scrambling up from my pile of pillows, I locate the source and gape at the number on the screen. The phone vibrates again in my hands, and I almost drop it, swiping with trembling fingers to answer.

"Hello?"

"Jaime, hello. This is Brad Longstead at KBCX. Are you free to talk?"

Leaping to my feet, I straighten my sweats as though he can see me. "Yes. Of course. Good to hear from you, Mr. Longstead."

"Please, call me Brad."

Standing in the middle of my room, pacing a small circle, I send out a plea to the universe as I wait for him to continue.

"I was very impressed with you during your interview, Jaime. I'd like to offer you one of our intern positions."

It takes everything I have not to squeal down the phone. Instead, I take a small breath and let it out as quietly as possible. "Thank you, Mr. Long—Brad. You won't regret this."

"I sincerely hope not." He chuckles softly. "My assistant will be in touch with your schedule and induction information. Don't let me down."

I swallow hard. "I won't. Thank you."

The line goes dead, and I stay standing in the middle of the room, the phone pressed to my ear for a few seconds. I did it. I got the internship.

Excitement bubbles over and I squeal, tossing my phone onto the bed and breaking into a celebratory dance. It's going to be a lot of pressure, juggling a part time job with my course and the responsibilities of being vice president of the Bees, but I'm more than up to the challenge.

When my phone buzzes again, I fall forward onto the

bed and scoop it up, half expecting it to be the email from Brad's assistant. It's not.

> Are you at the Hive? Have you seen Sasha?

My mood instantly drops as I type out my reply to Abi.

> Yeah. I'm here. I haven't seen Sash. Y?

> There's another post. She's not answering her phone...

I swear under my breath. If I ever get my hands on whoever stole her damn diary, I'll make them regret the day they were born. No one upsets one of my sisters like this and walks away unscathed.

> Shit. I'll check her room

Pushing back to my feet, I pad out of my room and next door to hers. The gold stars stuck to her door like it's Hollywood always make me smile, and I knock loudly.

"Sash?" I call. "You in there?"

There's no answer, so I grab my keys. Both Sasha and I have keys to each other's rooms for emergencies, and I knock one more time before unlocking the door.

"Hello? Sasha?"

It's dark inside, the curtains drawn, and I walk over and poke the pillows to make sure she's definitely not here before leaving and locking the door behind me.

> She's not here

Abi reads the text but doesn't reply, so I lie back down,

my phone loose in my hand. It's only as I'm lying there, I realize Abi never asked me how my interview went. Neither did Sasha. I spoke to them both the morning of, so they knew I was going.

In all fairness, Sasha has a lot of shit going on right now. Abi, however, has nothing but her course load as far as I know.

I slump down on my bed, the high of getting the internship quickly evaporating. How is it that I have no one to share this excitement with? My parents don't even know I applied, so there's no point calling them. The only other person that knows is . . .

My heart racing, I unlock my phone and swipe through my contacts until I find what I'm looking for. It takes me a minute because I forgot what I saved his contact under. Grinning, I type out a message.

> I got the internship

As soon as I press send, I contemplate deleting it before he sees. Honestly, I'm shocked Zak hasn't used my number beyond that first text. When I gave it to him, I expected to regret it almost instantly.

My phone jolts in my hand, and I smile as a second message joins my lonely first.

> Congrats, Kitty Cat! Never doubted you for a second

Closing my eyes, I smile to myself. In another life, I knew I'd have been happy with Zak. I can picture it vividly. My hand in his as we stroll through the common. Hanging out at parties and losing myself in his warm laugh and deep brown eyes. It would have been nice. Easy. Whether it would have matured past college, I don't know. But it's not worth wasting a brain cell on.

When my phone vibrates again, I assume it must be a message from Abi, or even Zak, and it takes a second to realize it's ringing.

A frown forms on my face as I stare at my mom's name on the caller ID before answering. "Hey, Mom."

"Pack a bag, honey. A car's on its way."

I blink, then push up to sitting. "Erm. Hi. What are you talking about?"

Mom makes a frustrated noise as though it's my fault she's talking in riddles. "The Chevaliers. They're coming over for dinner tonight. You have to be here."

My mouth falls open. "I have class tomorrow, Mom. Did you forget I'm at college? I can't just leave."

"You can and you will."

The finality in my mother's tone cuts me down at the knees, making me feel like a middle schooler instead of the almost twenty-two-year-old woman I am.

"Can't we just have dinner on the weekend?" I ask, trying not to sound like I'm pleading. If I had it my way, there would be no dinner. Ever.

She huffs again. "No. They're coming tonight and so are you. It's been six years, Jaime. They want to see you. *He* wants to see you."

My stomach rolls. Six years is a long time, but it's also nowhere near long enough. Nowhere near.

"A car will be with you in half an hour. No need to pack your outfit for tonight. I'll have something here for you."

I swallow around the lump in my throat. For a car to be here so soon, it's clear that informing me was more of an afterthought than a courtesy.

"Love you, bye!" She disconnects the call before I can say a word.

It takes me a minute, the phone still to my ear, before I finally let my hand fall to my side.

Even though I knew it was only a matter of time before he showed up and turned my life upside down, I didn't expect it to be so soon.

This was going to be my year, but I should have known better.

ZAK

Tugging off my helmet, I grab my towel and wipe the sweat from my face, breathing hard. I go to the gym four times a week, but it's nothing compared with the cardio of lacrosse practice. At my side, Sol pushes his hair from his forehead and tosses me my water bottle.

"That was intense," I wheeze, shaking my head as I gulp at the cold liquid. My phone sits on the bench next to my towel and I tap the screen, my heart sinking to see that Jaime hasn't replied. Not that she had anything to reply to. When her text had come through right at the end of a water break, I'd typed out my reply without thinking. A rookie mistake. I can't afford to miss opportunities like that.

Sol scoffs, tipping his head back and chugging his own water. Coach Pearson is working us harder than ever this year, and we've already played and won one of the preseason friendlies, with the next this weekend against Seattle. As much as I love lacrosse, I'm glad we only have a couple weeks of this. It's far too fucking cold for a start.

"It's just not the same when the grass crunches under your feet, is it?" Sol says, reading my thoughts.

I grunt in agreement and head in the direction of the locker room, steam rising from my body like I'm a freaking vampire in sunlight. Every step of the way, I feel Sol's questioning gaze on my back. He doesn't press me, though. In fact, he doesn't say a single word while we shower and change with the rest of the team. I know he's trying to do the right thing, but his thoughtful silence only makes things worse.

"Just ask," I snap as we trudge our way across the common toward the Den. "I can't take any more."

"Relax, man." Sol holds his hands up in mock surrender. "I know these early morning practices suck after having the summer off, but you're never usually this grumpy. I'm worried."

I shake my head. The truth is, I'm worried, too. Ever since I bumped into Jaime in Portland, she's been on my mind. My obsession might be a running joke, but I haven't actually spent every waking hour of the last three years thinking about her. Although, apparently, that *is* something I do now.

This must be what addiction feels like. I had one little taste, and now all I can think about is how to get more. It's a freaking minefield, though. After she gave me her number at the party, I was reluctant to text her in case I came on too strong and scared her away. So, when she messaged me first, to tell me about getting the internship, I couldn't believe it. And then I didn't give her a reason to text back.

Maybe I should text her.

Fuck.

"Seriously." Sol reaches out and clasps my shoulder. "Whatever it is, I promise I won't give you shit about it."

"You know what it's about."

He winces. "Jaime?"

"Jaime."

He doesn't say another word as we make our way up the winding gravel path to the Den, and I sigh in relief as I push open the door to be greeted by the warmth of the lit fireplace. I dump my kit bag unceremoniously in the entry hall and head through to our side of the Den. Both living rooms are free to be used by any of the twenty-one wolves, but one side is reverently left unoccupied for our triad.

Alex is already sprawled in his favorite chair, a laptop open on his thighs and a pensive frown on his face. I nod at him when he looks up and throw myself down in my chair, draping my legs over the arm and closing my eyes.

"Practice that good, huh?" Alex asks.

I grunt and he doesn't press any further.

A minute later, something hard smacks me in the chest and I open my eyes to find a packet of peanut M&Ms nestled in my sweatshirt. Looking up, I watch Sol settle into his chair, his phone in his hand.

"Thanks, man," I say, already feeling a little lighter as I tear open the packet.

Alex makes a gagging noise to my left. "It's not even ten in the morning and you're already eating that shit?"

In answer, I throw four of the brightly colored candies into my mouth and turn to face him, chewing with my mouth open.

Alex wrinkles his nose and turns back to his screen. "You're a fucking disgrace."

"You going to tell us or what?" Sol asks.

I turn my head his way, holding up the packet. "Is that what this was? A bribe?"

"Abso-fucking-lutely. Now spill."

I don't even know where to start. Staring at the flickering flames in the enormous fireplace, I try to sift through the reasons behind my mood but fail. In some ways I'm no closer to Jaime than I have been any other year, but at the same time, there's something different. I just can't quite put my finger on it.

"Has Jaime ever dated?" I ask, already knowing the answer.

Alex laughs, his attention never leaving his screen. "You're her stalker. If you don't know, no one does."

"Helpful." I scowl. "Thank you."

"No. She's never had a boyfriend," Sol offers.

"Yeah, but she definitely hooked up at least once."

My head whips to Alex. "She what now?"

He looks up, glancing between me and Sol. "Sophomore year, I ran into her in the hallway the morning after a party. Pretty sure she hooked up with Hodgson."

Hodgson graduated last year, so I can't kick his ass. My teeth clench. "Why the fuck don't I know about this?"

Alex shrugs. "Because I knew it would upset you."

I shake my head. "I can't believe this. I'm a big boy, I could have taken it. I was seeing Ariana that year."

"Exactly. This happened, like, a week after you broke it off with her."

I open my mouth to argue but snap it shut. As much as I hate to admit it, Alex is right. It would have destroyed me. It still fucking hurts now and the news is over a year old.

"Maybe it's time to admit that *you're* the problem," Alex says.

I don't even look at him. "Fuck off."

He laughs to himself, but his teasing words wedge themselves uncomfortably between my ribs. *Am* I the problem? Part of me says no because she hasn't had another boyfriend. Getting a little drunk and scratching an itch doesn't have to mean anything. I mean, I would have been more than willing to help her out, but clearly, she didn't take that avenue.

"Or maybe," Alex drawls. "Jaime is a distraction from a bigger problem."

"What are you talking about?" I turn my head toward him, shifting so he can enjoy the full force of my confused expression.

"I mean," he says, glancing at Sol again. "Maybe there's something bigger that you're avoiding by putting all of your focus on Jaime."

"I'm sorry," I say. "When did you change your major to psychiatry? Did I miss a memo?"

Alex shrugs and goes back to his laptop.

Angrily crunching on a handful of sugar-coated peanuts, and avoiding Sol's stare, I pretend Alex's words haven't wormed their way under my skin. My stomach clenches in a way that I don't think has anything to do with my sugar consumption as echoes of the conversation I had with Jaime at Joe For Joe sound in my head.

Am I really lacking direction? I guess I am. But having no plans after college is normal for a lot of people. Just because I'm not walking into a high-powered job doesn't mean anything. Lots of people haven't got it all figured out by twenty-two. I'm not worried.

I glare at Alex out of the corner of my eye. *Asshole.*

No. Any worry I'm feeling is solely about Jaime. And that's only because there's so much more pressure to make things happen. We're already more than halfway through September. There are only eight months left for me to convince Jaime that I'm everything she needs.

"Have you ever considered you might not actually get along?" Sol's voice breaks through my thoughts.

I turn my head to look at him. "What?"

"I mean, have you spent any time alone together? Do you even have anything in common?"

"We have lots in common," I retort. "And we actually had coffee in Portland last week."

Sol's eyebrows shoot up. "You what? Why didn't you tell me?"

I shrug. "I don't tell you everything."

"Yes, you fucking do. Even if it's shit I don't want to know."

Rolling my eyes, I return my gaze to the fire. I don't need dating advice from either of them. Alex is an unapologetic manwhore who I can't imagine settling down before he's fifty, if ever. And Sol hasn't had a relationship the entire time we've been at Franklin West. No. I need to trust my gut. It hasn't steered me wrong so far, and it's telling me to step things up. I've been biding my time, but that can't be my play anymore. No more waiting.

Tugging my phone from the pocket of my sweats, I pull up her contact.

> When can I take you out for a celebratory coffee?

I go to put it back in my pocket, but it vibrates in my hand, and I lift it back to my face in surprise.

> I'm on my way to the airport, so not anytime soon

> Airport? Where you going? Is it to do with the internship?

I watch the screen, waiting for her response. Where the hell is she going mid-week this early in the semester? A jolt of nervous energy shoots in my gut as I wonder whether something bad happened. Maybe it's something to do with her family . . .

> Florida. And no. I wish

She's originally from Florida, so maybe it *is* something to do with her family. If she wanted to tell me what was going on, she would have, so I resign myself to scowling at the screen as I hold back from pressing for more information.

> Any idea when you'll be back?

> As soon as I can

I blow out a slow breath. Vague as hell. I might be reading into things, but her response makes me think it's not a sick or dying relative.

> Well, let me know when you're back and we can celebrate. K?

She responds to my message with a thumbs up, and I sigh.

"Are you done?" Alex asks, his eyebrows raised as he peers at me from over his laptop. "That was like a lesson on the many ways to expel air."

"Fuck off."

Sol's questioning gaze bores into me like it has all morning, but I keep my attention on my phone, staring at our conversation. I know from articles in The Howl that Jaime's top of her class, winning some sort of award or special recognition every year. It really wasn't a surprise that she got that internship. I have no doubt that if she wants to take over the world, she will.

My gaze moves past my phone to Alex, who's frowning at his laptop again. His father owns half the East Coast, and I know Alex is going straight to a top-level position at his company after graduation—right into a world of board meetings and expensive suits.

I glance over at where Sol's tapping away on his phone. He's already applying to internships for next year where he'll train as a physical therapist for disabled athletes.

Goals. Dreams. And I have no doubt that my two best friends will make every one of them come true. Jaime, too. I'm happy for them.

But what about me? It's not that I don't have options. It's that none of those options make me feel . . . anything. Jaime's the only thing besides lacrosse that's ever made me feel excited, and even I know that's not enough.

My mood sinks further as I realize maybe I am a little more worried about the future than I thought. Being surrounded by people with such clear goals certainly doesn't help. Maybe I should just take my mom up on her offer and take a position at CHIPnique. Maybe I'll like it.

My fingers reach for another M&M, but then fall to my stomach, my appetite suddenly gone.

BE

Florida is humid as hell. It's been a while since I've been home at this time of year. Most of my summer was spent between Bali and the West Coast—totally not avoiding my family—and as I step out of the town car and my sunglasses steam up, I realize I haven't actually set foot in my family home since Christmas last year, because our family spent Thanksgiving at our cabin in Whistler.

Standing in the paved courtyard, staring up at the white pillars and foreboding black doors, I steel myself for what awaits me on the other side. I've barely taken a step forward when the doors swing open, and three women come rushing out.

"Miss Jaime! Hurry, hurry!"

Despite the horrors that lay ahead of me, I smile as Mary, my childhood nanny and housekeeper, comes hurrying down the steps, her long black hair piled into a messy bun barely touched by gray despite approaching sixty. Not far behind her are Lotta, our head of housekeeping, and Rosalita, who's responsible for looking after the women of the house. These three women have been more present in my life than my own mother, and my heart swells at the sight of them. Not that they give me chance to greet them properly.

"Too skinny, Miss Jaime," Mary chides as she wraps her hand around my arm and tugs me toward the house. She's worked for my family in the States for the last thirty years, but her thick Filipino accent remains unaffected.

In contrast, Lotta's German accent is a hilarious mashup of harsh Bavarian interspersed with rounded American vowels. "We only have two hours to get you ready," she clips as they usher me through the foyer. Despite her harsh tone, and the sharp angles of her face, her gray eyes are nothing but warm as she looks me over for signs of neglect.

"*Dios mío*," Rosalita mutters, and I stifle a laugh at the stress my mother appears to have put these incredible women under.

Rosalita was the last to join my mother's faithful team, appearing when I was nine. Her husband tends to our gardens and their son cleans our pools and maintains the sports facilities. My cheeks heat at the thought of Jordy. Watching him during high school as he cleaned the pool with his shirt off had been my sexual awakening.

As we ascend one of the sweeping onyx staircases that lead to the upper floor, I barely have time to glance around for any sign of my mother. She'll be here somewhere, though. The enormous chandeliers hanging between the staircases from the tall ceiling are different, I notice. No longer the dripping crystal that's hung almost to the floor since I was a child, but long shards of twisting blue and black glass, which I have to admit compliments the rest of the house's décor beautifully.

"Take a breath, ladies," I say, extracting myself from

Mary's iron grip as we reach the top of the stairs. "Two hours is plenty of time. I'm not that much of a mess."

My nonchalance is met with exasperated responses in three languages, and I roll my eyes again, allowing myself to be hauled into my bedroom and promptly stripped of the dove gray Alo Yoga cashmere set I'm wearing. I learned a long time ago it's easier to just let them do what they want and, seeing as all three of them have either bathed me or changed my diapers at some point in my life, I don't bat an eyelid as they all but throw me in the warm, lavender scented bath already waiting for me.

There's a long list of reasons I wanted to go to college at Franklin West. The top three being: it's as far away from my family as I can get without leaving the country, my dad is on the board, so my place was a given, and it's filled with the offspring of the country's elite.

It took me a while to realize that my family was different growing up—that the reporters hanging around the gated entrance to our estate and harassing my parents as we ate at exclusive Michelin Star restaurants wasn't normal.

I knew we were richer than most, of course. I just didn't know why. That, I discovered as a sophomore in high school, when Sebastian Cowling marched up to me in the cafeteria and threw a blueberry smoothie in my face. I'd been too shocked to respond. I may have been one of the most popular girls in school, but I was liked. Not only on the cheer squad, but on the debate team and an active member of the NHS, too. He'd yelled about how my family had ruined his life, and I'd just gaped at him in confusion.

Primus et Optimus Export Trading Company, or PEO, had always sounded boring to me, but that year, I realized that my father was one of the most influential and wealthy businessmen in North America. When I'd confronted my parents in tears after school, I'd discovered that the Cowling's company had been doing business with my father, but had been caught in an embezzlement scandal, so PEO had cut ties.

It was then, I started to dig. My ignorance to my own family history had astounded me. My father, Mason Smith, is a big deal. Like, a huge deal. His family can be traced back to the original families to make it big in America, his money coming from hundreds of years of tobacco and cotton exports before branching out after the 1800s.

Sebastian Cowling didn't come back to school after that day.

"*¿Cómo te sientes?*" Rosalita whispers in my ear as they scrub me within an inch of my life, preparing me for the hair and makeup crew I can already hear setting up in the dressing room.

"Nervous," I admit, before I can think better of it. It's the truth, though. "Where's Mother?"

"Terrorizing Francesca in the kitchen is my guess," Lotta grunts, holding up a large fluffy towel for me as I step out of the bath.

I smile, knowing she's probably right. It's not that I'm not close to my parents, it's just that . . . Okay, I'm not close to my parents. I'm almost one hundred percent certain they only had me to continue the family line. Dad's always been busy with work, barely in the same city, let alone country, and Mom is always busy with her various charities and events. Her own family is oil-rich from Texas, their marriage seemingly more strategic than romantic.

"Is Dad here?" I ask, realizing I might see him for the first time in months.

"Yes, Miss Jaime," Mary says, shooing me onto the stool

at my sprawling vanity. "He flew in from Hong Kong yesterday."

Huh. I hadn't even known he was out of the country.

I don't recognize the man and woman lunging at me with brushes and powders as I stare blankly at my reflection, but then, it's been a while since I've been subjected to this ridiculousness, so they might be new.

Behind me, I spot Lotta unzipping a garment case and I must admit, the dress my mother has chosen for me is stunning.

"It's bespoke Alberta Ferretti," Lotta says, catching my interested gaze in the mirror.

My eyebrows shoot up, causing the man currently painting my face to mutter under his breath.

It's gorgeous. Consisting of floor-length swathes of midnight blue silk and black lace, with a boned bustier, it's simple yet elegant. Almost something I would have chosen myself.

Unlike everything else in my life.

My fingers itch to reach for my purse to see if Longstead's secretary has sent through the email yet. If I'm supposed to start tomorrow, I'll scream. He's already made it clear he doesn't think I'm cut out for the internship, and if I have to call to say I can't make the first day because I'm across the country, it's only going to make him think he's right.

At the thought of my phone, my mind strays to Zak. I'd wondered if he'd message again after leaving the ball in my court. I can't decide whether his lack of forcefulness is intriguing or annoying. It's selfish of me to want him to chase me. I don't want to lead him on. It's the reason I've never let things progress past mild flirting. The kiss we shared in freshman year made it clear that Zak Aldridge is not someone I could just fuck out of my system. It would never be 'just' a one-night stand.

I get lost in my thoughts as people clean up around me and I'm fastened into my dress. It's only when Lotta coughs, that I blink and realize I'm standing in front of the mirror looking like a completely different person than I was when I arrived.

My hair has been styled into a chic chignon, my makeup flawless. I must ask them which lipstick they used because the matt plum compliments the golden tones of my brown skin perfectly. Of course, the dress fits like a dream. It was a risk ordering bespoke when I haven't seen them for so long, my mother assuming I hadn't put on weight since the last time I visited. Luckily for all of us, her gamble paid off.

I give a little twirl, momentarily forgetting the shit show that tonight will bring, and enjoying the feeling of being a princess for a heartbeat.

"You look stunning," Lotta says, her gray eyes a little glassy.

Beside her, Rosalita, and Mary agree, both gazing up at me like petite fairy godmothers. All too soon, their adoring expressions turn to concern, and they step away in a silent signal that there's nothing left to do but go downstairs.

My heart slams against my ribs as Rosalita and Lotta pull open the double doors and I step back out into the hallway, my blue velvet Manolo Blahnik pumps sinking into the plush carpet. Voices are already rising from downstairs, the familiar deep baritone of my father's voice mixed with unfamiliar laughter. My pulse kicks up a notch.

It's been so long since I saw my parents, and even though I knew entertaining their guests would take precedence, it still stings a little that they couldn't spare me five minutes to come and say hello.

Gripping the front of my dress in my fingers, I descend the staircase with the same dread I'm sure I'd feel if I were on my way to be sentenced for murder. The people waiting for me in our sixteen-seater dining room are simultaneously my future and the end of everything.

The voices get louder as a door opens and I blink in surprise to find my father striding to the bottom of the stairs to greet me. Someone must have informed him that I was on my way down.

His smile is warm as he watches me take the final steps, his arms outstretched. The black tailored suit he's wearing enhances his powerful frame, and I notice that his light brown beard and coiffed hair are speckled with gray. I can't remember if they were the last time I saw him. His skin is tanned, a little pink on the nose, which tells me he's been out on the water. Despite both me and Mom lecturing him on the dangers of skin cancer, he's always been awful at remembering to wear protection.

"You look stunning, darling," he says, pulling me to him and pressing a kiss to my forehead. "I'm sorry I haven't seen much of you lately. I feel like all I've done is blink, and you've turned from a teenager to a young woman."

I give him a small smile. "How was Hong Kong?"

"Sticky." He grimaces. "Much the same as here."

He links his arm with mine and steers me toward the dining room and it's hard to breathe. Panic rips through me and all I can think about is pulling from his grasp and running. Running through the doors and down the paved path and never stopping. I'd leave it all behind to escape this. I'd give up everything. I can't do this.

By the time we reach the door, I can hardly breathe.

Whether my dad notices, I have no idea. Either way, he doesn't slow, gently continuing to pull me forward.

A member of the hired waiting staff opens the door as we approach, and an almost inaudible whimper escapes my throat as everyone in the room stops talking and turns to us.

"Jaime!" Mrs. Chevalier steps forward, her white-blonde hair bouncing and her Botox-laced face stretching into what I think is a warm smile as her British accent echoes against the walls. "It's been an age, darling. Just look at you. You're simply stunning."

"Agreed," her husband says, looking me up and down in the same way I've seen my father appraise a racehorse. *"Vous êtes une vision."*

I try for as long as possible not to look at the third person, standing beside them.

"Jaime," my father prompts, squeezing my hand where it clutches his arm in a death grip. "Say hello to your fiancé."

BE

I was just six years old when my future was taken from me. Signed away with a handshake and a glass of expensive bourbon while I played with dolls in the garden.

Louis steps forward, his golden hair swept back from his face and his blue eyes wide as they meet mine.

"Jaime," he says, reaching for my hand and bringing it to his lips. "You look breathtaking."

I'm painfully aware that I haven't said a word, but I don't know what to say. I haven't seen Louis for six years. It didn't feel real back then—when I was sixteen and he was almost twenty—that one day we'd be getting married. Back then, I was crushing on the captain of the soccer team during the week and wearing skimpy bikinis around Jordy on the weekends.

He's very pretty. With neat blond hair, light blue eyes, and a square jaw, he's somewhere between Prince Charming and a Ken Doll. Sixteen-year-old me figured marrying him wouldn't be the worst thing in the world. But now, it's different. *Now*, it's real. Sixteen-year-old me was little more than a naïve child swept up in the romance of it all. A fairytale. I mentally scoff.

"Jamie?"

I blink at my mother's voice, turning to find her at my father's other side. It's only when I follow her pointed gaze that I realize I'm still clinging to his arm like a life raft. Reluctantly, I let go.

"It's a pleasure to see you again," I manage to force out, the words a little breathless.

"Shall we sit?" Mother gives me a look that might be concern but might also be a warning. It's hard to tell sometimes.

She looks stunning, as always. Her thin black braids are piled high on her head, accentuating her gold-dusted cheekbones and heavily lined eyes. Her deep red dress and matching lipstick bring out the rich umber of her skin. She looks like a goddess. Beautiful and powerful.

As I take my seat beside her at the long table, I try not to stiffen when Louis takes the seat to my right. At least sitting beside me, I don't have to look at him all night.

The server hands me a glass of champagne, and I take it and bring it to my lips, ready to down it in one go before Mother clears her throat, and I pause, realizing it's for a toast.

"Here's to new ventures," my father says, raising his glass at the head of the table.

Everyone raises their glasses, repeating his words. I down my champagne in one go.

"How was Oxford, Louis?" my mother asks.

He chuckles, low and warm. "Intense. In all honesty, I'm glad to see the back of it. Although, my MBA was very enlightening."

"We certainly have a lot to discuss while you're here," Father says, leaning back in his chair with a warm smile.

I resign myself to sitting back and staying out of it. I'm not a quiet person. I'm certainly not shy. Staying silent and sipping my refilled champagne goes against everything I love about myself, but I press my spine against the padded dining chair and suck it up.

Maybe that's why I am so outspoken at college. Perhaps I'm making up for the demure mask I'm forced to wear around my parents. The thought makes me half-choke on a mouthful of champagne. My future therapist will get a kick out of this.

Then a thought slams to the front of my brain and I tighten my grip on the thin stem of my glass. What if Louis likes this quiet, 'seen and not heard' act I'm putting on? What if he hates loud and opinionated? Panic seeps back into my veins at the thought of having to wear this mask for the rest of my life.

"Please, excuse me," I mutter, pushing away from the table. "I'll be right back."

Conversation halts as I stride from the room with as much calm as I can muster, but I only make it as far as the stairs before a hand grips my upper arm.

"Jaime," my mother hisses. "What are you doing?"

I pull out of her grip and turn to face her. "I'm going to the restroom, Mom. Is that okay?"

Her expression relaxes and she exhales. "Oh. I thought you were planning on disappearing."

"Disappearing?" I laugh. "Is that even an option?"

"Be quick," she says, ignoring my comment, and turning back toward the dining room. "They're serving the appetizers."

Instead of answering, I kick off my shoes, hitch up my

dress and jog up the stairs. I don't need the restroom. I need my phone.

Being here, with him, I feel untethered, as though I've woken up from a dream only to find myself in a nightmare. Franklin West feels like another life—another world—even though I was only there this morning.

A strangled laugh escapes me as I reach the top of the stairs. How is that even possible? Lying on my bed, daydreaming about a future that was never mine, seems like years ago.

My room is empty of people, no evidence to show that an entire production crew was ever here. My bag is still on my bed where Mary left it and I all but dive for it, digging out my phone. There are two missed calls from Abi and a text message asking me to call her when I see her message.

> Mom summoned me home. At awkward family dinner. I'll call later

My heart pounding, I pull up Zak's text thread and type out a message before I lose the nerve.

> Friday morning. Grinds?

It doesn't mean anything. We're just friends. Coffee isn't a date. My phone vibrates with a reply from Abi, and I huff a laugh.

> You're in ducking FLORIDA? WTH?

Smiling to myself, I send a shrugging emoji before forcing myself to put the phone back in my bag. Then, I take a breath and make my way quickly back down the stairs.

Although Mom gives me a stern look as I take my seat, no one else seems bothered that I disappeared for five minutes. Everyone's halfway through their steak tartare but I just push mine around my plate a little. I have zero appetite, even though I haven't eaten since grabbing breakfast at the airport.

Thankfully, Louis doesn't try to talk to me during dinner, allowing me to get quietly buzzed on the champagne while the men talk business, and the women talk charity work and holidays. It's all tediously cliché.

I'm so bored out of my skull that when Louis does eventually turn to me, it takes me a second to realize he's talking.

"Sorry," I say, blinking at him. "What did you say?"

He smiles, the corners of his eyes crinkling. "I asked whether you'd care to show me the gardens before dessert?"

I really don't want to be alone with him, but I'd also rather gnaw off my own leg than stay in this room, so it turns out, he's the lesser of two evils.

"Sure," I say, rising to my feet. "Let's go."

We excuse ourselves amidst a room filled with heart eyes and walk in uncomfortable silence toward the French doors that lead to the garden. It's still humid out, but the breeze from the ocean is cool and overall, it's bearable. Which is more than I can say for my company.

I lead him down the path toward the Japanese garden my mother had planted a few years ago, aiming toward the saltwater infinity pool. We're almost at the end of the gardens when he finally speaks.

"How's your final year of college going?" he asks.

I shrug, absentmindedly thinking that Abi would be drooling on her designer sneakers at his fancy British accent. "I've barely experienced it. Classes only started a couple of weeks ago and now I'm missing this week, so I'm already behind."

The words come out more bitter than I intend, and he draws to a halt, his eyes narrowing as he looks down at me.

"I know this is strange."

I huff a small laugh. "That's one way to put it."

He glances at me, his hair almost silver under the faint light reaching us from the house behind. "Yes, but this *is* happening. It's going to benefit both our families, which means it benefits us, too. We may as well embrace it."

I press my lips together. Are those his words, or the words his parents have recited to him since he was old enough to know what was going on? They sound eerily similar to the ones I've heard a thousand times myself.

"Sure."

I start walking before he can press the matter further.

The Chevaliers are the European version of us. Louis' mom is old money rich, her family involved in export trade dating back to the British Empire, and his dad is a mogul in the French textile industry, worth billions.

Even before I was born, my dad was trying to find a way to buy them out or forge a partnership, but the problem with old money is that they don't like to give up the legacy. Claude Chevalier would only merge companies if he knew his heir was still going to take over one day. My dad was of the same mind.

"I'm serious, Jaime," Louis says, reaching for my hand and tugging gently until I stop. "This doesn't have to be awkward. We don't have to be unhappy. Give us a chance. Please don't write this off before we've even got to know each other."

A twinge of guilt twists in my stomach. It's easy to feel like the only victim here, but he's in the same boat as me. It could be a lot worse, and I'm well aware there are hundreds, if not thousands, of women who would kick my ass for turning my nose up at a snagging a handsome billionaire.

I sigh, offering a small smile. "I'm sorry. It's just, this was all sprung on me this morning."

Louis' eyes widen and I realize again how my words must have sounded.

"Not the engagement, of course," I correct. "My mom sent a car for me at college and then several hours later I was here. It threw me for a loop and I'm still trying to get my feet back under me."

He smiles, squeezing my hand. "That's understandable. And I apologize for the abruptness. That's entirely my fault. We were planning on coming next weekend, but my schedule changed unexpectedly so we had to grab this opportunity."

I nod and he reaches for my other hand, his thumbs rubbing slow circles over my skin.

"I wanted to see you, Jaime," he says quietly. "I wish I could say I haven't looked at photographs of you on the internet like a stalker, but I'd be lying."

An unexpected laugh bursts from me and I look up to find him smiling. I don't say anything because I haven't googled him—I haven't looked for him—because I've spent the last few years trying to pretend that this wasn't going to happen.

"You're even more stunning in person," he says, drawing me closer. "I'm honored to call you my fiancée, Jaime, and I look forward to getting to know the brains behind the beauty."

My eyes widen as I look up at him. *My future husband.* No, I didn't choose this. Yes, I'm bitter as fuck about it. But he's right. Does it have to be so bad? Maybe not. It's a bitter pill to swallow, but maybe—just maybe—the aftertaste will be sweet.

As if reading my thoughts, Louis dips his head, slow enough to give me time to pull away or offer my cheek, but I don't. Our lips meet in a soft, barely-there kiss, and I let him linger a second before pulling away.

"I have something for you," he says, releasing my hands.

My heart picks up as he reaches inside his blazer and pulls out a small red box. I have a very good idea what's inside, and so many emotions slam through me in quick succession, my head spins.

"I hope you like it." Louis opens the box, revealing a beautiful Cartier engagement ring. "It was my grandmother's."

I have no idea what to say, so I say nothing as he pulls the ring free, slipping the box back in his pocket.

"This isn't a proposal," he says, slipping the ring on my finger. "Because our fathers already took care of that."

A soft laugh escapes me, and I stare down at the sparkling jewel on my finger, wondering how he managed to have it sized so perfectly.

"This ring is a promise," he continues, and I look up from the ring to meet his gaze. "I want us to have a relationship, Jaime. I want to be happy with you, and you with me. So, please wear this ring, knowing that I endeavor to make that happen for us."

I swallow, only managing to nod in response. What he's said makes sense and once again I'm reminded that he's had as little say as I have in this situation. His own future decided at ten-years-old. I remember playing with him back then. The little blond boy with the funny accent who liked to play hide and seek.

The difference is, while Louis has grown up being

groomed to take over the empire, my parents have sat back and let me do as I want. It's something I've been grateful for because I've never wanted to take the reins of PEO.

Now, I realize that was never an option. Perhaps it was when I was born, but ever since this alliance was decided between the Smiths and the Chevaliers, I've had one purpose and one purpose alone: To marry Louis, combining our empires, and produce an heir.

Maybe part of me has always known this, but I've pushed it down, convinced I can still have the life I want.

My smile is forced as Louis kisses my cheek and takes my arm, steering us back toward the house. He says that the ring on my finger is a promise, but it feels a hell of a lot like I've been sentenced.

ZAK

ΑΨΔ

Pouring another shot of the tequila I confiscated from Alex, I glance around for any sight of him. After a huge fight with Sasha, he spent most of the day in bed, only dragging himself out to find more booze. Alex hates tequila. I wince as I knock it back. I don't think I'm a big fan either.

It's not a big party tonight. The annual Thanksgiving Blow Out doesn't have caterers like the opening party. This is a good old-fashioned frat party. Franklin West has a longer break for Thanksgiving, thanks to the rich benefactors who moaned that the three-day weekend wasn't long enough to enjoy their ski chalets or desert islands. Either way, I'm certainly not complaining about a week off.

I spot Sol and call out to him. "Where's Alex?"

"He was right here a second ago."

Sighing, I put down my shot glass. "I'm gonna go look for him."

Of course, he's not the only one I'm looking for. It's been a fucking month since I've seen Jaime. When she got back from Florida, she sent me a message saying maybe coffee wasn't the best idea and we should leave it.

Leave it.

There's nothing to leave. It isn't like it was going to be a date. I analyzed our text thread until I was seeing double, but I have no fucking clue what I did wrong. I've even taken to waiting around in the common when I know she's due to finish class, but either she's leaving out of some secret exit I don't know about, or she's not going to class.

I have no idea if she's here tonight. If she's avoiding me like I think she is, she won't be.

Fuck.

I was getting so damn close. She might not be avoiding me, though. I can almost hear my dad's voice telling me 'it's not always about you'. He'd be right, too. I have no idea what happened in Florida. And that makes it worse. I need to know that she's okay.

Looping back through to the entrance hall, I spot Sol standing with Wes Bowers looking seven shades of awkward. I grin, feeling lighter than I have all week at the opportunity to be The Best Wingman Ever. Those two have been tiptoeing around each for weeks, and I'm just the man to give them a gentle shove in the right direction.

Tugging my sweater off, I shout to get my friend's attention. "Hey, Sol?"

He looks at me in confusion as I throw the balled-up clothing at him.

"Do me a favor and put that in my room for me?" I wink. "Not on my bed, though."

It takes everything I have not to laugh as Sol's face reddens, but I keep marching past, heading back to where Trey is on the decks, the music loud enough to vibrate my bones.

Pausing, I lean against a wall and survey the crowd. The good thing about being six-four, is I can see above crowds like a fucking periscope. I scan the heaving mass of bodies looking for one person and one person only. Determination settles in the slosh of tequila lining my gut. If she's not here, fuck it. I'm going over to the Hive and asking her what the hell's going on. I've got nothing to lose after—

My heart skips, my eyes widening as I spot her over by the kitchen chatting to a freshman I don't recognize. *Shit.* She's here.

Smoothing the front of my burgundy button down, I make my way through the party toward her, never daring to take my eyes off her, in case she slips away.

She doesn't see me coming until I'm less than a couple yards from her, and then her smile falls. That fucking kills me. My steps slow and I come to a stop. She doesn't want to see me. The freshman she's talking to hasn't even realized that Jaime's not listening to whatever she's jabbering on about.

A sense of finality washes over me like a tidal wave. I'm a fool. I've been chasing after this woman for years, pinning everything on the chemistry of a single kiss, and she's never going to be mine. She's fucking disappointed to see me. This is the wakeup call I needed back in freshman year. Has she always looked like this when I walk over? Have I been blind to it? Sol and Alex have been trying to get me to see sense all this time and I thought they were wrong. What if they're not?

I start to turn away.

"Zak?"

My eyes close briefly at Jaime's voice, raised over the music, then I paste a smile on my face and turn back around. "Hey."

The freshman looks between us and then says something to Jaime before disappearing into the crowd, leaving us alone. Well, as alone as you can be in a crowded kitchen filled with drunk college students.

"Enjoying the party?" she asks.

I shrug, all jokes and lighthearted comments just out of reach. The past month has exhausted me, and now, standing in front of her, it catches me up.

Jaime looks stunning as usual, in a black leather miniskirt, knee high boots and a cute little white cropped sweater. I stare at the strip of brown skin visible between her sweater and her skirt, wondering if it's as soft and warm as it looks. I swallow and force my gaze back up to her eyes.

"I haven't seen you around," I say, stepping closer so I don't need to shout over the music.

She drops her gaze to her drink, her hair falling over her shoulders in loose waves, and I reach out and touch her arm, causing her to look back up at me in question.

"Can we go somewhere and talk?" I ask.

Jaime stares up at me, her deep brown eyes searching my face, although I don't know what she's looking for. After an eternity, she nods her agreement, and I exhale in relief.

There's nowhere to talk downstairs and it's cold as fuck outside, so I snatch a bottle of vodka and two cups from the counter and head to my room.

Shit. I realize halfway up the first flight of stairs that I sent Sol there with Wes. I have no idea whether anything's happening between them, but I sure as hell don't want to walk in and ruin it for him. Sol's room is on the top floor, next to Alex's, so I decide to take her there instead.

By the time we start up the second flight, the music noticeably quieter up here, Jaime finally speaks. "Your room's on the top floor?"

I shake my head, glancing back over my shoulder at her.

"I'm on the second floor, but Sol's in my room. Long story. So, we're going to borrow his room."

"It's so weird," she says as we climb the final few steps. "Sol's room is my room in the Hive. I've never been up here before. I don't think I realized how similar it is. I should have. It makes sense given the rest of the house."

A rush of jealousy floods through me. She might not have been up to the top floor, but she's spent the night in one of the rooms in the Den. The fact that someone else got to have her, and it wasn't me, makes my blood boil.

Fishing my keys from my pocket, I find Sol's and slip it in the lock.

"You have keys to each other's rooms?" she asks. "Cute."

I push open the door and flick on the light, thankful that he's made the bed at least, as I gesture for her to come in. Honestly, Sol's room is always pretty tidy. Tidier than mine for sure.

I close the door quietly and watch as she pokes at the lacrosse gear and trophies scattered around.

"So, where have you been?" I ask.

Jaime turns and leans against Sol's desk. "My internship started the Friday I got back from Florida. I'm there three days a week."

I raise my eyebrows. "Three days? That's . . . a lot."

She unleashes a heavy sigh. "You're telling me. It's been intense. My professor has been super understanding and Wes is helping tons by taking notes and recording classes I miss."

"How's the internship going, though? Is it worth it?"

Something flashes across her face, but it's replaced by a smile before I can pin it down. "Yeah. It's tough but I love it."

The bottle of vodka I swiped is heavy in my hand, so I

walk over to the desk and place the red solo cups down beside where she's leaning. Unscrewing the cap, I pour us both a shot.

For a second, I think she's going to refuse, but then she picks it up and knocks it with mine.

"Here's to the gateway to adulthood."

I laugh. "Sure."

We knock back our drinks and I pour us another one. This time, she holds my gaze as she throws it back, and the anger in her eyes causes me to almost choke.

"What's wrong?" I ask.

She places her cup down and picks up the bottle, pouring a hell of a lot more than a shot. "Why would anything be wrong?"

I narrow my eyes, taking the cup she shoves at me. "Because you were okay a second ago and now you look pissed."

She takes a long sip of her drink, wincing as she swallows. It might be top shelf vodka, but it still packs a punch as it goes down.

"Maybe I am," she says, glaring at the clear liquid in her cup.

"Maybe you're what?"

"Pissed."

I shift awkwardly. I don't want to sit down on Sol's bed in case she thinks I'm trying to hint, and his desk chair is tucked in next to where Jaime's leaning. All I can do is stand in the middle of his room like a fucking tree, clutching my cup of vodka like a security blanket.

"Are you pissed at *me*?" I ask, already regretting asking the question.

She barks a laugh. "Definitely."

Even though I was expecting the answer, I frown. "Why? What did I do?"

"Nothing," she snaps. "Everything."

"Are you drunk?"

Her gaze locks on mine and she puts her cup down on the desk. "No. I'm not."

"Can I ask why you're angry with me? Considering you've been hiding from me since you got back from Florida." I try to inject a teasing tone into my voice, but even I can't hear it.

"Why won't you let this go?" She pushes away from the desk, stepping toward me. "It was one kiss, Zak. Why won't you leave me alone?"

Her words sting and I wince. "It wasn't just one kiss, Kitty Cat. It was a fucking great kiss."

Her gaze drops to my mouth, and I know she's remembering. But the same rush of guilt I felt downstairs washes over me again. How one-sided has this game of cat and mouse been?

I take a breath. "Jaime, if you honestly, truly, want me to stay away from you, I will. I'm sorry if I upset you. That's the last thing I would ever want to do to you."

She watches me, blinks, then lets out a loud groan. "Seriously? Can't you just stop?"

I place my cup down on the window ledge, starting to wonder whether bringing her up here was the world's worst idea. "Stop what?"

"Stop being, so . . ." She pauses, gesticulating at me wildly. "I don't know . . . Tall."

A laugh bursts from me. "Sorry, Kitty Cat. I can't do anything about that."

Jaime groans again. "You're making this so hard."

"I think you'll find that's the other way around."

She props a hand on her hip and glares at me in a way that's so freaking cute, I can't help but grin.

"Look, I'm not doing anything," I say, taking a step closer. "I'm just standing here trying to be your friend. You're the one making this hard."

I only mean to tease her, but her eyes shutter and she looks away.

"You have no idea what you're talking about," she says. "You know what? This was stupid. I should go."

She steps toward the door, but I block her way, my hands raised in front of me. "Say it, Jaime. Look me in the eyes and tell me you don't want me. Want this. That you've never wanted this."

Her breathing is quick as her gaze moves over my face before dropping to my chest, her tongue darting out to wet her lips. Maybe I'm cocky for thinking so, but I'm certain I'm not the only one feeling the chemistry between us.

Her gaze snaps back to mine, her brown eyes blazing, and I swallow. *Shit.*

"I don't want you," she grits out, stepping right up into my space, forcing me to drop my hands. Her fingers press into my solar plexus before smoothing out and palming my chest. "I don't want this."

I swallow again, too afraid to move as her fingers gather my shirt into her fist, shoving me backwards until my back hits the door. "I've never wanted this."

Jaime must be able to hear my heart hammering—feel it beneath her fist—and as I stare down into her eyes, I can hardly breathe as I wait for her to push me out of the way and leave.

Her grip tightens on my shirt, and she pulls, but instead of pushing me away, she yanks me down and presses her lips to mine.

JAIME

BE

For three years, I've both dreamed of and dreaded this happening again. Zak's lips are as soft as I remember beneath mine, but he remains frozen, probably wondering what the hell is going on. I know I am.

Without releasing the grip I have on his shirt, I reach up and slide my other hand around his shoulders, raking my nails through the closely shaved hair at the back of his head. It snaps him out of whatever trance he's in, and then I'm in trouble.

One of his hands cups my face as he deepens the kiss, the other pulling me against his chest. His thumb slides along my exposed midriff, and I melt against him with a moan. Nothing has ever felt so completely and utterly . . . Right.

Zak holds me to him like he's scared I'll run, but at the same time, with so much tenderness, tears prick beneath my eyelids. I shouldn't be doing this. Being trapped has made me reckless. Desperate for escape—to feel anything but the suffocating feeling of being lost in my own life. A lioness slamming herself against the bars of her cage uncaring of the broken bones it might cause.

My grip loosens on Zak's shirt and perhaps he takes it as a sign I'm going to put a stop to this epic mistake, because he pulls me even closer, a small groan of protest escaping him as he kisses me deeper.

I don't think I could stop even if I wanted to.

Which I don't.

Smoothing my hands down his broad chest, I slip my fingers up underneath his shirt and trace the warm, hard muscles of his stomach. Zak's hand drops from my waist to grip my ass as he flexes his hips, and my breath hitches when his hard cock presses into my stomach. *Fuck.*

My hands slide around to grip him, and he moans against my tongue, his hips grinding against me. Warmth builds between my legs, my body thrumming with need, but I know he won't take the lead. Not when I told him to his face that I didn't want this. Even though, it's clear it was a fucking lie.

Reaching between us, I flick open the button on his jeans and ease down the zipper. Zak's hands still, and he breaks the kiss, pulling back to look at me, his eyes searching mine.

"I want you to fuck me," I say, sliding my hand inside his underwear and wrapping my hand around his dick. My heart stutters in my chest. He's thick, long, and so fucking hard. My body aches for him.

I give him a firm stroke, watching as his eyes flutter closed, his chest heaving. But then he looks down at me, his lips pressed together.

"Don't overthink it," I say, rising onto my toes and brushing my lips against his. "We both want this."

But I know exactly what he's thinking. It's not that he

doesn't want this. He wants more. The problem is, a quick fuck is all I'm able to give him. And I shouldn't even be giving him that.

"Zak," I plead, easing his jeans and black boxer briefs down over his ass and setting his beautiful dick free.

Something settles in his gaze, and it breaks my heart. He'll accept this. He'll give me what I want, even though we both know he shouldn't.

Before I can let the guilt change my mind, I drop to my knees and push the head of his cock between my lips, causing Zak to gasp a curse. Gripping his base with one hand, I lick and suck at him, drinking in his groans and trying not to think about the tender way he strokes my hair as I take him as deep as I can.

"Fuck," he whispers. "Jaime."

The way he says my name wraps around my heart, and I slow, worshiping him with the care he deserves. My name becomes a pleading chant and need throbs between my thighs as I feel his entire body tense with the effort of holding back.

When his fingers gently grip my chin, easing me off and pulling me to my feet, the way he looks at me—the mixture of sadness and adoration—is almost enough to make me snap to my senses.

"Don't," I whisper.

Zak's jaw clenches and he spins us, pushing my back against the door. His touch is no longer gentle as he slides his hands up under my cropped sweater and tugs down the cups of my bra, thumbing my hardened nipples. I reach for his cock again, where it's hard and ready against my stomach, but he takes my hands and pins them above my head.

Holding me in place with one hand, he lifts my top with the other, dipping his head and sucking one of my nipples into his mouth. I moan, writhing against him as he teases me with his teeth and tongue, sliding his thigh between my legs.

Zak moves to pay my other breast equal attention, but his hand drops to stroke up my thigh, pushing up under my leather skirt. A whimper escapes me as his fingers brush the damp cotton between my legs, and he straightens, resting his forehead against mine, the sound of our breathless panting filling the room.

I close my eyes, leaning my head back against the door as he eases my panties down. Stepping out of them, I swallow, savoring the feeling of being at his mercy. With my wrists pinned almost painfully above my head, my breasts exposed, and my skirt hiked up around my waist, I'm his to take. His to claim.

But he doesn't move.

I make a small pleading noise, but still he stays, his head against mine, and his breath warm against my mouth. Opening my eyes, I find him staring at me with such intensity, I suck in a breath.

Before I can open my mouth to ask what he's waiting for, he slides his fingers between my legs, pushing one long digit inside. The deep groan that escapes his lips sends shudders through me, and I writhe against his hand. I need more. So much more.

His gaze flits to Sol's bedside table, and I can guess what he's thinking. I'm just as reluctant to break apart. "I'm on birth control."

His eyes meet mine and he swallows hard. "I'm clean. I haven't been with anyone since my medical."

I nod, the decision made, and he releases my wrists, gripping my waist and lifting me off the ground with an ease that pulls a gasp from my lips. Wrapping my legs around his waist, I expect him to walk us backwards to the bed, but he holds me pressed against the door, pushing the head of his cock between my spread legs. Something between a moan and a sigh leaves my lungs as he gently bucks his hips, working me down over his thick length. When I'm fully seated, his head falls forward, his chest heaving.

Then his mouth finds mine, a deliciously needy, frantic mesh of lips, teeth, and tongue as he starts to move. Each sure thrust of his hips sends jolts of pleasure through me, and I run my hands over every reachable inch of his body, wishing I'd taken off his shirt so I could fully appreciate him.

He shifts me in his arms, his fingers gripping my ass as he pounds into me, and the new angle hits a spot that has me crying out against his mouth. My head falls back against the door and Zak does exactly what I asked him to. He fucks me like he's trying to ruin me for anyone else. And maybe he is.

My moans turn to whimpers, and I'm glad we're on the top floor because I'm being loud as hell. "Fuck. Zak . . . I'm so close."

He grinds his hips with each punishing thrust and I gasp, clinging to him as my body explodes with pleasure, pulsing around him. Zak swears under his breath, his hips moving faster as he chases after me, but then his body tenses, his head dropping to my shoulder and his thick cock twitching as he empties inside me.

"Mine," he whispers hoarsely against my neck, the word so quiet I don't think he meant for me to hear it.

He holds me there as our breathing slows, his hips moving slightly as though he's hoping for another round, but then his grip tightens around me, and he releases me to the ground.

Adjusting my bra and tugging my top back over my

breasts, I wordlessly pull down my skirt and stoop to grab my underwear. One of the perks of a top floor room is the ensuite, and although I'm sure Sol will be pissed that his room stinks of sex, I'm grateful as hell. I don't look at Zak as I make my way into the small bathroom to clean up.

I can't.

Closing the door, I lean against it heavily and close my eyes, pressing my lips together to stem the burning that's building behind my eyelids. Having sex with Zak is the worst mistake I've ever made in my life. All it did was confirm what I've been trying to deny since freshman year. We're explosive.

Even though it was just a quick fuck against a door, it was easily the best sex I've had. My heart flutters at the thought of him taking me properly. Feeling his large, powerful body against mine, tasting every inch. Taking his time.

I push the thought away as I move to clean up. Because that can never happen. I've tasted Zak and never will again. I have to live out the rest of my life knowing what I could have had, if only things were different.

My stomach twists as I think of the ring hidden in my desk at the Hive. Will Louis touch me with such reverence? Will he look at me like I'm the center of his world? Will he light me up inside? Will he make me feel . . . I shake my head. Thinking about the way Zak makes me feel won't do either of us any favors.

Glancing in the mirror at my mussed hair and swollen lips, my heart sinks painfully, and I let out a deep sigh before heading back out into the bedroom. I'm a fucking idiot.

Zak looks up from where he's leaning against Sol's bedroom door, but the usual smile that lights his face when he sees me is gone—replaced by sadness. Does he regret what just happened? I suppose it doesn't matter whether he does or not. We did what we did and now we both have to live with it.

"I should let you get back to the party," I say, reaching around him to grip the handle.

His plump lips part with a small intake of breath, but then he nods and steps away, letting me leave. He lifts a hand as though he might reach for me, but I step past him out into the corridor, every step a lead weight. If he touches me, I might give in. I might forget that I belong to someone else. So, I don't look back.

When Zak doesn't follow me downstairs, I'm relieved. If nothing else, what just happened has made one thing perfectly clear. I need to stay as far away as possible from Zak Aldridge.

ZAK

A Ψ Δ

Peering through the tiny gap I've left between the narrow doors, I draw my knees up to my chest, and exhale. I love coming back to Chicago for the holidays, and Thanksgiving is always epic. Usually, I can play with my nieces for hours and enjoy every second of it. This year, however, my heart is only half in it.

Leaning my head back against the wall, half hidden behind a long winter coat, I close my eyes. I should be over the fucking moon. Just thirty-six hours ago, I had Jaime in my arms, tasting exactly the way I remember, but also so much more. Everything about her was incredible, a million moments from that evening now seared into my memory for eternity. Even if it didn't go down any of the ten thousand ways I've imagined it over the years.

She wanted me just as much as I wanted her in that moment. I could hear it in the way she chanted my name and feel it in the way she took my cock, but I'd be a fool to think we were feeling the same beyond our lust. The way she walked away without so much as a backwards glance made that perfectly clear.

It wasn't the beginning of something incredible, like it should have been. It was a moment of weakness on her part, and I've wondered more than a few times since that night whether I should have said no.

The thought is laughable. I could never say no to Jaime Smith.

I swallow down a groan. The feel of her under my fingers, the taste of her mouth. The way she'd dropped to her knees, her lips around my cock . . . I thud my head repeatedly against the wall.

I haven't told Sol or Alex what happened. Alex was dead to the world when I got up to go to the airport, and it just didn't feel like the right time to tell Sol. Okay. That's a bold-faced lie. I just know what he's going to say and I really don't want to hear it.

Fuck it.

Shifting a little amongst the boxes of musty smelling shoes, I tug my phone free from my jeans pocket and pull up Sol's number.

"Zak!" He answers almost immediately.

I smile, just the sound of my best friend's voice settling me a little. "Happy Thanksgiving, bro!"

"You enjoying yourself?"

I huff a laugh, looking around the cramped space and trying to rearrange my long legs so I don't lose circulation. "As much as I can. All six nieces are here, and I swear they think I'm some sort of jungle gym."

"Is that why you're calling me? Are you hiding right now?"

I laugh, opening my mouth to tell him that I want advice—that I want to know what he thinks I should do about Jaime. Should I call her? Text her? Ghost her? I've been chasing her for so long, I'm at a complete fucking loss of what to do now we've crossed that line. Sometimes I can't believe we did. It still feels like a dream.

"No," I find myself saying, pulling a hand over my face at my own cowardice. "I'm calling to see whether you've grown the balls to message Wes yet."

"You must be psychic." Sol laughs. "I literally just did."

That has me sitting up, a coat smacking me in the face. "Did he respond?"

"I don't fucking know because I'm talking to you."

I huff a laugh and lean back, trying to gather the nerve to steer the conversation back to my dilemma and failing. "How are you feeling about everything?"

"I'm okay," he says. "Is it a bit weird that I asked him to help with Jacey's fundraiser and then threw myself at him?"

"You didn't throw yourself at him."

"How do you know? You weren't there."

"I just know." I sigh. "And it's only weird if you make it weird. At least the fundraiser gives you an excuse to see him again."

"True."

It's the perfect timing to mention my own predicament. Sol might not have fucked Wes against a wall, but he does have the same awkward 'what now' situation that I'm trying to navigate. I'm just not sure why I can't seem to summon the balls to bring it up.

"Do you think it's gonna get serious?" I ask. "Like, are you going to have a boyfriend?"

"What the fuck kind of question is that?" Sol snorts. "Are you going to ask Jaime to marry you?"

My heart skips and I almost choke on my own saliva. "Fuck off."

"Exactly. Come on, man. We kissed once. I don't even know what happens next."

"Well—"

"Not like that."

The thunderous sound of six pairs of small feet approaching rattle the doors of my hiding spot. I'm out of time. "Shit."

"Oh my god." Sol's laugh is so loud, I have to pull the phone away from my ear. "You were actually hiding, weren't you? You're in a fucking cupboard right now, aren't you?"

I sigh, bracing myself for what I know is coming. "Under the stairs."

Sol's laughter fills the small space and I hang up, shoving my phone back in my pocket just in time, as the doors are flung open.

"Uncle Zakky!"

Before I can surrender, Lila, Skye, Talia, Noa, Petra and Dominique all cram into the already tiny space, crushing my lungs and pulling at my limbs like I'm the last human alive in a zombie apocalypse.

"Mercy!" I yell, but someone's braids fill my mouth, muffling my cry for help.

"Oh, no way. Nah-uh! Girls! Get off him! Now!"

I sag in relief at the sound of my eldest sister's voice, and one by one, the tiny terrors are hauled off me. Half crawling, half army rolling, I ease out of the under stair storage space and unfold.

"You okay?" Belinda asks, looking me up and down as though expecting to find another child clinging to me somewhere.

I stretch, my joints popping. "I am, thanks to you. You came just in time."

She reaches up and puts a hand on my arm. "You know me and the others appreciate you playing with the girls, but they're capable of amusing themselves. Or they can always go and annoy their fathers."

I give her a small smile and shrug. "I love playing with them."

"I know you do. But it's okay to take a break, too."

She pats my arm then hurries off in the direction the girls have sprinted. No doubt toward my mom in the kitchen if the smell of pecan pie is anything to go by.

Pulling my phone out, I contemplate calling Sol back, but I just can't bring myself to press the button. I know he'll be supportive, but I also know he has my best interests at heart. There's absolutely no way I can take anyone telling me that Jaime used me. Or that I need to walk away before I get hurt. That's the kind of defeatist shit, I just don't need to hear.

Even if it's the truth.

It's also one of the reasons I haven't called Alex. Sex is impersonal to him. He won't understand why I'm not just happy to get laid.

Heaving a sigh, I lean against the wall and tuck my phone back into my pocket. Why did she finally give in after three years? What changed? Not that anything's changed. The only difference is I know now that all this time, I was right. The chemistry between us is fire. We were made for each other.

A loud squeal has me straightening, my head snapping in the direction of the kitchen. It's not one of my nieces. With my long legs, it only takes me a few hurried strides to reach the source and my eyebrows shoot up as I find my mom jumping up and down, her phone in her hand, while my sisters, their husbands, and my dad look on in bemusement.

"What's going on?" I lean over and ask my other sister,

Melanie.

She shrugs. *Helpful.*

"Lauren," Dad says, reaching for Mom and gripping her arms. "Want to tell us what the hell is going on?"

"Dad!" Belinda snaps. "Language."

"I got in!" Mom squeals again, and this time Dad hollers and picks her up, swinging her round and almost knocking the pie off the counter.

"Will someone please explain what's happening?" I plead.

Dad puts Mom down and she beams at us, breathless, as she tries to fix her hair. "CHIPnique has been invited to the Winter Mingle."

I blink at her, glancing at my sisters for any clarification, but all three look as lost as me.

Melanie folds her arms over her chest. "Gonna need more words, Mom."

"Okay." She pulls up a stool and sits, her face glowing. "The Winter Mingle is a seriously big deal. It's essentially a meet and greet for companies that have been given the nod of approval by PEO. If you get an invite, it means you're one step closer to a deal. This could be CHIPnique's chance to break into the international market properly!"

While everyone else squeals in excitement, my stomach shrivels into a small uncomfortable knot. I know that name. PEO is Jaime's dad's company. It's just a weird coincidence, but I can't help but feel like universe is fucking taunting me.

"The chairman of PEO's daughter goes to Franklin West," Mom says, and what's left of my shriveled stomach proceeds to drop into my shoes. "Do you know her?"

I shrug, eyeing the pie on the counter and realizing my appetite has evaporated. "There are a lot of people at Franklin West, Mom."

Belinda laughs. "Mel and I can both vouch that you're talking out of your . . . butt. There's no way you don't know who she is."

My nieces snigger around my feet, and I roll my eyes. Both my older sisters graduated from Franklin West years ago. "It's changed since then, you know. Dinosaurs are also now extinct."

Belinda tries to smack the back of my head, but I'm too tall and too fast, and her palm meets nothing but air.

"That's great news, Mom," I say, forcing a smile. "When is it?"

"December twenty-first." She claps her hands together. "How about we celebrate with pie?"

The crowded kitchen cheers and I take a step back, letting everyone gather round the island. I am pleased for my mom. CHIPnique is essentially her company. She's the Chief Operations Officer and has been since it was little more than a startup, making integrated circuits for vehicles, specifically high spec cars and airplanes. The company does really well, but they've been trying to break out of the US market for the last few years.

"Hey. You okay?"

I blink to find my mom in front of me, her dark brown eyes narrowed.

"Yeah," I lie. "Just tired from dinner and playing with the girls."

She places a hand on my arm in a way that tells me she's not buying it. "You'll come with me, right?"

It takes me a second to figure out what she means and, when I do, my heart sinks. "To the Mingle thing?"

"Of course." She nods. "I know you're not sure whether you're going to join the company, I think it'll be good for you to get some experience on the schmoozing side. See if you like it."

The corner of my mouth kicks up, ignoring her comment about joining her company. "Schmoozing?"

"You know what I mean. You'll come, right?"

I glance over at where Dad's talking to Belinda's husband, Mike. "What about Dad? Don't you want to take him?"

Mom smiles and shakes her head. "You know your dad hates that kind of stuff."

She's right. Dad's an engineer, and although he understands the technical side of her work, he's a huge introvert and hates the office politics she has to deal with.

"Please," she pleads, trying to give me puppy dog eyes.

I heave a sigh. "Mom. That's not playing fair."

"Don't you want a little winter holiday? Some winter sunshine?"

My eyes narrow. "What? Where is it?"

Mom's face lights up. She thinks she has me. But that's not it at all.

"It's in Florida, at Mason Smith's mansion."

It takes a lot of self-control to hold in my groan. Do I want to go to Jaime's house? No. Yes? Fuck knows. Will she even be there? As much as I pride myself on knowing about all things Jaime Smith, I don't know her winter break plans.

I also don't want to give my mom false hope. I haven't committed to joining CHIPnique after graduation and I'm nowhere close to making up my mind about it.

"Sure," I say, smiling as my mom squeezes my hands with a grin.

I am kind of curious, though. I guess, this could be a taster of what life could be like in the corporate world.

It could also be awkward as fuck.

BEA

Our table overlooks the ocean as the sun sets on the horizon, casting the sky in pinks and golden yellows. The private room is cozy, with soft chairs and exquisite food. Louis is charming and attentive, living up to his promise to get to know me with thoughtful comments and insightful questions, but it feels wrong.

It's not him. He's still every bit the dream man. Not too short, not too tall. Dark blond hair and bright blue eyes, golden skin, a strong jaw, and straight nose. As I get to know him, I can't even find fault with his personality. He's quite funny, sweet, and intelligent. He's the perfect man.

Just not perfect for me.

Not that it matters.

As he tells me about the charity work he's been doing recently in Pakistan, I start to wonder whether the problem is me. I mean, it has to be. Or not me, per se, but what I've done.

A prickle of guilt twists in my gut as I pick up my glass of sauvignon blanc and take a sip, my engagement ring catching the light. As far as I know, there were no specifics in the contract drawn up when we were kids. I've never had a boyfriend because I've known since I was old enough to be interested in boys that my husband had already been picked out. But no one ever told me I couldn't fool around with anyone.

Although, it's not like I asked. I mean, how would you even start that conversation?

"Hi, Mom, Dad. You know how you promised me to a stranger? Am I allowed to sleep with other guys until I have to marry him?"

Nope. Screw that.

I eye Louis over the rim of my glass. There's no way he's a virgin. Surely, he's not expecting me to be. I mean . . . it's not like they'd check. Right? I push the thought away as soon as it manifests. This isn't sixteenth century Europe for fuck's sake.

Avoiding Zak since that night has been exhausting. I've had to stay behind after my classes, waiting until he's no longer lingering outside, or taking the back exit and walking through the parking lot instead of the common. It all feels very childish, but it's still better than the alternative. I can't see him. That moment of weakness has flipped my world on its head, and I need to get things right again. Not to mention all the shit that's been going down at the Hive.

I take another long sip of wine. More of Sasha's diary got posted online and it turns out she's been lying to us since the first week of college. With everything else that's going on, I don't even know how to begin processing the idea of losing one of my best friends. I wanted to go out with a bang this year but I didn't count on that bang being everything I've ever known exploding around me.

At least my internship at KBCX is going well. I rarely see Brad, and the other intern tends to stay out of my way.

It's busy, and involves a lot of grunt work, which I was expecting, but I'm getting to see how the station is run and that experience is invaluable.

"Is that all right?"

I blink, my skin heating as I realize Louis asked me a question and I haven't got a clue what he said. "I'm sorry. I was still thinking about those poor families in Balochistan."

"Understandable." Louis gives me a sad smile. "I was just asking whether it's okay if my lawyer drops something off for you to take a look at."

"Lawyer?" My heart speeds. "Sure. What kind of thing?"

Louis motions to someone behind me, and I turn to find a woman walking toward us, a file in her hands and a tight smile on her face. Her heels echo on the marble floor as she crosses the room, her ash blonde hair bouncing on the shoulders of her expensive pant suit.

"Good afternoon, Mr. Chevalier. Miss Smith." She hands the file to Louis, who takes it with a warm smile.

"Thank you, Maddison. That'll be all."

Maddison turns and strides away, leaving me wondering what the hell is in the beige file Louis has started leafing through.

"It's all fairly standard," he says, pulling out a sheath of papers and handing them to me.

I push my abandoned salad to the side and waiters immediately swoop down and remove our plates, giving me room to spread out the mysterious papers.

Although, they don't remain a mystery for very long.

"A prenup?" I ask, my eyes widening in disbelief as I scan the first page. "You can't be serious?"

Louis eyebrows rise, and he leans back, resting an ankle against his knee as he sips his wine. "I'm not sure why you're surprised. Prenuptial agreements are commonplace when you have as much money as our families do."

"Exactly," I say, still shaking my head. "I'm worth more than you, so surely it should be me asking *you* to sign."

Louis stares at me for a moment as though figuring something out and I force myself to meet his gaze.

"Your father's lawyer worked with Maddison on this. The agreement keeps both parties safe."

My heart sinks. Of course, my dad is part of this. My already molten skin heats further as Louis' eyes soften with what had better not be fucking pity.

"I assumed he'd spoken with you," Louis says gently.

There's nothing to say. It's clear that he didn't. So, I just keep my eyes down and concentrate on reading the document. It's complicated as hell, which is not surprising, because this whole deal is a shit show.

Both my dad and Louis' want to ensure that their respective money stays in the family, all while getting even richer. Which means, the hypothetical child that Louis and I haven't had yet, is mentioned throughout the entire contract.

I'm glad I didn't do more than pick at my salad, because by the time I'm ten pages in, I'm ready to hurl.

"May I take this and read over it with my own lawyer?" I ask, finally looking up to find Louis on his phone, his brow furrowed.

He puts the phone down and smiles. "Of course. There's plenty of time before the wedding."

My blood runs cold. "Excuse me?"

"The wedding," Louis repeats, his eyes narrowing. "Jaime, I don't mean to sound rude, but you understand we're getting married, don't you?"

"Of course," I say, shuffling the papers and slotting them

back into the folder. "It's just the way you said it, it sounded like a date had been set."

Louis stares at me for long enough that I shift uncomfortably on my chair. The sinking feeling in my gut tells me I already know what's coming before he opens his mouth.

"The date has been set for December twentieth next year." Louis scratches his jaw, looking more uncomfortable than I've seen him. "Please tell me your parents consulted you on this."

I push back my chair and stand. "I'm sorry, Louis. Lunch has been lovely. However, I have a few matters to take care of at home."

He exhales softly and moves around the table. My eyes burn and I'm not sure how much is anger and how much is sheer mortification that the virtual stranger standing in front of me knows more about my future—my life—than I do.

"Jaime," he says, taking my hands. "I'm so sorry. I had no idea."

I huff a laugh. "No. *I'm* the one who has no idea."

"Speak to your parents, but please know that throughout this, I'm on your side."

His words cause me to look up at him, and the sincerity in his gaze causes me to pause. He tugs at my hands gently and leans forward, pressing a soft kiss to my temple.

"This might be a deal thought up by our parents, but we're the ones getting married. You're going to be my wife, Jaime. I meant what I said when I gave you that ring. Please know that I will always put you first."

Staring into his sky-blue eyes, I swallow. "Thank you."

"There's no need to thank me for doing what I should." He brushes his thumbs over the tops of my hands, squeezing once more before letting go. "I'm going with your father to

Hong Kong tomorrow, but I'll be back next month. I hope I can see you then."

I nod, still reeling from the revelations of the last few minutes. It's not surprising I didn't know Dad was heading back to Hong Kong tomorrow. He's never included me in any details regarding his business before, so it's not like I'm expecting him to start now.

The journey back down to the ground floor is a blur, spent lost in my own thoughts. Part of me is outraged that so much has been decided behind my back, but another, larger, part isn't the least bit surprised.

When we reach the valet, Louis turns to me and takes my hand once more. "I meant what I said. I know this might not be conventional, but I honestly believe we could make each other very happy."

I give him a weak smile, saved from giving a response by the valet pulling up with the BMW 8 I've borrowed from my parents' garage. "I guess I'll see you next month."

Louis smiles warmly, closing my car door and waiting until I lower the window before replying, "I look forward to it."

I'm barely a block away before I dial my mom's number through the Bluetooth. It rings for so long, I'm on the verge of hanging up when it finally connects.

"Hello?"

"Mom?" I grip the steering wheel, all the rage I felt during dinner rising to the surface again. I don't want to do this over the phone, though. "Are you at home?"

"No, darling. We're at the airport. Is everything okay?"

My eyes narrow as I mentally flick through our conversations, trying to recall any mention of travel, but coming up blank. "Why are you at the airport?"

"Your father has a meeting in New York, so I thought I'd

join him for some shopping. He'll leave from there for Hong Kong tomorrow morning, but I'll stay a few days." She pauses, as if remembering that I never call her. "Is everything okay, Jaime?"

I almost hang up. What's the point? I'm starting to think my mom has the emotional intelligence of a slug. How have I never noticed before?

"Jaime?"

Taking a shaky breath, I decide to at least try to get some of the answers I'd hoped for. "I just had dinner with Louis. He showed me the prenup Dad's lawyer helped draw up."

"Oh, good." Mom pauses, speaking to someone in the background, and I grip the steering wheel tighter. "I hope you signed it."

"I did not."

Silence fills the line for a moment. "Why not?"

"Because I didn't get a say in signing my life away, so I'm sure as hell going to make sure I read the contract."

She tuts, my attitude clearly not acceptable to her. Her airs and graces bug me sometimes. Mom's not old money like Dad. Her father worked his way up from practically nothing to get to where he is now. And there might not be any proof that I've found, but if Grandpa's thick Texan accent is anything to go by, Mom hasn't always been so soft spoken.

"Jaime," she says, her voice warning. "I hope you were nice to Louis."

A laugh bursts from between my pursed lips. "Of course, I was. Louis isn't the problem."

"I hope you're not insinuating what I think you are?"

My heart is racing, and as I change lanes, almost clipping a white Tesla, I'm reminded why I didn't want to do this while driving. "I don't know, Mom. What do you think I'm insinuating?"

"Jaime, I'm not going to play these childish games with you."

My finger lifts to press the button to end the call, but Mom's tired sigh causes me to pause.

"You know, sweetheart," she says quietly. "My wedding to your father was strategic. Not quite in the way yours is, in that we met as adults, but believe me when I tell you I know how you're feeling."

Silence fills the car as I let her words settle. They don't bring me the comfort I think she hopes they will.

"I love your father," she continues. "Marrying him was the best thing I ever did, and not just because it gave me you. You'll learn to love Louis, and I really think you'll be happy with him."

I nod, even though she can't see me, and exhale with resigned acceptance. "I hope so, Mom."

After wishing her a safe flight, I hang up, feeling more miserable than I've felt in a long time.

ZAK

I've had enough. Pulling the hood of my sweatshirt down further over my head, I wrap my jacket tighter around me and breathe into my gloves. There are barely two weeks between Thanksgiving and winter break thanks to Franklin West's five-day weekend. Some students don't even bother coming back, taking the full month of December off instead.

I know Jaime's back, though. Even though she's ignored the text I sent, asking her if she wanted to go and get coffee, both Sol and Alex say they've seen her. Which can only mean one thing. She's avoiding me.

After what happened at the party, I knew things would be awkward. I told her we'd just be friends and, although what we did was more than friendly, I'm pretty sure that's not what Jaime meant. Maybe she thinks I'm done with her —that I got what I wanted and now I can graduate happy. Well, I'm not. Far fucking from it.

Which is why I'm camped out in the woods behind the Hive, waiting for her to get back from class like a goddamn stalker. I figure, if she spots me on the front steps, she'll turn and run. The same with the car park and the path from it to the Hive. Which leaves me in the fucking woods.

The sound of footsteps crunching on gravel carries across the crisp afternoon air and I freeze, watching as Jaime strides down the path, her eyes on her phone. I press my lips together. It would seem she didn't lose her phone, or her sight, in a freak accident, preventing her from returning my text.

She looks amazing, as always. With a knitted hat and her hair loose around her shoulders, the dark orange dress she's wearing brushes her knees beneath her woolen coat as she walks. She's fall personified.

I think she's wearing the same ankle boots she wore to the party, and I swallow hard at the memory of them digging into my ass, my dick attempting to cheer from where it's hiding from the freezing cold.

When she gets inside, I'm not planning on knocking. I have no idea whether she's told the Bees what happened between us, but I'm not risking being turned away. The way I see it, I have nothing to lose. She's already ignoring me, so why not go for broke.

Which is why I cross to the side of the sorority house and start to climb.

The Hive and the Den are almost identical, so I've had plenty of time and opportunity to plan how to do this. The only problem is, thinking about it and actually doing it are two very different things. Especially when everything's covered in fucking frost.

Because Jaime's room is on the very top floor, I climb up onto the top of the bay window on the side first, then up onto the second story window to get to the lowest point of the sloped roof. From there, I just have to get to her skylight and hope she lets me the fuck in. She has a window on the side of the house, but I can't figure out a way to get to it from the roof. I may or may not have sat in Sol's room for a good hour trying to figure it out.

The skylights aren't original to the house, apparently, and are some fancy ones that open with some sort of remote. Sol was buzzed about his when he moved in this year, and I can't pretend I wasn't a little impressed.

I'm well aware this is desperate, and I'm kind of waiting for someone to call campus security, but as my feet slip for the ninth time on the tiles, I realize I've gone too far to turn back now. When I finally reach her skylight, I exhale in relief to find the light on. If she'd stayed downstairs, I'd have been left sitting on the roof like fucking Santa.

My heart hammering in my chest and my breath in thick clouds around me, I pull off one of my gloves and knock on the glass. After a few seconds, I knock again, sounding out a pattern so there's no doubting that it's a person and not just a bird or the wind.

When Jaime appears below, her big brown eyes wide in horror, I regret every decision I've ever made. What the fuck am I doing on her goddamn roof? How is this going to make her want me? If I wanted to drive an even bigger wedge between us, I've definitely done it now.

Hanging my head in shame, I wait as she presses the button to open the high skylight, bracing myself for the onslaught of abuse I suspect is coming.

"What the hell, Zak? Get in here before you get yourself killed!"

I blink, staring down into her room as she gestures frantically for me to come inside. She doesn't have to ask me twice. Easing my body through the gap, I grip hold of the frame and lower myself down until I can let go, dropping onto her carpet.

Jaime immediately smacks me in the chest. "What the hell were you doing on the fucking roof?"

"You ignored my text."

She stares up at me, blinking. "Climbing onto the roof and coming through someone's window is not the appropriate response to having a text ignored. I think you need professional help."

Rolling my eyes, I shove my hands in my pockets. "What I need is for you to talk to me, Jaime. You said we were friends, and then you ghosted me."

All concern drains from her face, her features tightening. "I've had a lot of shit going on, Zak. My world doesn't revolve around you."

"I never said it did, Kitty Cat. All I wanted was a response. Common courtesy. Even if it was a text saying, 'leave me alone'."

Jaime marches over to her desk and snatches up her phone, unlocking it and tapping at the screen. A few seconds later, my phone vibrates in my pocket.

I narrow my eyes. "Hilarious."

"You got your text. Now you can leave. Through the door this time."

I make no move to go. "How was your Thanksgiving?"

She stares at me as though I've lost my mind. Maybe I have. I've never been able to think clearly when it comes to her.

I take the silence as an excuse to look around her room. The layout is identical to Sol's, but it's pretty much how I imagined it. Not cluttered, with lots of earth tones and shiny bits. Shrugging off my jacket, I sit down on the bed, scooting back until I'm leaning against the wall.

Jamie huffs through her nose. "Make yourself comfortable, why don't you?"

"I'm very comfortable. Thank you."

Her growl of frustration is fucking adorable, and I can't disguise my grin.

"You like making my life difficult, don't you?" she asks. "Do you get some sort of kick out of it?"

I shake my head. "I don't want to make your life difficult. I want to make it easier, but you keep trying to push me away when I'm trying to help."

"I don't need your help," she snaps. "If I wanted help, I'd ask for it."

I chuckle softly. "You know that's not true."

"Fine." She folds her arms across her chest. "But you can't help me. There's no one that can help me."

There's a pain lacing her words that has me sitting up, my heart quickening. "What are you talking about?"

"Nothing." She turns away, placing her phone back down on her desk.

"Jaime." She stiffens at my firm tone, and when she turns around, I pat the bed next to me. "Come here."

I half expect her to tell me to fuck off, but she walks over and climbs onto the bed, settling a foot away from me. Huffing through my nose, I reach out and wrap an arm around her, dragging her closer until she's leaning against my chest. She doesn't fight me, and I close my eyes as she relaxes against me, her hand resting over my stomach. She smells wonderful. I don't have a clue about flowers, but it's something heady and rich that makes me want to bury my face in her hair and inhale.

"You can tell me," I say quietly, rubbing my hand up and down her arm. "Whatever it is."

She shakes her head slightly. "No."

I don't push. I'm not sure whether she's saying she can't or won't tell me, but no means no. All I can do is show her that she can trust me and maybe one day she will.

Jaime turns her head, looking up at me. "Why are you doing this?"

"What?" I raise my eyebrows with a grin. "Stalking you and climbing in through your window? Isn't it obvious?"

She stares at me, her eyes narrowing slightly. Then she looks away. "I thought after the Thanksgiving party you'd be over it."

My heart surges in my chest and I sit up a little straighter, pulling Jaime from my chest and cupping her face as I stare into her eyes. "This is not an infatuation, Kitty Cat. The very first time I laid eyes on you, I knew. I knew you were perfect for me."

She scoffs and tries to pull out of my grip, but I hold her firm, stroking her jaw with my thumbs. "It's the truth. Don't ask me how I knew—how I still know—but I feel it, right here in my chest. So, in answer to your question, Jaime. I'm doing this because my heart has been laid out before you for three years. That hasn't changed because we fucked. I'm yours. I always have been. I'm just waiting for you to wake up and see it. I'm not going to give up on you. On us."

"There is no 'us,'" she says, tugging free of my grip. "You're delusional, Zak. And you *need* to give up on me because we're not going to happen. The party was a mistake, a lapse in judgment that won't be happening again."

Her words hurt just enough to make me pause, but then I shake them off. "That's bullshit. It might not have been my best work, but you sure as hell felt the same connection I did."

She looks away and I know I'm right. But then, she stands and walks over to her door.

"You need to leave."

I fold my arms across my chest, tempted to tell her to make me, but she stares at me in a way that makes me shuffle to the end of the bed and stand.

"You know," I say as I pull on my jacket, "Thanksgiving wasn't a fair trial. You should give me a proper try, Kitty Cat. Maybe you wouldn't be so quick to write me off."

I swear her lips almost pull into a smile, but she manages to squash it, her glare narrowing as she puts a hand on her hip.

"Out, Aldridge."

Holding up my hands in surrender, I grin at her. "Okay. Fine. But just know that you might be getting rid of me, but I'm not giving up."

I pause by the door, and she stares up at me, her glare faltering just enough that I reach for her face again. When she doesn't stop me, I lean down and brush my lips against hers. As much as I want to push, to kiss her until she feels what I feel, I force myself to step back.

"Reply to my text," I say, ducking a little under the doorframe. "We'll have coffee."

Before she can refuse, I turn and jog down the stairs. What her sisters will say about me leaving when they didn't see me come in, I have no idea. Jaime will have to deal with that one. If I had my way, I'd have stayed all night and sneaked out either at dawn or when everyone was in class.

One day, I tell myself as I close the front door and step out into the cold, zipping up my jacket. *One day, she won't want to let me leave.*

BE

My jaw aches as I force yet another smile for the rude as fuck anchor sneering at the coffee I've placed in front her. It's the third one she's rejected and I swear if she asks for a fourth, she'll be wearing it.

Roxanne Sawyer is simultaneously the best and worst thing about interning at KBCX. On camera, she's poised and perfect, and she works damn hard behind the screen, too. She's fascinating to watch. But she's such a fucking bitch to everyone, including Derek John, her co-anchor.

Simeon, the other intern, told me they were having an affair last year and it ended badly, so now the tension is unbearable. Personally, I think she's just rude as hell.

"It's too cold," she snips, flicking a hand at the coffee. She doesn't even turn from her dressing room mirror to address me, instead returning to inspecting her long red nails.

My lips press together as I reach and pick it up. The heat immediately seeps through the cardboard sleeve, causing me to swap hands. If I threw it in her face, she'd get first-degree burns, it's that hot. "This is the hottest they can make it. Shall I find a thermos for you? Maybe it cooled a few degrees on the walk back."

Her hazel eyes narrow as they meet mine in the mirror, and she slowly pushes her thick brown hair over her shoulder. "I'm not sure I like your attitude, Janet."

I honestly don't mean to, and I try to hold it in, but I laugh. She's so childish it's ridiculous. Shaking my head, I head to the open door of her dressing room. "I'll get you another one."

And I hope it burns your vicious tongue.

As I walk back out into the hallway, I can practically feel her glare trying to set me on fire, but I just smile and keep on walking.

Everyone else at the station is okay. Even Simeon has started treating more like an ally than a threat, which is nice. Above everything else, I love how busy it is here. There's no time to stop and think. From the minute I set foot in the building until I drag myself to my car, it's a hundred miles an hour.

Thanks to Roxanne's diva tantrum, I'm now late to pick up and deliver the script revisions to Derek's dressing room, so I decide to get that done before I try to find her a coffee that's hotter than the sun.

My heels echo down the hallway as I make my way to the producer's office, and for a brief second, I let my mind wander. Instantly, I regret it. It's been four days since Zak climbed the goddamn roof of the Hive to sneak into my room, and I haven't heard from him since.

I know he's waiting for me, but he's going to be waiting a long time. There's no way I can play this game with him. Not while I'm arranging to see Louis when he comes back from Hong Kong. My stomach dips at the thought of my fiancé. I had a lawyer go through the prenup and it's airtight. It seems Louis was right, it's not even about me or him. It's all about the money and a child who hasn't been born yet.

I mean, what if I don't want kids? What if one of us is infertile? My chest tightens and I take a deep breath, blowing it out slowly. This is exactly why I try not to think about anything other than the internship or my classes.

It was far too easy to lie there in Zak's arms, breathing him in and forgetting about the world. I smile to myself. He always smells amazing. A rich woodsy smell, laced with the sweetness of chocolate—probably from the M&Ms he's always inhaling. My eyes close briefly and I take a breath.

It's easy to pretend that I haven't paid much attention to Zak Aldridge over the last few years, but I'd only be lying to myself. When I've attended lacrosse games with the Bees, my attention has always been solely on one player. I've watched him around campus, too. Always big, bright smiles, and booming laughter as he hangs out with Sol and Alex. He's a joker, but he's also fiercely loyal and kind. I know in my bones he's a good man.

Whoever ends up with him will be a lucky woman.

I could have told him the truth. I thought about it. It would have been so easy to tell him I'm engaged. But I have no idea how to even begin to explain how I've been promised to another man since I was a child. It's the same reason I haven't told my friends. They wouldn't understand. Sure, they all come from places of privilege, but it's just different. Maybe Alex would get it. I've heard his family's name come up during conversation with my dad sometimes.

Even still, I'm . . . tired. I don't want to have to face the indignation and horror that would follow the revelation. Maybe it's cowardly, but it's so much easier to just slip away after graduation and get married. Apparently, next Christmas.

Swallowing down a groan, I shove all thoughts of men from my mind, and raise my fist to knock on the producer's door. It opens almost immediately, a black file thrust in my face with so much force, I stumble backwards.

"You're late."

I take the file before offering an apologetic smile. "Sorry. Roxanne had coffee issues."

Matt, the producer, stares down at me through his thick, black-rimmed glasses, but doesn't berate me any further, instead huffing through his nose and closing the door again. I blink, already accustomed to his brusque manner, and turn on my heel to head back down the hallway toward Derek's dressing room.

He and Roxanne will read the script from the teleprompter but, even though it might change between now and when they go live in an hour, Derek likes to run his eye over what they have beforehand.

When I reach his door, I raise my hand to knock, but pause at the sound of Roxanne's raised voice.

"I can't stand her! I want her gone!"

My stomach drops, and my breath catches. *Please* don't be talking about me.

"Roxy," Derek soothes. "Jaime's harmless."

Fuck.

"No. She's not. She's after my job. I know she is."

"She's a college student, Rox. You've got nothing to worry about."

I lower my hand, my heart racing. I should walk away. They could open the door at any second, or someone could come along and find me standing here. But I can't.

"Well, I'm going to talk to Brad," she continues. "You

didn't see how rude she was to me just now. There are a million others who'd kill for an internship here. He can find someone else."

I swallow, panic causing my blood to run cold. I can't lose this internship. There's no way I'll find another one with such short notice. Not to mention, I like it here, and I'm damn good at my job. Surely Brad wouldn't listen to her? He can't let me go for laughing at the fact she called me the wrong name just to be petty. Can he?

"Save your breath, Roxy. She's not going anywhere."

"What do you mean?"

Yeah, what *does* he mean? I step closer, glancing up and down the hallway to make sure no one is witnessing my eavesdropping.

"She's the boss' son's fiancée."

I almost choke on my own saliva.

"What?" Roxanne barks, her outrage matching my own. "Brad has a son?"

"Not Brad. I'm talking big boss. Like, the company who own the station."

I stagger away from the door, bile rising in my throat. Surely, it's not true. The Chevaliers don't own the station. I'd know if they did. I was aware they owned businesses in the States, but I've never bothered finding out which ones, because they're usually product based. Certainly not media companies.

Any interest I had in listening to their conversation has evaporated and I turn, all but running to the nearest restroom. The door slams against the wall as I rush in, exhaling in relief to find the other stalls empty. My lungs are so tight, I can't breathe, and I place my hands on the counter by the sinks and try to suck in gulps of air.

Is that the reason I got the job? After my interview, I

was sure Brad wasn't going to give it to me. Is this what changed his mind? My eyes burn, and I press my lips together.

This is exactly why I didn't tell my parents about the internship. I wanted to do this by myself. Now, staring at myself in the mirror, in my black, designer pant suit, my hair up in a stylish chignon, I can't see anything but a fraud.

Pulling my phone from my pocket with trembling fingers, I type out a message to Lydia, Brad's secretary and the woman responsible for handling the interns, and tell her I've come down with some sort of stomach bug and I'm going home.

For a split second, I worry about losing the internship for being unreliable. Then, I bark a cold laugh. Apparently, that's not going to happen.

Straightening, I take a breath and hold my head high. Perhaps I didn't get this internship completely on my own merit, but I know I'm worthy of it. I've done the work. I do everything that's asked of me and more. I'm the best damn intern they have.

Repeating the mantra in my head, I keep my chin held high as I march to the elevators and swipe my pass, pressing the button for the basement parking. I manage to stay that way until I'm settled, hidden, in my car. Then I crumble.

Tears gather in my eyes, and I sniff, trying not to let them fall, because if they do, I won't be able to stop the disappointment from drowning me.

ZAK

I swear I've never seen my mom so happy. The huge smile on her face is literally the only reason I'm doing this. Winter fucking Mingle. Even the name is lame as hell.

"Zakary Aldridge, you look so handsome!" She pats down the lapels of my tux before reaching up and cupping my face. "I'm so happy you agreed to come."

"Anything for my favorite mom." She rolls her eyes and I grin. "You look gorgeous, too, by the way."

Gripping the skirts of her flowing red dress, she does a little spin in the lobby of the hotel we're staying at, and I laugh. I definitely take after her. She lives life loud and unapologetically, whereas Dad is quiet and reserved. They're chalk and cheese, but they somehow make loving each other look effortless.

"Come on," she says, linking her arm through mine and pulling me toward the entrance. "We don't want to be late."

I feel sick. It's been so hard not to text Jaime, but I've forced myself not to. As much as I'm not giving up, I also have to leave the ball in her court for a while. I climbed a damn house for her. It's her turn. Although, if she doesn't text me, I'm not sure what my next play will be.

Every five minutes I change my mind on whether I want Jaime to be there tonight. If she's not, it'll be a hell of a lot less awkward. If she is, I get to see her and maybe even dance with her. Nope. I hope she's not there. It's too much pressure. *Fuck.* I'll probably meet her parents, though.

"Are you okay?" Mom asks as the driver PEO sent opens the door for us.

I hadn't even noticed the car arrive. "Yeah. Sorry. I just spaced."

Even though she smiles, I can tell she doesn't buy it, but I'm not going to explain. I'm aware that when I voice the situation aloud, it sounds ridiculous.

"So," I say, forcing a grin. "Is this a Cinderella type deal? Do we have to be back by midnight? Or are you going to give me a glimpse of your college rave days?"

Mom throws back her head and laughs, her diamanté earrings brushing her shoulders. "College rave days? Oh, honey. No. What kind of party do you think this is going to be? It's going to be a bunch of old guys drinking champagne with someone playing piano. If we're not home before midnight, I'll be shocked."

Shaking my head, I watch the Miami skyline twinkling in the distance over the water. When I found out Jaime's family lived on Fisher Island, I wasn't surprised. Even still, I'm a little blown away by the sprawling mansions. Our own brownstone in Chicago is impressive, but it might as well be an apartment in Ford Heights compared to these.

When we join a line of similar black town cars, my eyebrows shoot up. "What? We're here already? We could have walked."

"In these heels?" Mom scoffs. "I don't think so, baby."

We wait patiently as cars deposit the guests out front, and a fresh wave of nerves washes over me when I see people taking photos like it's the goddamn Oscars.

Mom reaches over and squeezes my hand. I think for a second, she's reassuring me, but one look at her face tells me she's nervous as hell.

"Relax, Mom," I say quietly, squeezing back. "You look stunning and it's going to be a great night."

She nods, giving me a tight smile, and I decide right there and then, I'm going to put all my own personal bull-shit aside, and make sure tonight is the best night of her life.

My heart thunders as the driver opens the door and I get out, extending a hand to my mom. She's a natural, smiling at the cameras and posing on my arm. I'd be worried about people thinking I'm her date if I didn't look so much like her.

The Smith mansion is spectacular, with a Christmas tree out front the size of the one at Rockefeller, and a million twinkle lights coating every palm tree in a way that should be tacky, but just kind of looks magical.

"Wow," Mom whispers as we make our way up the steps to the front doors.

I nod, trying not to gawp at the glass light fixtures drip-ping from the ceilings, the fifteen-foot windows and the sweeping staircases. There really are different levels of rich. My family is rich, but this is . . . something else entirely.

There are another two Christmas trees in the entrance hall, enormous blue, silver, and white baubles hanging at varying lengths throughout the space. I wonder if there's a personal one somewhere with presents underneath it. How many trees does one family need?

"Good evening, Mrs. Aldridge, Mr. Aldridge."

My head snaps to the side to find a waiter standing there with a tray of champagne.

"Thank you," we both mumble, taking a glass each.

As he moves away, I lean down to my mom. "How the hell does he know our names?"

She shakes her head and takes a sip of champagne. "I was wondering the same thing. Maybe there's a book with photos and they make the staff memorize them. Maybe there's a quiz."

I cough to hide my laugh and we make our way along with the mingling crowd into a large room filled with tables. A quick count tells me there are eight tables, each with six places.

"It's smaller than I thought," I say.

"Are you joking right now?" Mom's eyebrows arch. "There's nothing small around here."

I shake my head. "No. I mean, there are only forty-eight people invited. I was kind of expecting hundreds."

"That's what makes it exclusive," she says, pulling me over to the seating chart discretely displayed at the entrance.

It hits me then, what an important thing this is for Mom. She really has been personally selected. A wave of pride washes over me and I smile down at her as she finds us on the list.

"We're sitting next to the owner of a tech company and his husband, and sisters that own a textile export company," she says, glancing around the room. "I'm so intimidated right now."

"You belong here just as much as anyone," I reassure her. "I'm really impressed, Mom."

She smiles and gently pushes my chest. "Oh, hush."

Mom called it with the piano and lots of old guys. The

small crowd is pretty mixed, but I'm definitely the youngest here by a good decade. Also, possibly the tallest. I'm used to being the giant in the room though, just as I'm used to the basketball jokes.

"Are you gonna be okay if I go find a restroom?" I ask, placing my already empty glass down on a passing waiter's tray.

"Sure. Just don't get lost."

I laugh, but it's a real possibility. This place is freaking huge.

So far, I haven't seen any of the Smiths. I know what her parents look like, thanks to Google, and they're not here. I'm assuming they're going to make some sort of grand entrance once all the guests have arrived. It must not be far off, because the room is already pretty full.

I don't make it far before a man in a black suit stops me.

"Can I help you, sir?"

"Just looking for a restroom," I reply noting the subtle earpiece. I suppose this many millionaires in one place requires private security.

"Just down that hallway, sir," he says, pointing me in the opposite direction.

I thank him and head that way, taking in the incredible house. Is this where Jaime grew up? I did my research but only surface stuff. I don't know how long they've lived here. The thought of her childhood bedroom being here somewhere has me staring up at the double staircase curiously. Is there a living room somewhere with framed pictures of her from school? Her high school graduation? There's certainly nothing personal out here.

The restroom is empty, and I take a second to check my hair and adjust my bowtie after taking care of business. I made the decision to cut my hair before tonight, taking it back down to the shorter length it was last year.

Taking a deep breath, I head back out, mentally preparing myself for a couple of hours of engaging in conversation about things I really have no interest in, with people I'll probably never see again.

I'm relieved to find that the guests are still milling around when I reach the dining room, and I spot my mom right away chatting with a small group. When I see who's in the group, however, my stomach drops to my polished black shoes.

Fuck.

Mason Smith laughs at something Mom says and his wife reaches out and puts her hand on Mom's arm as though they're long-lost friends. But it's not them that has my heart racing. Standing beside them is Jaime, looking beyond stunning in a floor-length silver dress. It shimmers and sparkles with a pattern made of pearls and crystals, her hair pinned back with matching clips. She looks like a goddess.

For a second, I consider turning and walking in the other direction, but there's no way I can abandon my mom. I just have to suck it up. Swallowing hard, I will my feet to move forward until I reach them.

Mom's eyes light up as she spots me, reaching immediately for my arm. I can't look at Jaime, so I focus on Mason instead.

"This is my son, Zak," Mom says. "Zak, this is Mason Smith."

I extend my hand, shaking his firmly. "A pleasure, Mr. Smith. Your home is stunning."

"Thank you," he says, his blue eyes crinkling. "Nice to meet you, Zak. This is my wife, Melanie."

I take her proffered hand with a smile. "A pleasure to meet you."

His next words are barely audible over the thundering of my heart.

"And this is my daughter, Jaime."

I finally allow myself to look at her, completely unsurprised by the barely concealed horror on her beautiful face.

But Mason isn't finished as he gestures to the man beside her.

"And her fiancé, Louis Chevalier."

And just like that, five words cleave my world to pieces.

BE

I can hardly breathe as Zak shakes Louis' hand. His smile is tight, pain clear in his brown eyes, but I'm sure I'm the only one who notices. Although, when I tear my eyes from the car crash happening right in front of me, I find his mom eyeing him with concern.

This shouldn't be happening. Zak shouldn't be here. Seeing him in my house is so jarring—my two worlds colliding in a way I never imagined. He looks handsome as hell in his fitted tux, his hair shorter than it was when I last saw him, and it takes a hell of a lot of willpower not to let my gaze linger.

"Surely you two must have crossed paths," Zak's mom says, looking between us before turning back to my dad. "They're both seniors at Franklin West."

Louis' arm slides around my waist and it takes far too much effort to stay still and not move away.

"Is that so?" he says. "What a small world."

"Small world indeed," my mom agrees.

Zak's smile is tight, his gaze dropping to Louis' arm, but thankfully, any explanation is cut short by dinner being announced, and a request for everyone to take their seats.

As Zak and his mom move away, I exhale.

"Are you okay?" Louis asks, his grip tightening on my waist.

Forcing a lightness into my tone, I turn and give him a bright smile. "Of course. Why wouldn't I be?"

His blue eyes search mine, and my heart races as though he might be able to find the lie on my face.

"You tensed up when he came over. Is he an ex?"

I blink, unsure what to say. Does *he* have exes?

"I've been engaged since I was six-years-old," I say quietly, discreetly checking that my parents have moved away. "I've never had a boyfriend, so I don't have any exes."

Louis' eyes widen, and I get the answer to my question. He definitely hasn't been saving himself for me either.

Turning me to face him, he places both hands on my hips as he leans a little closer, his voice dropping to a whisper. "You're not—"

"A virgin?" I hiss. "No. Are you?"

His laugh is loud enough that the nearest table look up in interest. My cheeks burn.

"Come on," I say, moving out of his grip. "We're almost the last to sit down."

I move through the tables, smiling at semi-familiar faces, losing Louis at some point as he stops to talk to someone. When I reach our table, my parents glance up, but before they can say anything, I strike up a conversation with Louis' mom.

Louis and my dad only arrived back from Hong Kong yesterday afternoon, so I haven't had a chance to talk to him yet about the fact that he set a date for the wedding without consulting me. Sure, I could ask Mom, but after our last conversation, I've been avoiding her like the plague. Part of me can't even be bothered to fight it. It's set. Just like everything else in my life.

As Louis' mom proceeds to tell the whole table in great detail about the yacht Claude bought her for Christmas, I let my gaze drift to the table on the other side of the room. I can see Zak's profile as he talks to a woman wearing an emerald satin turban, and I take the opportunity to look at him properly.

I saw him in a suit at the opening party, but there's just something about a tux that hits different. He looks gorgeous, and I can't stop myself from thinking how, in another life, I'd be the one to watch him take it off for me. I press my thighs together under the table at the thought, trying to pull myself back to the talk of reputable yacht maintenance companies, but I can't. Not even when Louis returns and sits beside me.

I don't look at Zak again, for fear of someone noticing, but I'm dying to know what he's thinking. Is he angry with me? Almost certainly. There's no way he'll be climbing roofs for me anymore, that's for sure.

My heart sinks as I realize how selfish I've been. Even though I've always known I can't have him, I've let him chase me. Sure, I've always said no, but I could have just told him the truth. I could have been firmer. I know that if I'd shut him down properly, he wouldn't have pursued me the way he has. I certainly shouldn't have kissed him. Or fucked him.

Without thinking, my eyes flit to his table, my body stiffening as I find him staring at me. I don't think I've ever seen him look so angry. I swallow and look away.

All through my dad's welcoming speech, I sit, staring at my empty side plate, my champagne untouched. I can't do this. I can't sit here, in the same room as him without explaining. Without . . . apologizing.

The second the servers start bringing around the appetizers, I push back my chair.

"I'm sorry. I'm not feeling great. I'm going to get some air."

Louis stands too, his brow creasing with concern. "Do you want me to come with you?"

"No." I shake my head and give him what I hope is a reassuring smile. "I won't be long. I think my dress is just a little too tight."

Avoiding my mom's eye, I turn and walk away, heading for the exit. She knows this dress fits perfectly because I was measured for it the last time I was here.

As I move away from the table, I hear Louis convincing my mother not to go after me, and I exhale in gratitude. I just need a little space to breathe. Although, I have a feeling I'm not going to get it.

I'm barely ten feet out of the room when I hear footsteps behind me on the polished marble floor and my eyes close, ready for what I'm sure is about to come.

"Jaime!" Zak hisses.

I take a deep breath and turn, trying not to shrink under his furious stare. "Not here. Come with me."

His jaw clenches, but he nods, and I lead him past one of the security guards to the glass doors that lead out to the gardens. I close them behind us, trying to decide what to say, but Zak beats me to the punch.

"What the hell, Jaime? You're *engaged*?"

I wince. "I can explain."

"I should fucking hope so!" He pushes his fingers through his short black curls, his eyes wide. "Why the hell didn't you tell me?"

"I . . ." My breath leaves my lungs in a heavy exhale, my shoulders sagging. "I didn't know how."

He barks a laugh. "It's really fucking easy. Zak? I'm engaged to another man. See? See how easy that was?"

My nose itches as tears start to form against my will and I press my lips together, looking away. "I'm sorry."

Zak groans before sinking down to the stone step with a sigh. "I just don't understand why you didn't tell me. When did it happen? Over the summer? Last year? How long have you been with him?"

"Since I was six."

Zak's head snaps up as he stares at me. "What? Like some childhood sweetheart? You've been with him the entire time I've known you?"

My lip trembles as his head drops to his hands, but I don't answer. I don't know how.

"I'm such a fucking idiot," he mutters.

Staring down at him, I know this is how I should leave it. It would be so much easier with him hating me—being disgusted by me. Everything tells me I should walk away. But I don't.

"I don't want to marry him," I say, instantly wincing as the words leave my lips. It's the first time I've voiced the thought aloud, and I hate myself for it.

Zak slowly lifts his head, his brow furrowed. "So, why are you?"

"Because I have to."

Perhaps realizing that I'm not going to sit down, Zak pushes to his feet, towering over me once more, even in my heels. "What does that even mean?"

I look away, regretting not walking away when I had the chance. This is exactly why I never told him. I can barely explain it to myself, let alone to someone else.

Zak reaches out and takes hold of my chin, gently tilting my head to look at him. "Is he forcing you, Jaime?" he asks softly. "Is he blackmailing you or something? You can tell me. Maybe I can help, or—"

"He's not forcing me," I say, turning my face out of his grip. "It's just always been this way."

Zak pulls a hand over his face and takes a deep breath. "Maybe I'm being fucking stupid here, Jaime, but I don't get it. If you don't want to marry the guy, don't."

"This is exactly why I didn't tell you," I say, frustration taking my despair and molding it into something sharp and jagged. "I knew you wouldn't understand."

"Then help me," he grits out. "Help me understand why you didn't just fucking tell me you were taken."

"I don't know!" I glance over my shoulder at the doors as my voice rises, but there's no one there. "But now you know. I'm marrying Louis next December and there's nothing either one of us can do about it."

Zak stares at me, his eyes wide. "You're serious, aren't you? You honestly think you can't get out of this."

"I can't." I take a step toward the doors.

He reaches for my arm, but I twist away. "Jaime. This is the US. No one can force you to get married. That kind of shit doesn't happen here."

"Enough, Zak." I open the door, aware I've been gone far too long.

He rushes forward and blocks my way, ignoring my answering scowl. "Say no, Jaime. It's that simple."

"I can't!" Reaching out, I shove him out of the way and step back through into the house. No footsteps follow and I sag with relief. It's done. My secret is out. Maybe I should tell Abi and Sasha, too. After all, I'll want them at the wedding.

When I reach the dining room, I find Louis waiting outside. He straightens, looking me over as I approach.

"Are you feeling better?" he asks.

I nod, forcing a smile. "Much. Thank you."

He offers me his arm and I take it, thankful that Zak didn't follow me back. I should feel relieved that he knows, but I don't. It's not even that I couldn't make him understand. The problem is the words I voiced that I shouldn't have. It doesn't make them any less true, though. I don't want to marry Louis.

In the sixteen years since the arrangement was made, I've never allowed myself to consider not going through with it. It's been a part of my story for as long as I can remember.

When she was in town, Mom would read me bedtime stories, and whenever there was a prince involved, she'd say 'just like Louis'. The phrase 'when you marry Louis' has been commonplace my whole life. Of course, as soon as I got to middle school, I realized it wasn't normal. But it made sense. I understood why our families would want a union.

But now . . . Now I'm starting to wonder just how much my life would fall apart if I did what Zak suggested. What if I said, 'no'?

ZAK

She's engaged. *Engaged.* I wince as the bourbon burns down my throat, and open the top button of my shirt, regretting not changing into sweats before heading to the hotel bar. This time next year, Jaime will be married. To Louis *fucking* Chevalier.

I googled him. After she left me outside, I searched up everything I could find on the guy. It turns out Billionaire Ken is on every list of 'most eligible bachelors'. I scoff to my glass. Not so eligible apparently.

Sitting through the rest of the Winter Mingle was sheer hell. Being in the same room as Jaime knowing the blond-haired billionaire beside her is the reason she isn't mine. It doesn't make things easier that she doesn't want to marry him either. The real kicker is that she won't do anything about it.

Closing my eyes, I breathe in a deep breath, exhaling slowly as I try to quell the building rage. At least Mom didn't seem to notice things were off. I managed to talk with the people on our table and held my own as she went off to mingle and make connections that would benefit her company.

Although, when she called it at eleven, the Mingle was still in full swing, so maybe she did notice. I saw her to her room before heading straight to the hotel bar, because there's no way I'm sleeping any time soon. Not with hurricane Jaime raging in my head.

I wish she'd told me.

Raising my glass, I tip it back, emptying it, before signaling to the bartender for another. Would it have made it easier if she'd told me from the start? Definitely. If she'd told me straight up in freshman year that she was engaged, I'd have stepped down. No eighteen-year-old wants to get tangled up in that shit.

If she'd told me *this* year . . . No. I don't think things would have changed. I can't decide whether I'm pissed or disappointed. Maybe both.

Does Billionaire Ken even know her? Have they been meeting up during holidays? The thought of him fucking her sends waves of nausea through me, and I clench my fists. Does he know she cheated on him with me? My stomach rolls. I'm definitely pissed about that. Cheating is never acceptable, and she made me part of that without my consent. If I'd known she was taken, I'd never have let it get that far.

"Zak?"

My entire body freezes at the sound of Jaime's voice, as if my own thoughts have conjured her. Slowly, I turn around to find her standing a little way away, her expression cautious, as though I'm a wild animal she doesn't know how to approach. Her hair is still pinned back with pearls and diamonds, her make up flawless, but her dress has been replaced by black velour sweats, her heels for slides.

She still looks like a dream even if she's a fucking nightmare.

I have no idea what to say, so I say nothing, turning back to the bar and the fresh glass of bourbon that's appeared in front of me.

"Zak," she tries again. "Can we talk?"

"Shouldn't you be with *him*?" I snap, fingers gripping the glass as I glare at the amber liquid.

I don't dare breathe as she sighs, wondering whether she'll do us both a favor and leave. But the footsteps don't get quieter, they grow closer, and she pulls herself up onto the barstool beside me.

"Please? Zak?"

Turning my head to look at her, I raise my eyebrows. "Please, what? Did you tell him? Did you tell him you cheated on him with me? Did he kick you out? Is that what happened? Is that why you're here?"

She winces but doesn't look away. "I haven't seen Louis in six years. When I came back to Florida for that family emergency at the start of the year? That was to meet him."

"It doesn't matter," I say, shaking my head. "You're still engaged. You belong to someone else."

"I don't *belong* to anyone," she snaps. "I'm my own damn person."

A cold laugh escapes me. "Oh, really? If you were your own person, you'd be able to tell Louis that you don't want to marry him."

Her lips part to argue, but then she closes them, her gaze dropping to her hands. The huge diamond ring she was wearing at the Winter Mingle is missing. I snort and take a swig of bourbon.

"You should have told me," I say into my glass. "You led me on."

This time, it's her bitter laugh that fills the space between us. "I've been telling you we can't happen for three years, Zak. I've always been perfectly clear that there's no chance of us."

"Yeah. Shoving my cock in your mouth definitely hammered that home."

She looks away and I almost feel bad.

"I never asked for this," she says quietly, her voice breaking a little. "I didn't ask for any of it."

Fuck. Throwing back the rest of my bourbon with a wince, I stand and swipe my bowtie off the bar. "If you want to talk, let's talk. But not here."

She looks up, her brown eyes shimmering with unshed tears. "Where?"

I pull my room key out of my pocket. "Privacy. Come on." When she doesn't move, I sigh. "You think I'm going to try anything now that I've met your fucking fiancé?"

My words are harsh, and I'm not even sure if they're true. But I wouldn't try anything. No. If Jaime were to make a move, however, there's no universe that exists with a version of me strong enough to say no.

Her nose wrinkles like she's about to start crying, and I shake my head, moving away. If she wants to start crying in a hotel bar, that's her call, but I'm heading to my room.

After a second, however, I hear her footsteps behind me, and breathe a sigh of relief. We ride to the third floor in silence, and I watch Jaime in the reflection of the polished elevator doors as she wraps her arms around herself, her head down. There's nothing I want to do more than to pull her into my arms and hold her—tell her everything's going to be okay. But I don't. I can't.

Housekeeping has tidied my room, which I'm grateful

for, because when I left for the Mingle, the bed was unmade, my clothes all over the floor.

"Drink?" I offer, gesturing to the mini fridge.

She shakes her head and sits down on the foot of my bed, her eyes fixed on the carpet. I watch her for a second, before sighing and stooping to take off my shoes and socks, figuring I might as well be comfortable for what is likely going to be an uncomfortable discussion.

"Okay," I say, leaning against the desk and folding my arms. "Tell me what's going on. Properly this time. How are you engaged to a man you don't want to be engaged to?"

Jaime groans and flops back on the bed, her eyes falling closed. Her zippered sweatshirt rides up as she does so, revealing a delicious slice of soft brown skin. I tear my gaze from it, forcing myself to look at her face.

"So, in case the house wasn't a big enough clue, my family is rich," she says.

I bark a laugh. "Yeah. It was subtle, but I got that."

"Yeah, well, the Chevaliers are the European version of us. When my dad met Claude, Louis' dad, years ago, they bonded over the fact they had small children. Dad really wanted to partner with the Chevaliers to take a bigger slice of the European market, and Claude wanted more of North America, but they were reluctant to risk so much of their own business." Jaime sighs and drapes an arm over her face. "The next time they met, they brought their wives and kids with them. Somewhere along the negotiations, they decided it would be mutually beneficial to merge their businesses, but only if they could be sure that the wealth would stay in the family."

I can't keep in the noise of disgust that escapes me. "So, your dad sold you as part of a fucking business deal?"

"Not quite," Jaime says with a sigh. "But yeah. They agreed to merge their companies after Louis and I were wed, ensuring that their combined wealth would transfer to their joint heir."

I stare at her, laid out on my bed, my head spinning. "That's ridiculous."

"It's my life, Zak." She shifts an arm and opens her eyes to look at me. "It's all I've ever known."

"That doesn't mean you have to accept it," I say, pushing off the desk and stalking toward her. "If you don't want to marry Louis, just say so. Tell him. Tell your dad."

She shakes her head. "It's not that simple."

"It really fucking is," I say, my voice raising. "You're not a piece of property to be used in business negotiations, Jaime. He can't farm you out to produce heirs."

My stomach turns at the thought of her with him. His hands on her. I wince and turn, sitting down beside her, my head in my hands.

"It's not like that," she says quietly.

"It's exactly like that. What do you think's going to happen if you say no? You'll get sued? Disinherited?"

When Jaime doesn't answer, I turn and look at her. She's staring up at the ceiling, a defeated look on her beautiful face.

"Jaime," I try again, gentler this time. "No one can make you do anything you don't want to do. If you're worried about money—"

"I'm not," she huffs. "I don't give a crap about the money."

"What, then? Are you just brainwashed by this whole thing? Is it some sort of Stockholm Syndrome? Because I'm sure you could seek some help with that."

Jaime turns her head and narrows her eyes at me. "You're a dick."

"I'm being fucking serious." I hold up my hands. "Because from where I'm sitting, you don't have to sign your life away for no reason."

When she says nothing, I sigh. Lying back on the bed beside her and staring up at the ceiling. After a few minutes of silence, she takes a breath to speak.

"It's not for no reason."

She doesn't elaborate and as much as I want to push, I don't. It's so fucking frustrating. I'm not a black and white person. I'm a big fan of the gray in between. But this whole situation seems so cut and dry. It's just another giant glaring reason, set out in fucking neon, telling me to get the hell out of here.

Alex and Sol have been gently pushing me to let her go for years, and if this wasn't the shove that I needed, I don't know what is. But how can I walk away and leave her to marry some guy she doesn't want? Yeah, she's a big girl and can stand up for herself, but for some reason, she's not. And it doesn't sit well with me.

I scrub my hands over my face, and when I drop them back to my side, my fingers brush against hers.

When she doesn't immediately pull away, I close my eyes, the barely-there touch of her fingers against mine burning hot. This is why I don't walk away. I'm addicted to this woman. She was made for me, and I know, in the deepest part of my soul, more certain than anything, I'm the only one that can make her truly happy.

If only she'd let me.

When her fingers move, a wave of disappointment crashes over me. But she doesn't pull away. Instead, she brushes her hand against mine, as though seeking the contact I'm craving just as much. Before I can question whether it's a good idea, I take hold of her hand, lacing our fingers together.

Maybe it's because this feels like the end—like goodbye—that I don't just lie there and take it. Instead, I open my stupid mouth.

"Have you picked out a wedding dress yet?"

Jaime turns her head to face me but doesn't pull away. "Not yet. I'm going this weekend. Want to come with me and give your opinion?"

Frowning at her serious tone, I turn my head to look at her. "What?"

She narrows her eyes. "Ask a stupid question, get a stupid answer."

Glowering back at her, I can't help but notice how close we are. I can feel the warmth of her breath on my skin as her eyes burn into mine.

We stay there, staring at each other, hands intertwined, a million unspoken words hanging between us. Just when the tension builds to an unbearable level, Jaime rolls onto her side, moving her even closer. Reaching up, she rests the fingers of her free hand against my chest, the touch burning through the fabric of my white shirt.

"I'm sorry," she says quietly. "For not telling you. I didn't want anyone to know because I knew they wouldn't understand. Back in freshman year, I didn't know you well enough to know that you wouldn't have told anyone if I'd asked you not to."

I roll onto my side, too, wondering if she has any idea what she's doing to me. Being this close, smelling the way she does. My dick is growing harder in my pants and as her fingers remain, resting so lightly on my chest, I can't do anything to stop it. All I want to do is roll on top of her and make her mine. Take her in the way I didn't get a chance to in Sol's room.

"I'm not going to forgive you," I say, my voice rough. "You know that, right?"

She drops her hand from my chest, her fingers pulling free from mine, and I reach for her, cupping her jaw and holding her in place before she can pull away.

"How can I?" I ask, staring into the depths of her dark brown eyes. They're darker than mine, like polished mahogany. "How can I forgive you when you've towed my heart alongside yours all this time, and you could have set me free with two words?"

Her breathing quickens, her wide eyes dropping to my mouth, and I swallow at the knowledge that even now, as I tell her that I can never forgive her, she wants me as much as I want her.

"This is why, isn't it?" I ask, stroking my thumb over her full lower lip. "This is why you didn't let me go. Because you want me. You want this."

The faintest whimper falls from her lips, and I reach for her, grabbing a handful of her ass and pulling her flush with my body, letting her feel every inch of the effect she has on me.

"Say you don't want this," I say, flexing my hips just enough to drive my meaning home as I repeat the ultimatum I've given her before. "Say it. Then leave and don't come near me again."

Jaime's eyes flutter closed as she presses against me, and my teeth grind at the effort of holding back.

"Say it." I grip her chin a little tighter, causing her eyes to open. "Tell me we're done."

Even as the words leave my lips, I realize I'm asking her

to end something we've never even started. Not really. My heart slams against my ribs as I watch her mouth, waiting for the end. I've put the ball in her court again, and this time, I don't think I'm ever going to get it back.

BE

I'm on fire. Burning under the intensity of Zak's gaze, every inch of me alight at the feel of his hard body against mine. I shouldn't have come to his hotel. I shouldn't have come up to his room. Did I want this to happen? Had I known this might be a possibility? How am I supposed to pull away from something I want this badly?

Zak's grip on my chin is almost painful, his own jaw clenched as he stares at me, waiting for my decision. How can I end something that never began? My mind flits to the prenup sitting on my bedroom dresser, still unsigned, my ring beside it. Is it as simple as he says?

I can't just walk away. Not from Louis. Not from my family. And apparently, not from Zak. But I can't have it all.

I honestly don't mean to, but my hips move against my will, seeking out friction from where his cock is trying to break free of his tuxedo pants. He groans and drops his forehead to mine.

"Jaime," he breathes, the smell of bourbon brushing over my skin. "You're killing me."

He's so close. So goddamn perfect. I tilt my head,

rubbing my nose along his, our lips barely touching. My body aches as though I might just die if I don't have him, the throbbing between my thighs almost unbearable.

"I want you so badly, Zak," I whisper.

He groans in response, his hips shifting and drawing another whimper from me. "I told you before. I'm yours, Kitty Cat. I've always been yours."

My heart aches as I part my lips, taking his mouth with mine, and it's as though I've opened the cage and set him free.

Zak rolls us with a rumbling growl, settling on top of me as he kisses me breathless, and I melt beneath him. My hands roam over his broad shoulders, exploring his back and untucking the white shirt from his pants to grasp the warm skin beneath.

I don't get far before he pulls away, breathing hard. For a moment, I wonder whether he's come to his senses as he slides off the bed and stands. But then, he reaches for the waistband of my sweats and pulls them down, dragging them along my legs before dropping them to the floor, leaving me in my white lace thong.

His eyes are molten as he stares down at me and I squirm under his gaze. Just as I go to reach for him, he drops to his knees at the foot of the bed and drags me toward him.

I gasp as he parts my thighs, burying his face between my legs and running his nose over the scrap of material covering my throbbing core. He slides the material to the side, and I can barely breathe, fisting the sheets as his breath ghosts over my skin in teasing waves.

"Zak," I whine, my hips canting.

He slowly pulls my thong down and off, before extending a single finger, sliding through the slick want between my legs until he comes to my clit, where he begins to rub tortuous circles. It's not enough, and my body pulses with need.

As I open my eyes, I find him watching me, his expression dark and unreadable. Then, I realize. This is punishment. He's going to give me everything I want—everything I need—but he's not going to make it easy. He's making a fucking point. Making sure I remember how much I want him.

And I'll take it.

Gladly.

I deserve every ounce of punishment he can give me, and I'll receive it gratefully if it means longer with him. Perhaps he sees the acceptance in my eyes, because the second I lie back and take a breath, his tongue licks a sure stripe through me, and I cry out.

Zak groans, his hands gripping my inner thighs, spreading me almost painfully wide as he devours me, alternating between licking and sucking, fucking me with his tongue before teasing my clit. Every time I get close, he pulls back, pressing kisses to my inner thighs until my breathing evens out. Then he repeats the process.

After the fourth time, I'm almost sobbing, his name a pleading loop on my lips. I'm so resigned to what he's doing, that when he pushes two fingers inside me, sucking hard on my clit, I cry out as I come immediately, clenching around his fingers in pulsing waves, my legs trembling.

My eyes open as the bed dips, and I find him leaning over me, his eyes roaming my face. He presses two fingers to my lips.

"Open," he murmurs. "Taste how much you want me, Kitty Cat. How much you want this."

I do as he says, and he pushes his fingers inside, stroking my tongue as I suck him clean.

Then he reaches between us and takes hold of the zipper on my black velour hoodie. He pulls it down slowly, swearing under his breath as he realizes I'm not wearing anything underneath.

My dress was boned in a way I didn't need a bra, so when I threw on my loungewear to come and find him, I didn't think past needing to see him.

Zak runs his fingers down between my breasts, shaking his head, before pulling my arms free of the sleeves and dropping the hoodie to the floor, leaving me naked beneath him. He's still fully dressed, his shirt only partly untucked from our initial kiss, and my heart speeds at being so exposed for him.

As if realizing the same thing, he stands and stares down at me, his rich brown eyes slowly moving over every bare inch of me, drinking his fill. I try not to squirm, letting him know that I submit. I'll take everything he has to give and more.

Slowly, Zak unbuttons his cuffs, his eyes continuing to look over me, leaving trails of burning desire in their wake. He moves onto his buttons, each one exposing another inch of hard, brown skin, and my breathing becomes little more than breathy pants. The visual is too much, I'm aching for him, and I press my thighs together.

Zak pauses, then reaches out and grips my knees, tugging my legs apart until I'm completely exposed to him.

"I want to see," he says, his voice gruffer than usual. "I want to see how much you want me."

It's too much. My nipples are hard, my breasts aching, as need throbs in time with my heartbeat between my legs. I've never been so turned on in my life.

Far too slowly, Zak shrugs out of his shirt, his muscles contracting, and I drink in the definition of his abs and the vee that disappears beneath his snug black pants. I swallow hard, and I swear for a split second, I see a glimpse of Zak's usual cocky grin. But then it's gone. Replaced by the hard, scorching glare I've accepted I deserve.

"Move up the bed," he commands, reaching for the button on his pants.

I swallow, watching him track the sway of my breasts as I do as he says. When I'm settled amongst the pillows, he unzips his pants and hooks his thumb inside the waistband, pushing them down along with his black boxer briefs. My mouth runs dry as his long, hard cock springs free, and I marvel at the sight I've imagined for years. Zak Aldridge, naked and ready in front of me. Six foot four inches of hard, brown muscle—a body crafted by the fucking gods.

He reaches for his cock, tugging it roughly a couple of times before climbing up on the bed between my open legs. I'm so ready for him. He pauses in front of me on his knees, his expression hardening as he looks me over, and a trickle of panic settles in my chest. Is he having second thoughts? A small noise escapes my throat at the thought of him stopping this, and he blinks, snapping out of whatever thought spiral he'd been in.

"Sit up," he says, his voice rough.

When I do as he says, he reaches for my hair, touching his fingers to the pins keeping it off my face.

"Take these out," he says. "You dressed up for him. I don't want you like that."

My heart twists, and I almost open my mouth to tell him that he's wrong—that I dressed up for me, not for Louis. Never for Louis. But I don't. Instead, I give him what he needs, and reach up to tug out the pins, placing them on the nightstand as my hair falls back around my face.

"Better," he breathes.

I sit, waiting for his next instruction, not daring to reach for him in case he changes his mind. I need this. I want this. Even if it's selfish and wrong, because it really can't happen again. That's why I submit, when what I really want to do is push him to the bed and ride his dick until I see stars.

Zak pulls me to my knees, roughly turning me to face the wall, and places my hands on the padded headboard. Nudging my legs apart with his, I moan as his hands reach around to squeeze my breasts, his fingers pinching my hardened nipples. His dick presses against my back as he kisses and nips at the skin along my shoulder and neck, and I grip the headboard until my fingers ache.

Just when I think I can't take anymore, he shifts, his hands gripping my hips tight as he lifts me slightly, positioning me over his cock. I really hope his mom isn't in the room next door, because I moan loud enough to wake the dead as he thrusts into me hard; his thick length stretching and pushing me to my limits. Before I can take a breath, he snaps his hips again, slamming into me with such force, I fall forward, bracing myself on the headboard.

Zak holds onto my hips, fucking into me relentlessly, using me for his pleasure, and I love every second of it.

My body clenches around him as I reach the edge and I already know it's coming when he pulls out of me, breathing hard. I don't move, my head bowed, body trembling as I wait for him to take me again.

But he doesn't. Instead, he presses a kiss to my shoulder and lifts my hands from the headboard, laying me on my back amongst the pillows. Before I can question what's happening, he settles over me, caging me between his arms as he slowly eases back into me.

Carefully, I reach for him, tracing every inch of available skin with my fingers, memorizing the feel of him as he moves in me. Zak dips his head, taking my mouth in a tender kiss, and I wrap my legs around him, digging my heels into his firm ass, urging him deeper. As though there might be some way to meld us together so I don't have to let him go. So I can keep him always.

Zak's steady thrusts pick up as the need between us grows, our kisses becoming breathy and sloppy, punctuated by moans and gasps as we both chase our release. When I arch beneath him, my body throbbing with bliss, he pushes deep inside me, his hips falling off rhythm as he follows after with a rumbling groan.

I cling to him, burying my face in his neck and feeling the pounding of his heart against mine as the aftershocks of my orgasm flicker through my body like sparks.

"You might not want to admit it," he says, his voice still breathless against my skin. "But just as much as I'm yours. You're mine."

Squeezing my burning eyes closed, I hold him tighter, wishing it was that simple.

"I'm going to find a way to get you out of this," he says, pulling back to look at me. "You're not marrying Louis."

My heart throbs with hope, but I shake my head. "I don't need a knight in shining armor, Zak. I'm not a princess in a tower who needs saving."

He pulls out of me, dropping to the side, and I immediately mourn the loss. "What if I want to do it anyway?"

"You can't save me, Zak." I turn and face him, tucking an arm under my head. "This is real life. There are no happily ever afters."

He sighs deeply, turning to face me, and I'm hit with how we've ended up exactly as we started. Minus clothes.

He reaches out and tucks my hair behind my ear. "That's the most depressing thing I've ever heard."

I shrug as best I can in this position. "The truth usually is."

We stare at each other for a minute more, then I push up and roll off the bed to clean up in the bathroom. I don't look at myself in the mirror. I don't want to see what waits for me there. As long as I'm here, in his room, the guilt and regret can be held at bay.

When I step back into the bedroom, I'm not sure what to expect and I eye Zak warily, finding him under the covers, his arms behind his head.

"Come here," he says. It's not a question.

I eye my clothes, knowing I need to get going. I didn't tell my parents I was going out, and even though I'm a grown woman, I know they'll freak out if I'm not there when they wake up.

"I'm not asking you to stay the night," he says. "Just a few minutes."

Ignoring common sense for the hundredth time tonight, I climb onto the bed beside him, sliding down under the covers. He's still naked and, despite being completely sated, my body thrums as he pulls me to his chest.

"I hope you're ready for my white horse, Kitty Cat," he says, pressing a kiss to my forehead and pulling me tighter. "Because if you're not willing to save yourself. I will."

I want to tell him no, but it appears I've used up all my 'nos' when it comes to Zak Aldridge, because I say nothing as I wrap myself around him and close my eyes.

ZAK

"Fuck!"

I groan, opening my eyes to find the room lighter than I expect. It takes me a second to remember where I am, and another to take in the fact that Jaime Smith is naked and swearing angrily in my room.

Sitting up with a sleepy grin, I watch as she frantically searches for her underwear, pulling the scrap of white lace up and making me wish I'd torn it instead of taking it off carefully. She might be freaking out, but she looks like a fucking dream.

Yawning, I palm my hard cock as I watch her full breasts swing with the movement of searching for the rest of her clothes, her dark nipples tantalizingly tight, calling out for my tongue. My mouth salivates at the thought of tasting her again.

"You're already late," I say, my voice still thick with sleep. Throwing back the covers, I fist my cock lazily. "You might as well have a little morning work out before you leave."

Jaime turns, her beautiful face twisted into a scowl, but

as her gaze falls on my hard dick, lust clearly passes over her features for a second.

"Stop it," she says, turning away. "I can't believe I fell asleep. My parents are going to be pissed as hell."

Swinging my legs off the bed, I walk over to where I dropped my pants and pull my phone from the pocket. "It's six a.m.," I say. "They won't even be awake yet. Relax."

Jaime shows zero signs of relaxing, so I take hold of her shoulders, turning her toward me. She huffs, looking adorably disgruntled for someone wearing nothing but a thong.

"Take a second," I say gently. "Your house is like, two minutes away. Your folks were up until at least one in the morning. You really think they're going to be awake so early?"

Her lips press together as though she's going to argue, but then she sighs. "Probably not."

"There we go." I stroke down her arms, gathering her hands in mine. "Now get your ass back in bed and I'll order us some breakfast."

As much as I'd have loved for a repeat of last night, I know it's not going to happen, and my dick slowly deflates in reluctant agreement.

"Zak . . ."

"Look," I say, letting go of her hands and reaching for the room service menu on the desk. "I'm going to take a shower. Order some coffee and whatever else you want. Give me until six fifty. You can still be home before seven."

Jaime sighs, taking the menu from me, and I turn and head into the bathroom for the world's quickest piss, shower, and tooth clean in history.

I'm being selfish. I know I am. But I want a few more precious minutes with Jaime like this. Where she's mine, and only mine. A few minutes pretending I don't have to hand her back to someone else. My muscles tense at the thought. Is Louis staying at her house? They're clearly not sharing a room if she's not worried about him noticing she's gone. Have they slept together yet? I push the thought away as my stomach rolls.

I'm in the bathroom for all of eight minutes but when I step out, a fluffy white towel around my waist, the room is empty.

Slumping against the doorframe, I stare at the menu abandoned on the bed, and the floor empty of clothes. She even picked up my tux and draped it over the chair.

A little part of me knew this might happen, but I really hoped it wouldn't. If it wasn't for the state of the unmade bed, I'd think she'd never been here at all.

My good mood obliterated, I tug on some clean underwear and pull a pair of jeans and a sweatshirt from the closet. When my phone bleeps, my heart skips. But when I pick it up, it's just my mom asking what time I want to go for breakfast. Why she's up this goddamn early, I have no idea.

Sinking to the bed with a sigh, I plug it in and tell her I'm ready whenever she is. It's then that something catches my eye. Lying on the bedside table, are the sparkling pins from Jaime's hair. I pick one of them up, watching how the sunlight catches on the tiny crystals. I'm still staring when a knock sounds on my door.

Tossing the pins in my toiletry bag, I open the door to find my mom standing there in a long blue t-shirt dress and gold hooped earrings, looking fresh as a daisy.

"Who the hell pissed in your cereal?" she asks, frowning up at me.

My eyebrows shoot up and I choke on a laugh. "Mom!"

She reaches up and cups my cheek, her eyes searching mine. "Seriously. What happened?"

"Nothing happened." I swat her away. "It's really early, and I'm a twenty-one-year-old athlete who hasn't eaten since the tiny food last night."

She hums, clearly not believing me, but lets it drop, not speaking again until we're seated at a table with fresh coffee and orange juice in front of us.

"Are you hungover?" she asks.

I raise an eyebrow over the rim of my coffee cup. "No. Are you?"

"Is it something to do with Mason's daughter?"

I groan, putting my coffee down on the table. "Mom, I thought we'd dropped this. I'm just tired and hungry. That's all."

"Yeah," she mutters, standing to go and fill her plate at the buffet. "And you're a big fat liar."

For a second, I consider telling her, but I don't want what's happened between me and Jamie to taint whatever relationship she's building with the Smiths. A partnership with PEO could mean huge things for her company and I don't want to jeopardize it.

Sitting back in my chair, I watch the ocean outside the window and replay the events of last night. Did I push her? Did I make it too hard for her to say no? I don't think so. *Fuck.* I told her there was no way I'd touch her knowing she was engaged to someone else, but she proved me a liar. I guess Mom's right.

I don't regret it, though. It easily replaced what happened in Sol's room as the hottest night of my life. Jaime is just as perfect as I imagined, and the memory of her laid out, naked and begging for me, is going to be one I never forget.

I meant what I told her, too. She's mine. The second she kissed me, she claimed me. No backsies. And I'm not going to let her go without a fight. She said she doesn't need anyone to rescue her but damnit, I'm going to try.

How, I have no fucking idea.

For the hundredth time, I consider calling Sol or Alex but my phone is still charging up in my room. Besides, Alex is all loved up, and Sol is going through whatever messed up shit he has going on with Wes. I don't want to bother them with my stuff. Or maybe I still don't want to hear what they have to say.

Either way, it's going to be two weeks until I see Jaime again. We fly back to Chicago today for Christmas, and I won't be back in Oregon until January second. A lot can happen in two weeks. I'm pretty sure nothing physical has happened between her and Louis yet, but what if it does? What if she falls for Billionaire Ken?

On paper, he's a better match for sure. They have family history. They're both stupid rich. He's annoyingly good looking. I can practically see them on a yacht somewhere, laughing and enjoying life while sipping champagne.

I hate it.

My muscles tense as something Jaime said in Joe For Joe echoes into my memory. *Lack of direction.* Fuck. Louis Chevalier has more direction than most people on the planet. A goddamn empire to head. It's almost laughable that Jaime finds me even the smallest bit tempting. I have nothing to offer her. No big career plans. No sparkling future. All I have are more lacrosse trophies than I have room to display and a reasonable inheritance.

Frustration builds and builds until I'm ready to throw my empty coffee cup across the room. Why the hell haven't

I spent more time trying to figure shit out? I couldn't care less about economics, and I know last night's dinner wasn't the best showcase of the business world, but I know in my gut I don't want to join Mom's company. Which leaves me . . . Absolutely nowhere.

Slumping in my chair, I pinch the bridge of my nose. I might be lacking in direction, but I'm a good person. I know that. And I also know that Louis might be a perfect match on paper, but no one will care for Jaime better than me.

I may have chased her time and time again, but last night it was Jaime who came to the hotel looking for me. It was also Jaime that kissed me first in Sol's room. Who asked me to fuck her. For all the pushing from my side, Jaime's also done more than her fair share.

She says she doesn't want rescuing, but she also said she doesn't want me. One of those is clearly a lie. But what if it's both? For the first time, I can't see the right play.

If I step back, will she find her way back to me? Or will I end up seeing her wedding photos in magazines next year, wondering whether I could have stopped it? Does she even want me to? No one can make Jaime Smith do anything she doesn't want to. Surely if she really didn't want to marry him, she wouldn't?

By the time Mom gets back with a plate laden with fresh fruit and pastries, I'm more confused than ever.

BE

Walking down the steps of Franklin West Hall, I cast a worried glance at Abi beside me. "Are you sure you're okay?"

She sucks in a breath, tucking her dark blonde hair behind her ear and nods. "Yeah. It's just a lot."

I hum in agreement. After everything that happened with Sasha's diary before winter break, she decided to step down as president. Usually, it would be down to me to take her place, but with the internship and everything that's going on with my family, I couldn't even begin to entertain the idea of taking something else on. Abi was the natural choice.

"The dean might be good looking as hell," I say, looking out over the common. "But there's something off about him. I don't like it."

Abi chokes on a laugh. "There's nothing 'off' about him."

I shoot her a look, but before I can argue, my phone chirps in my purse, and I pull it out.

Hey, Kitty Cat

My eyes roll and I fight the smile trying to curve my lips. I felt awful running out on him at the hotel, but I couldn't stay and pretend. The night with him was hands down the best of my life and the rest of that day was a blur of blushes and heated skin with every aching muscle and memory of what he'd done to me.

Luckily, Louis was tied up in meetings with my dad and his father all day, so I didn't have to face him. And no one's pressed me about the prenup. I guess because it's pretty much a given.

What happened with Zak is a very morally gray area and it makes me uneasy. Yes, Louis and I are engaged, but we haven't even kissed properly yet. Is it still cheating when it's little more than a business transaction?

Zak didn't text me that day, leaving me to think I'd finally broken whatever it was between us by running out on him. It would have been for the best. But then, he messaged me on Christmas Day and again on New Years'. Nothing more than a friendly greeting, which I returned.

"Who's got you smiling?" Abi asks.

I blink, shoving my phone back in my purse. "No-one."

"It's Zak, isn't it?"

We reach the turn off for the path to the Greek houses and I turn to face her. "What makes you say that?"

Abi shrugs, linking her arm with mine and tugging me with her as she starts walking again, her big blue eyes sparkling. "You have a Zak Smile."

"Fuck you."

She laughs. "It's been three and a half years of flirting. If you think you don't have a Zak Face, you're delusional."

I raise my eyebrows. "Is it a Zak Face or a Zak Smile? Make up your damn mind."

Abi laughs and my phone chirps again, but I ignore it.

"I'm kind of nervous," she admits. "What if the party sucks? What if everyone thinks it's because of me?"

I roll my eyes. "A Hive party *never* sucks."

This weekend it's the annual 'welcome back' party to kick off the new year. The responsibility alternates between the Wolves and the Bees, and it's our turn this year. We've been planning for it since November, as the Wolves got the Thanksgiving party, so everything is more than ready.

"Just because you're President doesn't change anything. Sasha and I still have your back." We reach the steps to the Hive, some of the Freshman Bees already setting up the fire pits ready for tomorrow night. "It's going to be a great party."

She takes a breath and nods, following me through the front door, but when I make to head upstairs, she stops me with a hand on my arm.

"If you ever want to talk about stuff," she says. "I'm here. Okay?"

I frown. "I know. What's wrong? Do *you* need to talk about something?"

She shakes her head. "No. I'm just saying."

It doesn't escape me that I'm keeping something from her after almost losing Sasha for doing the same thing to us. "Damnit."

Abi looks at me questioningly and I nod my head toward the living room. No one's in there and I take off my coat, settling down in one of the chairs by the fire. Abi does the same, taking the one opposite.

Glancing around to make sure no one is anywhere near, I lean forward. "I'm getting married."

Abi's mouth forms a perfect 'o', her blue eyes wide. It would be funny if my heart wasn't jackhammering in my chest. "What the hell, Jaime? Who to? Zak?"

The suggestion should make me laugh, but instead, it hurts. I shake my head. "No. Not to Zak."

"So, what? You have a secret boyfriend? Is it someone from back home? Spill!"

Leaning back in the chair, I heave a sigh, trying to decide how much to tell her. "His name is Louis. He's the son of one of my dad's business partners."

Abi continues to gawp at me. "Okay, number one, how long has this been going on? And number two, I need pictures. Stat."

Rolling my eyes, I take my phone from my purse. I forgot I got a text and my heart stutters at the notification from Zak on my screen.

See you at the party tomorrow

There's no way I can avoid him. I can't not go to the party when it's at my own damn house. Clicking out of the message, I bring up a browser and type in Louis' name. Immediately, the screen fills with press shots and the Forbes magazine cover he apparently did last year.

I hand the phone to Abi. "We've known each other forever, but we only got reacquainted as adults recently."

Abi stares between me and the phone, her mouth still open. "He's gorgeous."

I shrug.

"Holy shit," she says, scrolling through the phone. "He's number two on the world's most eligible billionaires, Jay!"

Is he? I watch her scroll, grateful that she's not pressing for more details, although I'm sure it'll come.

"I have to admit, I'm surprised," she says eventually, handing me back my phone.

"Oh?"

"Yeah. I didn't think you were the 'get married young' type." She kicks off her ankle boots and tucks her feet underneath her. "And although he's gorgeous, he's not what I expected your type to be."

This time I laugh. "Oh, really? And what's my type."

"Zak."

I groan. "If Zak's my type, I wouldn't have been saying no to him for the past three years."

"That's just it," Abi says, eyeing me carefully. "I never understood why you kept saying no. He's hot, funny, sweet, and completely smitten with you. Is it because of this Louis guy? Have you been holding out for him?"

Let's go with that. "Sort of, yeah."

"I have questions, though." She raises an eyebrow as she starts braiding her hair over her shoulder. "How did he propose and why aren't you wearing a ring?"

My mouth opens to reply, that the ring is upstairs in my jewelry box, but she cuts me off.

"You are actually getting married to this guy, right?" she asks, narrowing her blue eyes. "This isn't a fake fiancé type thing?"

"Why the hell would I need to invent a fake fiancé?"

Abi raises an eyebrow. "I don't know. You tell me."

"Screw you." I roll my eyes. "I don't need a fake fiancé. My ring is upstairs. It's a vintage Cartier, and he gave it to me in the garden of my home in Florida. Okay?"

She watches me carefully, but I have no idea what she's thinking. I'm not sure I want to know.

"Do you know what you're wearing to the party tonight?" I ask.

My question does the trick, and the conversation moves to hosting the first party as the official new President of the Beta Epsilon Deltas.

I smile and nod, making all the right noises, but my brain is firmly lodged somewhere else. The same place it's been since the Winter Mingle.

Christmas was strange. Louis and his family went back to Europe, maintaining the tradition of Christmas Eve in Winchester and Christmas on the French Riviera. It was hinted at very strongly that I'd be joining them next year before leaving for our honeymoon.

A shudder runs through me. Is this what it felt like for princesses back in the Middle Ages? Shipped off for alliances and then expected to produce an heir? At least I don't have to worry about being beheaded if I don't.

Louis has only tried to kiss me once since that first time in the gardens. When he left for Christmas, he leaned in as we said goodbye, but I turned my head, offering my cheek instead. I'm hoping it was subtle enough that he didn't realize it was on purpose.

As much as I'd never admit it, kissing Louis would feel like cheating on Zak. Which is literally ridiculous. How can you cheat on a man you're not dating with your fiancé?

Not only that, but if I actually try to form some sort of relationship with Louis, it would make things . . . official. I don't want this to be real. If I can pretend for as long as possible that it's not really happening, that's good with me. The problem with pretending, however, is that you can only do it for so long before reality comes knocking.

ZAK

Things are different this year. It's subtle, but I feel it like a splinter, digging under my skin. For the last three years, me, Sol and Alex have been inseparable. But right from the opening parties this year, shit started to go differently than before. Which is why I find myself at the welcome back party with neither of my guys in sight.

Exhaling loudly, I scan the crowd again. I arrived with both Sol and Alex, but neither of them is anywhere to be seen.

Even before his relationship was official, I've seen less and less of Alex. And now that the eternal bastard bachelor has gone and settled down, becoming disgustingly loved up, he may as well have graduated early. And fuck knows what's going on with Sol and Wes, because I keep asking, but he's keeping his cards close to his chest.

A wave of sadness crashes in my chest. I have no doubt we'll stay close after graduation, but in just a few short months, we won't be housemates or teammates anymore. It's going to take actual effort to see each other, and I hate the thought of it. Not bumping into Alex when I raid the kitchen . . . No early morning gym sessions with Sol, or runs with Alex . . . No crashing weekends at Sol's parents' place for home cooked food.

I'm not an idiot. I know part of the reason I'm not feeling as close to them is because I'm keeping a huge fucking secret. They may have accepted that Jaime is end game as far as I'm concerned, but they think I'm still pining from afar. Fuck. I *am* still pining from afar.

The Hive is packed to bursting, with students spilling out to the fire pits outside despite the freezing cold. It's one of the few parties hosted where everyone on campus is invited, and people make the most of it.

I haven't seen Jaime yet, but I know she's here. There's no way she'd leave Abi alone on her first party as President. As for how I'm going to play it tonight, I have no idea. I wasn't even going to text her after she skipped out on me, but I decided to take the high road. The idea of not wishing her a happy new year was too bitter a pill to swallow, even if she was probably kissing Louis at midnight.

Sucking in a deep breath, I push the image from my mind. It would be different if she actually wanted to marry the guy. If she did, I'd step back, no questions asked. But she told me she doesn't want to. The fact that she feels like she has no choice has my fingers forming a tight fist around my beer bottle. I just don't understand why she feels so fucking obligated. Why she can't just say no.

The anger builds and builds until my body is practically steaming, but then I see her, and it evaporates with a single exhale. Dressed in skinny ripped jeans and a gold halter neck top, her hair swept into a high ponytail, she looks perfect. She always does.

My eyes never leave her as she moves through the crowd, smiling at everyone and talking to most. My mouth twitches as she gives a passing group of Wolves a dirty look. It's one of the many things I love about Jaime. She's so unapologetically her. If she doesn't like you, she'll tell you and list the reasons why to your face.

Which is why I just don't understand why she isn't fighting this engagement. No one makes Jaime Smith do something she doesn't want to do. I should know.

I don't need to approach her. Leaning against the wall, on the outskirts of the crowd, it doesn't take long for her eyes to find me. She's still too far away for me to read her expression when she does, but when she starts walking toward me, I smile, my heart skipping a beat.

By the time she reaches me, my smile is a full-blown grin. Jaime's not a short girl, but she's not tall either, and even with her spiked heels, she still has to tilt her head back fully to look up at me, and I love it.

"Hey, Kitty Cat," I say. "Great party."

Her eyebrows arch and she folds her arms. "Where are your minions?"

"I'm pretty sure Sol and I are the minions." I chuckle. "And our illustrious leader is probably balls-deep in your former leader right about now."

Jaime pulls a face and kicks me in the shin.

"Ow! What the fuck?"

"Do not mention the words 'balls-deep' and my best friend in the same sentence ever again."

Grinning, I bring my beer to my lips and take a sip, my eyes never leaving her. "We need to talk."

"Do we?"

"Yes. We do. Can we go somewhere where I don't have to shout?" I glance over to where Joy Blake is DJing. "I have a fear of saying something embarrassing right as the music cuts out."

Jaime's lips twitch as though she's holding back a smile. "That only happens in cheesy teen movies, and Joy never leaves gaps between songs."

"It doesn't have to be between," I argue. "It could be right before a beat drops."

She rolls her eyes and turns, moving through the crowd, and I push away from the wall to chase after her.

"Whoa! Where you going?"

"You wanted to go somewhere quiet?" she calls over her shoulder. "I'm going somewhere quiet."

My heart speeds as we approach the foyer, but instead of heading upstairs, she pushes through the front door and steps out into the icy evening air.

The night is filled with the sounds of people laughing and talking amidst the backdrop of crackling fires and music leaking through open doors from the party inside.

Jaime wraps her arms around herself, shivering slightly. "What did you want to talk about?"

"It's too cold out here." I frown. "You'll freeze."

"Talk fast, then."

A growl of frustration builds in my chest, but I swallow it down, forcing a laid-back smile. She knows we can't talk out here, but she doesn't know me at all if she thinks that's going to stop me. "I want to take you for that coffee this weekend."

She stares up at me, her eyes narrowed, and I take the opportunity to drink in the dark eyeliner she's wearing and the gold powder on her lids. *Mine.* The thought echoes through my body like a drumbeat.

"Coffee?" she repeats slowly.

I grin. "You know? The brown stuff that gets you through the day?"

"I don't think that's a good idea," she says, carefully.

"Thanks for asking, though."

She's moving, walking back through the front door before I can stop her, and it takes my brain a second to tell my feet to move. I catch her just inside, grabbing her shoulder and hauling her into the corner. She squawks in protest, but I crowd her in, blocking her from the rest of the party, making sure I'm the only person she can see.

"It's a *great* idea, Kitty Cat," I say, resting my forearms on either side of her, leaning close so she can hear me over the music. "Friends go for coffee together all the time."

Jaime stares up at me, her chest rising and falling rapidly, her eyes hard and her mouth in a firm line. "You have lots of friends. Ask one of them."

I lean a little closer, inhaling her perfume. "But why would I ask someone else when I can ask you? Besides, I think you owe me after running out on me."

Her eyes widen, as if she'd expected me not to bring up what happened over winter break. If Jaime thinks I'm going to forget the best fucking night of my life, she's got another thing coming.

"Is it him?" I ask, dipping my head until my lips brush the shell of her ear. She trembles and my eyes fall closed for a second. "Do you have plans with *Louis* this weekend?"

Her fingers press to my chest as though she's going to push me away, but then her palm flattens, smoothing over my shirt and resting above my heart.

"Do you?" I ask, aware of the quickening thudding beneath her splayed hand.

She nods. "Yes."

The single word is a knife through my heart, and my hand grips my beer bottle so tightly I think it might crack. I lean closer, dipping my mouth to her ear. "Have you let him fuck you, Kitty Cat?"

Her breath catches and she leans back against the wall in a half-hearted attempt to put distance between us. But she still doesn't push me away.

"Tell me," I press, my words little more than a growl. "Has he tasted you yet, Kitty Cat?"

I don't know why I'm pushing it. If she says yes, if she tells me she's let him into her bed, it will cleave me in fucking two.

"No," she whispers.

My head falls forward against the wall, my eyes closing as I suck in a breath, not caring that she can see my relief. I've never hidden my feelings for her and I'm not about to start now.

"Are you going to let him?" I ask, not sure why I'm insisting on torturing myself. "Are you going to let him into your bed?"

Jaime looks up at me and I swallow hard at the emotion in her eyes. I'm not being fair to either of us.

"Come for a coffee with me when you get back, Kitty Cat." I shift so I can wrap my fingers around the end of her ponytail, tugging gently. "As friends."

She swallows, her tongue darting out to wet her lips, and my body sways forward as though beckoned by her siren's call. I inhale her scent, pressing our bodies together, and she sucks in a breath, her fingers tensing against my chest. Dipping my head, I ghost a kiss against her neck.

"As friends," she whispers, the words breathless as she tilts her head, granting me better access.

I run my nose along her jaw, pausing above her lips, before dropping my arms and stepping back.

"Of course, Kitty Cat." I wink at her before raising my near-empty beer bottle in a salute as I walk away. "What else?"

JAIME

BE

The sunlight catches on my engagement ring as I raise the strawberry mojito to my lips. As always, it feels heavy in a way that has nothing to do with the sparkling two-karat diamond.

I've already been back to Fisher Island more times this school year than the last three combined, and I'm not happy about it. There are precious few weekends left of college and I want to enjoy them. I want to go out with my girls and have fun. If I'm going to be chained to Louis and his family for the rest of my life, I think it's only fair I get to enjoy my last few months of freedom first.

Mom does not agree.

When I told her as much, she told me in no uncertain terms that I was coming home because Louis had flown all the way from Italy to spend a rare free weekend with me. When she'd suggested he could come to Oregon if I was unwilling to travel to Florida, I booked my own flight. The idea of Louis at Franklin West—of everyone finding out—causes me to shudder.

A shadow falls over me and I look up to find a sweaty Louis staring down at me as he grabs his water from the table. "Are you all right?"

I smile from under my sunhat, trying to muster *something* at the sight of him shirtless and glistening with sweat from his tennis session. Sure, he's got a great body. I'm not blind. I'm also not interested.

"I'm fine," I reassure him. "Nice serve."

Louis smiles and swaps his water for a towel, patting his face. "Thanks. I think I'm about done. I'll grab a quick shower then come out and join you."

I watch him head back up the path toward the house, towel slung over his muscled shoulder and wish I did feel something. It would make things so much easier.

My phone vibrates on the wrought iron table, and I pick it up, expecting it to be one of the girls. My pulse skips at Zak's name.

> How's your weekend going?

Before I can think better of it, I take a selfie with my mojito and send it in reply. He starts typing immediately and I sip my drink with a smile waiting for his response.

> Not as good as the oat milk vanilla latte
> you could be having right now at Joe
> For Joe

I shake my head, about to put my phone down when I see the dots appear again.

> You look gorgeous btw

My smile widens, and even though I know I shouldn't engage in this conversation while I'm waiting for Louis to return—or ever, if I'm being honest—I type out a response.

> Thank you. So do you

Grinning at my own hilariousness, I take another sip of my drink. Louis asked whether I wanted to go into Miami or somewhere else to spend the day together, but honestly, the whole thing's so awkward, I figured it would be better to stay here. The house is big enough that there's no chance of driving each other up the wall, and I have no idea if my parents are actually home. Not that it would matter if they were. It's not like Louis and I will be doing anything that requires privacy.

Butterflies swarm in my gut as I recall Zak's whispered words at the Hive, my heart squeezing at the way he'd clearly been so relieved to hear I haven't been intimate with Louis yet.

Yet.

My phone buzzes on the table and I scoop it up, thankful for the distraction. *Holy shit.* I sit up, lifting my sunglasses as I stare at the photo Zak sent through. I figured from his last text that he was out in Portland, but clearly not.

Laying on his bed, he's shirtless, one arm bent behind his head, every muscle is on display as he smirks at the camera. It's the kind of smirk that should make me roll my eyes—that should make me dislike him. But it doesn't.

> Thx

Biting back my grin, I type out a reply.

> What you up to today besides sending thirst traps?

> Got a paper due. What u doing with him?

An unexpected rush of sadness steals my breath and I put the phone down, my smile a distant memory. I get what he's doing. It's not like we can forget it's happening. And apparently, we're 'friends' now.

"I brought you out a fresh one."

I turn at the sound of Louis' voice to find him approaching the table, two mojitos in his hand. He hands me the strawberry one, keeping the regular for himself, as he sits down opposite me.

"Thank you." I return his smile. "Feel better?"

"Absolutely," he says, running a hand through his still-damp hair. "Sunshine, exercise, and beautiful company. Life couldn't be better."

I look away, hoping he thinks I'm being demure. He looks like he's just stepped out of a country club magazine in pressed shorts and a pale blue shirt. Is it bad I wish he was an asshole?

My phone buzzes and I glance down at the notification. It's from Zak, but it's just a single emoji. I frown at the screen. Why would he send me a carousel horse?

"Everything okay?" Louis asks.

My skin heats and as I pick the phone up and turn it face down, another message comes through.

> Just say the word

I'm half tempted to text him back to ask him what the hell he means, when it clicks.

A white horse.

Putting the phone down, I smile at Louis. "Everything's fine. When do you have to go back to Europe?"

He sighs and takes a sip of his drink, crossing his ankles. "First thing Monday morning, unfortunately. I would have liked longer."

"Well, I have class on Monday morning, so if you stayed, you'd be by yourself."

Louis gives me a lopsided grin. "You wouldn't have blown off class for me?"

"Sorry, I'm just not that kind of girl." I laugh. "Besides, it's not just class. I can't miss work."

Louis turns to me, his dark blond eyebrows raised. "Work?"

"Yeah. I intern three days a week at KBCX," I explain. "It's acting as course credit for my degree."

I hold his stare as I sip my drink, wondering if he'll mention the coincidence that his family own the station, but he looks more confused than anything.

"Why would you do that?" he asks.

I blink. "Because it's invaluable experience. If I want to own my own network one day—"

"Excuse me?" Louis sits forward, a deep frown creasing his handsome features.

Unease settles in my stomach, and I straighten, taking off my sunglasses and placing them beside my drink. "That's my goal," I say carefully. "I want to run my own television network."

Louis rubs his chin, his frown showing no sign of leaving. "I didn't realize."

"Realize what?"

He continues to frown, and I shift on my seat. Surely, he knows I have no plans to take over my father's business. It's never once been an option. And I'm glad of it. I've sat through enough conversations with business partners he brought home for a 'family dinner' to know that it doesn't interest me at all.

"This won't do," he says, almost to himself. "I'll have to check the agreement."

"What?" I snap, no longer able to hide my irritation. "What won't do?"

Louis's features pinch as he looks at me. "I didn't realize you thought you'd be working."

"What else would I be doing?"

"Well." He makes a vague gesture with his hands as though it's obvious. "You'd be traveling with me most of the year. At least at first. I'd need you on hand to attend events and dinners with me. And, if we're going to conceive, it helps if we're on the same continent, right?"

All the blood drains from my face. "What?"

He smiles, reaching out and covering my hand where it's gripping the table. "Of course, once we start having children, you'd stay in London with them."

What the actual *fuck?*

"London," I echo.

"Naturally." Louis squeezes my hand. "It's all in the prenup. Did you give it back to the lawyer? I haven't checked."

Apparently, it's me who should have checked. I hired a lawyer to look it over for anything that sounded out of place, but perhaps I should have been more specific. I realize now, they were thinking about protecting my money. What I should have asked them to look for was whether it was protecting my fucking life.

"Just how many children are we having?" I ask through gritted teeth.

"Four would be wonderful," he says, his smile growing. "I always wanted a big family."

I can't breathe. Pushing back my chair, I stumble to my feet. "Sorry. I think the sun and the alcohol has made me a little queasy." My hand moves to my chest, where my heart slams beneath it.

Louis stands, too, his smile fading as he looks at me with concern. "Let me walk you inside."

"No. Please." Stepping away from him, I snatch my phone from the table and back away. "I'll be fine."

He opens his mouth to protest but, before he can utter a single word, I turn and walk as fast as I can back down the path.

My feet move quickly, pulling me toward the house and through the doors, not slowing until I reach my bedroom. Closing the doors behind me and flicking the lock, I stand in the middle of the room breathing hard.

This can't be happening.

Storming over to my dresser, I wrench open the top drawer and pull out the unsigned prenup. Leafing through with trembling hands, I scan for words like 'employment' and 'career' but I'm not entirely sure what I'm looking for and the words blur before me.

Tossing the papers back down on my dresser, I collapse on the bed as my tears threaten to overflow. Just when I think I can make the best of the situation, life throws another wrench in.

I can't. I can't be one of those wives who just follows her husband around, smiling and hanging on his arm between popping out kids. *Four* apparently. I'm not even sure I want *one*.

Rolling onto my side, my phone digs into my hip and I tug it free. Zak's notification is still there, and I stare at the little white horse through blurry eyes.

Maybe I do need rescuing after all.

ZAK

The door to my room pushes open and I look up from my bed at Alex with wide eyes. "Hey, man. Won't you come in?"

"I'm here to tell you to stop." He folds his arms and stares pointedly at the yellow lacrosse ball in my hand. "And put a shirt on."

Keeping my eyes on him, I toss the ball to the wall, catching it effortlessly as it bounces back. "Why?"

"Because it's cold and your nips are going to poke my eyes out."

I roll my eyes. "Why do I need to stop with the ball?"

"Because you can hear it throughout the entire fucking house."

He strides forward and tries to snatch the ball from my hand, but I leap to my feet and hold it against the ceiling, just out of his reach.

"Sorry," I say, swatting away his attempts to grab my arm. "I didn't realize someone had called the fun police."

"Smashing a ball against a wall for two fucking hours isn't fun," he snaps. "For anyone."

Two hours? I glance at my watch in surprise.

Alex gives up and sits down on my desk chair with a sigh. "Want to tell me what's got you holed up in your room, pissing everyone off?"

Sinking back down onto my bed, I turn the ball over in my hands with a frown. "Nothing. I'm just bored."

"Bored?" Alex's laughter fills my room. "Never once in the years I've known you have I heard you utter those words. You don't know how to do bored."

The corner of my mouth kicks up. "Fine. I'm thinking."

"About?"

"Stuff." I move to toss the ball again, but Alex leaps out of the chair and snatches it before it can leave my hands. "Fucker."

"Talk to me," he says, placing the ball on my desk behind him. "I know I've been busy lately, but you know I'm here for you, right?"

Leaning back against my bedroom wall, I close my eyes. "You haven't been busy; you've been *getting* busy."

"Stop deflecting."

"Fine." I open an eye and peer at him. "I guess I'm a little stressed out about after graduation."

Alex sits forward, resting his arms on his knees. "What do you mean?"

"You know . . . Life. You and Sol have shit sorted out and I . . . Don't."

"Do you need to have shit sorted out?" he asks. "Is anyone expecting that of you?"

It's the same internal conversation I've had since the start of the year, but things have changed. Before winter break, I'd have said 'no', and breathed a sigh of relief. But now . . . Now I'm competing with a fucking billionaire, I kind of feel like I have to up my game.

But am I really competing? Jaime said she'd go for coffee with me next week but I'm not expecting her to keep to it. Fuck knows what's going to happen this weekend. When she told me she was spending it with him, I swear I almost cracked a molar. Even the fact that she hasn't slept with him yet holds little relief, because it's only a matter of time before she does. What if he's fucking her right this very second?

"Zak?"

I blink, meeting Alex's blue stare. "What's going on? I don't think I've ever seen you angry off the lacrosse field. It's terrifying."

For a second, I consider telling him everything. But I can't. If I did, I'd be breaking my promise to Jaime, and that's something I'd never do.

"What if I never find something?" I say, the words surprising me as they trip from my lips.

Alex frowns. "What do you mean?"

"Like, my calling," I explain. "What if I never find something I really love?"

"There's got to be stuff you love already," he says. "Start there. What brings you joy?"

The name that jumps straight into my head isn't a surprise, but I shove it to the side before it makes itself at home.

"Lacrosse," I say without hesitation. "Peanut M&Ms, sex, hot showers, fall, and playing with my nieces."

Alex stares at me for a solid minute, then blinks. "Okay. Unless we're going for a sex worker paid in chocolate, or a nanny, I guess we're looking at lacrosse."

"Or porn star," I muse, making my pecs dance.

"Zak." Alex gives me his 'president' stare, but it doesn't work on me the same way as it does the freshmen.

"What?" My shoulders rise in a shrug. "Lacrosse isn't a real option. I've left it too late to go down the PLL route."

Alex eyes the trophies scattered around my room before looking back at me. "I've watched almost every game for years. You're damn good, Zak. It's never too late."

Holding his stare, I try to muster some sort of feeling about playing professional lacrosse, but it's just not there. I freaking love the game, but playing it somewhere else, without Sol? It just doesn't hold the same appeal.

Alex shakes his head. "Don't worry about it. You'll find something you love. And even if you don't right away, you've got time. I'm not excited about going to work for my dad, but I'm excited to enter that world so I can find my own place within it. Maybe that's what it'll take for you. Find something . . . lacrosse adjacent."

Chuckling softly, I open my mouth to make a joke about lacrosse themed porn, when my phone vibrates obnoxiously on my desk.

Alex turns to look, his head snapping back to me immediately, eyes narrowed. "Who's Kitty Cat?"

"What?" My heart leaps into my mouth as I stand and snatch up the phone. Why the hell is Jaime calling me? I turn away from Alex's curious stare and swipe to answer. "Hey. You okay?"

A faint sob sounds down the line followed by a sniffle, and I freeze, my heart rate kicking into overdrive.

"Jaime? What happened? Are you okay?"

I'm vaguely aware of Alex's eyebrows hitting my ceiling, but I wave my hand in a gesture somewhere between 'see you later' and 'fuck off', and he takes the hint, closing the door behind him as he leaves.

"Jaime?"

Sniffles sound down the line, and my chest tightens. I

hate that she's somewhere I can't get to. If I could only see her . . . Pulling the phone away from my ear, I click the FaceTime button.

"You don't want to see me right now," Jaime says through a forced laugh.

"There is no scenario that exists where I wouldn't want to see you."

Watching the screen, I smile as the video loads. But then my heart sinks as I see Jaime's beautiful face, her mascara a little smudged and her eyes still shiny with tears.

"Hey," she says, her smile small and unsure. "I'm not sure why I called you. Sorry."

Climbing onto my bed, I lie back against the pillows. "You called me because I'm your friend. And because I know your big bad secret."

"I told Abigail."

My eyebrows shoot up. "Did you tell her everything?"

"No."

A small ember of pride sparks in my gut before concern extinguishes it. "Maybe you should. It's good to have people to talk to."

"I have you."

"Yeah? Are you still going to call me when you're married to Billionaire Ken?" I know I shouldn't, but the truth is as painful to me as it is to her.

Jaime's face shutters and the camera moves further away from her face. "I shouldn't have called. You're right. I—"

"Stop," I snap. "You did the right thing to call. Now, tell me why you're upset or I'm getting my ass on a plane and turning up on your doorstep."

Jaime's lips quirk and she swipes her fingers under her eyes. "I was talking to Louis."

Even though I know she's there with him all weekend, the sound of his name causes my jaw to clench, my fingers tightening their grip on the phone. I have to take a deep breath to force a relaxed, open expression back onto my face.

"I mentioned the internship," she continues. "And he said he didn't realize I had plans to work."

My face falls into a frown. "What? Like, during your senior year?"

"No. Like ever."

The anger I pushed down into the pit of my stomach comes roaring back to the surface. "What the fuck? He wants you as what? A trophy wife?"

A wry smile curves her lips. "Pretty much."

"I hope you told him to go fuck himself."

Jamie's laugh momentarily causes me to forget why I'm so angry, and I smile at the way her brown hair splays across the bedspread beneath her, her eyes crinkling.

"No," she says. "Although, I should have. He started talking about how many kids he wanted, and I said I was feeling a bit queasy and left."

This conversation is the sweetest torture. Jaime is confiding in me, she chose to call *me*, but she's telling me about the man whose children she's going to bear. Well, not if I have anything to say about it. That's for damn sure.

"Speaking of queasy," she says. "Could you put a shirt on?"

I laugh, lifting the phone to give her a full view of my chest as I flex my muscles. "You say queasy, but you mean horny, right?"

"You keep telling yourself that." She smiles, but then it fades, the haunted look seeping back into her features. "I can't do this, Zak. I don't want to follow him around the world while he lives his life until he knocks me up."

"How about I murder him?" I suggest. "I have no plans after college, right? I'd be more than happy for my 'direction' to be a life sentence for voluntary manslaughter."

"I'm pretty sure voluntary manslaughter is first degree murder," Jaime says, her smile returned. "And no. You can't murder him."

"Fine." I pout. "But you said it, Kitty Cat. That life is not you. Have you tried speaking to your parents? Surely, they know you well enough to know that would be hell for you?"

Jaime sighs and closes her eyes. "I'm not sure they care."

"Well, you won't know unless you try."

I wish I knew what she was so scared of. Having met her parents, they do seem slightly terrifying in a rich and powerful way, but not in an evil villain kind of way. Surely, she must be able to talk to them about her life?

Jaime opens an eye. "Don't think I didn't notice your little self-depreciation back there by the way, Mr. Aldridge."

"My what?"

"About having no plans after college." She sits up and the camera moves around, giving me a dizzying glimpse of what looks like her bedroom as she moves to a sitting position at the head of her bed. "I'm sorry about what I said at Joe For Joe."

I shrug. "No idea what you're talking about."

"Don't ever lie to me, Zak," she says quietly, her brow knitting together slightly. "Not everyone has their life figured out by the end of college, and I'm nothing but envious that you have the space and time to do so."

"I already found out," I say, giving her a lopsided grin. "I'm going to be a nanny by day and a porn star by night."

Jaime's eyes bug out of her head. "What the actual fuck?"

"Well, that's an option on the list," I clarify. "I'm still working on it."

An expression I can't decipher crosses Jaime's face, but then she smiles. "Thank you for making me feel better, Zak. I appreciate it."

"Any time." I wish so much I could reach through the screen and touch her. I'd give everything I owned to be able to hold her in my arms right now. "What are you going to do?"

She sighs heavily, dropping her head back against her headboard. "I'm going to speak to my mom. I should probably also speak to Louis. And I'm going to give the contract back to my lawyer and get her to check for clauses about my employment."

I sit up so fast I get a head rush. "Contract? You've got a fucking contract?"

Jaime's eyes widen, her lips parting. "It's just a prenup."

"A prenup?" A huffed laugh of disbelief leaves my mouth. "I'm not an idiot, Jaime. Prenups are about money and property. So, unless you're the property in this fucking contract, it can't stipulate whether you can work or not."

"Maybe you should look into becoming a lawyer," she grumbles.

Leaning back against the pillow again, I push my fingers through my hair, missing the longer length I would be able to tug in frustration. She's only joking, but I'm definitely going to look into the technicalities of this. I'm really fucking certain Mason Smith can't contractually force his daughter to marry someone she doesn't want to.

Although, I'm certain Jaime knows that, too.

"I should go," she says, pulling me from my thoughts.

"Do you have to?"

She nods. "Yeah."

"We still on for coffee when you get back?" I ask.

Jaime's lips curve into a small smile, and my heart thuds an extra beat in response. "Yes. I have too much course work on Monday, but Tuesday, I could meet you on my lunch from KBCX?"

"Sounds good, Kitty Cat." I give her my brightest smile, and it works because her eyes gain back a little light.

As soon as she hangs up, my smile fades. It doesn't sound good. I want so much more than a coffee, and I hate that she's going to go and spend more time with *him*. Who the fuck does he think he is? Jaime was put on this planet to take it by storm, not to breed tiny billionaires.

Tossing my phone down onto my bed, I take a deep breath and reach for my laptop. Jaime might be reluctant to fight for her freedom, but I'm sure as hell not going to sit around and wait for her to disappear into the sunset with Louis. Even if she doesn't choose me—even if what we have now is how it ends for us—I'm not going to let him have her. She deserves so much more, and I'm not letting this go without a fight.

JAIME

BE

Swiping my card, I stab the button for the fourteenth floor of KBCX, feeling a little lighter than the last time I was here. Although I didn't get an opportunity to speak to my parents this weekend, because it turned out they'd decided on a last-minute trip to their house in the Hamptons to give Louis and me some space, it's still going to happen this week. I've also given the prenup back to my lawyer and she's working her way through it again.

I'm not even going to pretend that Zak doesn't have something to do with my lifted mood. Calling him on Saturday might have been stupid, but it was exactly what I needed. The two-hour-long conversation we had last night, too.

The elevator makes an abrasive sound, the card reader flashing red, and I frown. I swipe my card again and the same thing happens. *Weird.* Shrugging, I press the button for the lobby instead and it flashes green, immediately whisking me away from the underground parking.

Checking my reflection in the mirrored doors, I smile to myself. As promised, I'm meeting Zak on my lunch break at

Joe For Joe. I figure, if we only have an hour, I won't be tempted to do something stupid. You know, like drag him to a hotel or something. Because I totally have self-control. I smile to myself at the blatant lie.

Maybe it's because he's been around for the last few years, but I feel so comfortable with Zak. In just a few months, he knows more about me than my friends, and he's somehow become the person I go to before anyone else. Which is ridiculous. It's something I shouldn't have let happen, but it did. And I can't bring myself to walk away.

The elevator doors ping open and, as I step out into the sparsely populated lobby, my heart swells at the thought of being greeted by his dimpled smile at lunch. The next four hours can't go fast enough.

My heels click on the marble as I cross the lobby with my access card in my hand, smiling at the woman behind the desk. "Morning, Sophie. My card isn't working for some reason. Can you let me up to fourteenth, please?"

Sophie's warm smile fades, and she glances at her computer before turning back to me. "I'm sorry, Jaime. I can't."

"You can't?" I frown, watching as her eyes dart to Stuart, the security guard, over by the front doors. "Why not?"

She swallows. "You don't work here anymore."

My mouth drops open. "Excuse me?"

I'm vaguely aware of Stuart's broad frame moving toward us, but I'm too busy processing the rush of emotions slamming through me to think about why.

"Let me speak to Brad," I demand, holding out my hand.

Sophie looks like she's about to be sick and I honestly feel sorry for her. If Roxanne has somehow managed to get me fired, Brad should at least have the fucking balls to tell me to my face. Not get poor Sophie to do his dirty work.

"I . . . I can't," the poor woman stutters, her eyes flitting between me and Stuart, who's made his way over to my side.

There are a few people in the lobby watching curiously, and I take a breath, flashing a woman I recognize a warm smile before turning and glaring at Stuart.

"Any thoughts you have of dragging me out of here, you'd best forget them. Fast," I hiss. "I'm calling Brad."

Stuart holds my stare but doesn't make a move as I grab my phone from my purse and find his number. I keep staring at the security guard, ignoring everyone else, as the phone rings against my ear.

"Miss Smith." Brad sighs as he answers. "How can I help you?"

My eyebrow arches. "You can help me by letting me up so I can do my job."

"I'm afraid that won't be possible." He sighs again. "Your contract has been terminated. Effective immediately."

A lump forms in my throat, but I swallow it down, my fingers holding my phone in a death grip. "Why? If Roxanne has—"

"It's nothing to do with Roxanne," he says, his voice frustratingly calm. "This request has come from the top."

The top? I frown, an unease beginning to fill my gut as I shift my purse on my shoulder, still staring at Stuart's frowning face. "What does that mean?"

"It means, Miss Smith, if you want to take this up with someone, speak to your father-in-law."

The lobby sways, and I lean against Sophie's desk as I the phone falls away from my ear. This has nothing to do with my future father-in-law. This is Louis. I know it. He didn't want me working, so he's taken care of it himself.

"Don't you fucking dare," I snap at Stuart as he takes a cautious step forward. "I'll see myself out."

Avoiding Sophie's eye, I turn and walk back toward the elevators with my head held high as people turn, their whispers too loud despite the blood roaring in my ears.

I can't fucking believe this. My eyes burn as the doors slide shut and I descend back to the parking lot. How dare he? I swipe through to Louis' contact and then stare at my phone with trembling hands. I don't want to speak to him. I can't.

I'm too angry. Too sad. Too . . . everything.

Dragging in deep breaths to calm my racing heart, I make my way over to my car and climb in. What the hell do I do now? If I go to class, I'll have to tell my professor what happened. Mortification heats my skin. No. I need to fix this. I'll speak to Louis and get him to undo this. He has to.

Once my hands stop shaking, I put my car in reverse and make my way out of the garage. I'm not really aware of the drive back to Franklin West, and as I leave Portland behind for the quiet mountain roads, I retreat further into my head, going over things I could have done differently.

There's no way I could have known Louis would do that, but I still mentally kick myself for telling him about the internship. I realize it doesn't really matter, though. Even if I'd managed to keep it a secret, there's no way I could have held down a secret job after graduation. Not when he expects me to travel the world with him, warming his bed like a little portable incubator.

My stomach rolls. This isn't what I signed up for. All this time, despite my reservations, I pictured living my life alongside Louis, both of us following our own paths, pursuing our dreams. Never once did I imagine him stomping on them until they drew their last breath.

When I pull into the Den parking lot, I blink in surprise. I hadn't meant to drive here. Why didn't I go to the Hive? My hand goes to put the car in reverse but stills. I came here for Zak—my brain subconsciously steering me to the place I feel safe and unjudged.

Shaking my head, I put the car in reverse and press on the gas. I should go to Abigail. Together we can bitch about Louis and drown my sorrows in wine and ice cream.

But I don't want that.

Sighing in frustration, I pull back into the parking spot and put the car in park. Reaching for my phone, I tap out a message.

> You home?

He sees it instantly, the dots dancing at the bottom of our thread.

> Yeah. You okay?

> I'm at the door

Climbing out of my car, I cross to the pebbled path leading to the Den. I don't even care if the Wolves see me. Let them think what they want. Besides, it's this or climbing through a fucking window, and that's not happening.

Zak's already at the door, looking like sin, barefoot in dark gray sweatpants and a white t-shirt that might as well be painted on. As I draw closer, his eyes meet mine and the concern etched across his handsome features almost breaks the dam I've walled my tears behind.

"What's up, Kitty Cat?" he asks as I climb the steps.

I shake my head and move past him into the Den, heading for the stairs. He doesn't question me, instead closing the door and following behind, taking my hand when we reach the landing and steering me toward his room.

It occurs to me then, that I've never been in his room, and as he opens the door I peer around in curiosity. It's neater than I expected, smelling of the woodsy cologne he wears and a little sweat. I don't hate it.

"Jaime?" he says softly.

I stare at the lacrosse gear littering the corners, my gaze flitting to the trophies on the window ledge from his past three seasons. Anything to not look at him. Not when I'm this close to breaking.

"Want me to leave you alone?" he asks. "If you just want to hide out, that's fine by me."

I let out a breath, knowing he means it. That he'd let me just sit in his room if I needed it. I'm pretty sure Zak would give me anything I needed. It's one of the things that makes him so damn dangerous.

"Stay," I say softly, shrugging off my jacket and hanging it on his desk chair before sitting down on the bed.

After a minute, I glance up. He's still leaning against the closed doors, his arms folded across his chest, and his eyes fixed on me.

"What?" I ask, kicking off my black patent Jimmy Choos.

He raises a dark eyebrow. "Nothing. Just thinking how good you look on my bed."

Despite the shit show that has been this morning, a laugh rises in my throat. "You're a dick."

"Yeah." He sighs and crosses the room, pulling out his chair and sitting down on it. "But I'm *your* dick."

It doesn't escape my attention that he hasn't sat on the bed, and I wonder whether it's for my sake or his. He leans forward, resting his forearms on his knees, studying me with a half-smile that makes me regret coming here, yet somehow also confirms that this is exactly where I'm meant to be.

"I got fired," I say on an exhale.

Zak's eyes widen, his mouth falling open. "Why? What happened? Was it that fucking bitch Roxanne? I always hated her."

I smile despite my misery. "What are you talking about?"

"She looks like a piece of work," he says with a frown. "Fake as fuck. I don't know how Derek puts up with her."

My eyebrows shoot up. "Since when do you watch the news?"

"Since you started working there." He shrugs, meeting my gaze with a look that says, 'what else did you expect?'

"You're ridiculous," I mutter.

"No. What's ridiculous is that they fired you. They can't just do that. Is there some sort of process to follow? Can you dispute it?"

I shake my head, my stomach rolling as I prepare myself to say the words I still can't quite believe myself. "No. It wasn't even the station. It was Louis."

"Louis?" He frowns. "What the hell does Billionaire Ken have to do with this?"

Shuffling back on his bed, I lean back against the wall and close my eyes. "His family own the station."

Silence fills the space between us as my words sink in, and I wait. But instead of the slew of cursing I expect, the bed dips, and before I can open my eyes, Zak folds me into his arms.

I frown against his chest, opening my mouth to ask what

he's doing, but then I hear his heart hammering rapidly beneath my ear. It's so at odds with the slow, rhythmic movement of his hand across my back. Then, I realize. He's furious. Seething. But he's not shouting. He knows this is what I need.

My eyes brim with tears and I hold him closer, burying my face in his t-shirt as my dam finally breaks. Zak presses a kiss to my head, his arms holding me tighter as I sob, not only for the loss of my job, but of my future. Everything is a huge fucking mess, and I can't even begin to see my way out of it. Especially when the only thing that makes sense is being here in another man's arms.

ZAK

I'm going to fucking kill him. Who the fuck does he think he is? My heart slams against my chest as I picture smashing that pretty face of his in with my lacrosse stick and then finishing him off with my fists. Exhaling, I try to breathe out my anger, instead focusing on the woman in my arms.

She came to me. It doesn't even matter why. The fact that she was upset, and she chose to come here, means everything. I hold her tighter, murmuring that everything's going to be okay.

And it will. I fucking swear it. Jamie is too bright a flame to be extinguished. She's the kind of spark that burns, scorching her mark into the world for all eternity. She needs to shine, and the fact that Louis fucking Chevalier can't see that means he's not the right man for her.

But Jaime knows that.

If he was the right man, she wouldn't have fucked me at the beginning of the year. She would be proudly wearing his ring. And she certainly wouldn't be crying in my arms.

"What am I going to do?" she asks, her tears soaking through my t-shirt. "I don't know what to do."

"Yes, you do," I whisper against her hair.

She pulls back and my chest tightens at her tear-stained face. Although she's dressed to kill, in a pinstripe skirt and crisp white blouse, she looks so fucking vulnerable as she looks up at me through damp lashes. I glance around for tissue but there's none in sight, so I grip the back of my t-shirt and haul it off. Her big brown eyes widen as I use it to carefully wipe away her tears, taking the time to try to fix her makeup a little.

"Your shirt is going to be ruined," she mutters.

"Don't care," I say, sitting back to admire my work.

She shakes her head, and I smile, tossing the t-shirt to the floor. I want so much to reach for her, to touch her in some way, but ever since she left my hotel room, I've been trying to walk the 'friend line'. So, I move away a little and lean against the other wall by my pillow, drawing my knees to my chest. It physically hurts to put distance between us, but I have to, or I'll do something stupid like kiss her.

"I'm sorry." She pulls her legs up underneath her. "I'm sure the last thing you wanted this morning was me crying on your shirt."

"Oh, Kitty Cat." I shake my head. "It's like you don't even know me. Of course, I'd rather you weren't crying, but I'm here for you always. I'll take the good, the bad, and the ugly when it comes to you. I'll take it all and I'll cherish every fucking second of it."

She looks at me, and my shoulders tense, wondering if I've gone too far, but then she raises her eyebrows and pins me with a stare. "Are you saying I'm ugly right now, Aldridge?"

I bark a laugh and exhale in relief. "Abso-fucking-lutely not. The situation is ugly as hell, but it's physically impossible for you to be ugly in any way, shape, or form, Kitty Cat."

She rolls her eyes and leans her head back against the wall, allowing me to look at her properly. I haven't seen her since the welcome back party, which may only have been four days ago, but things feel different since then. All year, we've been on this back and forth, but since Friday night, we've spoken every day, which is a first. It's also the reason I'm sitting as far away from her on the bed as I can.

"You're wrong," Jaime murmurs.

"About?"

"Knowing what to do." She turns her head and looks at me. "I'm so lost, Zak. I feel like I'm drowning."

The agony on her face is too much, and I roll forward until I'm on my knees before her. Dipping so we're eye to eye, I reach out and cup her cheeks.

"You do know," I say softly. "You're Jaime Smith. The world is yours to take. I know you're not telling me everything—why you're so sure you can't change the path you're on—but I promise you, you can; because there's nothing you can't do, Kitty Cat. Not if you want it."

She blinks, her expression unreadable as her gaze flits between mine, and I carefully stroke the soft skin of her cheeks, my heart rate spiking as I realize just how close we are. So much for keeping a friendly distance between us. But that's what Jaime is: a damn magnet, always pulling me toward her.

"That's not fair," she says, pulling out of my grasp. "You've put me on a pedestal and there's no way I can live up to the way you see me."

I laugh softly. "There's no pedestal, Jaime. I've watched from the sidelines for years. Watched you speak your mind. Watched you excel at everything you try. You're unstoppable, baby. You know this." I reach out and tap her chest above her heart with two fingers. "You've just forgotten. All I'm doing is reminding you."

She shakes her head, but I can tell my words are starting to seep in. Taking a chance, I reach out and slide my hand around her neck, pulling her forward until her forehead meets mine.

"You have too much faith in me," she says, her breath warm against my lips.

"No." I shift and press a kiss to her forehead. "You don't have enough faith in yourself." Her eyes fall closed, and I brush my lips against her cheek. "You've got this." I kiss her other cheek. "You do." I kiss the tip of her nose. "And if you don't, I'll be right here to catch you."

Her eyes open and I reluctantly start to pull back, aware that every brush of my lips is crossing the line that she's drawn between us, but her hands reach up, fingers sliding against the back of my head, holding me in place. I don't dare breathe as we stay there, a breath apart and so many words between us.

"Say it again," she says, so softly, I barely hear it.

I swallow, my body aching with the effort of holding back. "I'll catch you, Kitty Cat."

Her eyes flutter closed and her exhale brushes over my skin. I go to move away again, but her grip gently tightens on the back of my neck, pulling me closer. Her lips meet mine and although my heart sings, I don't push, waiting for her to take things further.

It's only when she leans into me, an urgency mixing with the gentle kisses, that I let myself go. Sliding my fingers into her hair, I deepen the kiss, licking into her mouth and pulling her against me. She comes willingly, pushing me backwards onto the bed and climbing on top of me as her fingers roam my bare chest. I smile against her mouth. I love this Jaime—the fierce woman who takes what she wants. Especially, when what she wants is me.

My dick is already half-way to stone when she presses our bodies together, and I groan at the delicious feel of her against me.

"You're wearing too many clothes," I mutter, my fingers sliding up her thighs and under her tight, sexy skirt.

She stills, and when she climbs off me, I press my lips together, cursing my big mouth. But then, her fingers move to the buttons on her blouse. *Yes*.

Pushing down my sweats and boxers, I kick them off and wrap a fist around my dick as Jaime flicks open one button after another. Her eyes move to where I'm slowly stroking myself, her tongue darting out to wet her lips, and my dick jerks in my hand, as though it's eager to feel the warmth of her perfect mouth again.

Jaime drops the blouse on my floor and, standing there in her sexy skirt and a pale pink bra, her dark nipples just about visible through the lace, I can't help the needy groan that leaves my throat.

She's so fucking perfect.

I'm transfixed as she reaches around and unzips her skirt, shimmying out of it in a way that has me gripping my cock instead of stroking it. The all-consuming *need* I have for this woman blows my mind.

"You look fucking incredible," I murmur, drinking in the swell of her breasts and the way her pink lace thong sits on her curvy hips.

I go to sit up, no longer able to resist the temptation in front of me, but she steps forward and places a hand on my chest, pushing me back down. My heart hammers beneath her palm, my eyes wide as she climbs on top of me, and I wonder for the millionth time how I got this lucky.

Jaime dips her head to kiss me, her hair a curtain of gold and brown around us, and I reach up to trail my fingertips down her back, smiling as she shivers. My smile is immediately wiped from my face, however, as she reaches between us and slides her thong to the side, pushing the tip of my aching cock inside her. I barely have a second to catch my breath before she slides down with a moan, sitting back and flicking her hair over her shoulder.

My hands go to her thighs, my jaw slack at the sight of her sitting on top of me, her heat like heaven around my cock, looking like a fucking goddess.

Words she's nowhere near ready to hear queue on my tongue, but I swallow them down, sliding my hands up her body instead and tugging down the lacy cups of her bra. Her head falls back as I roll her nipples between my fingers, my hips shifting as they harden at my touch. She's driving me over the fucking edge and she's not even doing anything.

"You need to move," I grit out.

Her eyebrows raise and she rolls her hips once, pulling a groan from deep in my chest. "Oh, really? And why's that?"

I drop my hands from her breasts and grip her waist tight. "Because if you don't, I'm going to flip you over and fuck you so hard, every student at Franklin West is going to hear your screams and know that you're mine."

Just to prove my point, I hold her in place as I snap my hips up, and she gasps, her fingers digging into my chest.

"Ride me, Kitty Cat," I say, releasing my grip and pinching her nipples. "Give me everything."

And she fucking does.

With a smile on her face, she undulates her hips, gradually building speed until her smirk fades and she's grinding against me, her eyes half closed and her mouth open as she uses me for her pleasure.

It's everything.

"Fuck." She gasps. "I'm so close, Zak."

Her brown skin gleams with the effort of riding me, and as I reach between us and rub her clit, her rhythm stumbles, her moans loud enough that, if any of my brothers are home, there's no fucking question I'm getting laid.

It's something that pulls me in two directions. I don't want anyone hearing my Kitty Cat's moans, but I also love the idea of everyone knowing what I do to her. For a split second, I imagine filming her, writhing on my cock, and sending it to fucking Louis, but I push the thought away. I don't want to think about that asshole.

"ZakZakZakZak . . ."

Her pleas pull me from my thoughts and I concentrate on rubbing her clit as I sit up and suck her nipple into my mouth. Almost instantly, she clenches around me, her entire body trembling as she moans through her release. I'm addicted to the feeling of her pulsing around my dick, and I grip her hips, fucking up into her fast and hard as I let myself hurtle toward oblivion.

"Fuck!" My orgasm hits me so hard, my entire body tenses, the edges of my vision darkening as I hold Jaime down over my cock with enough force, I'm sure I'll leave marks. My dick pulses over and over, the sensation so fucking intense I swear I might pass out.

But then Jaime's lips find mine and it's like coming home.

Releasing my punishing grip, I wrap my arms around her and pull her flush against my chest, pouring everything I feel for her into each tender swipe of my tongue against hers.

After a while, she pulls away, resting her head against my chest, and we lie there, the rest of the world slowly creeping in. There is literally nowhere else I'd rather be.

"Do you have class?" she asks.

I press a kiss to her head, my hands running up and down her spine. "Doesn't matter if I do or not. I'm not going."

She lifts her head to look at me. "You have to go."

"No. I don't."

We stare at each other, and I raise an eyebrow to let her know she can't push me on this. Eventually she returns to my chest with a sigh.

"I'm going to order pizza," I say. "You want?"

She nods, and I hold her tighter. We need to clean up at some point, but I'm not going to move until I absolutely have to. I've never been jealous of Alex and Sol's ensuite rooms until this moment. The idea of being able to shower with Jaime, and maybe go for a second round while we're in there, has my dick waking up. But there's no fucking way we can do that in the shared bathroom on my floor.

One thing is for certain, though. I'm not letting her leave my room today. As long as she's here in my arms, the rest of the world can fuck right off. There's no Louis, no marriage, no life after college. Just us.

It's a shame we can't stay here forever.

BE

Lips press to my forehead in a barely-there kiss and, as the bed dips, I pry my eyes open to find Zak pulling on his dark gray sweats. I watch him for a moment as he searches for a t-shirt, enjoying the view before he realizes I'm awake.

Yesterday was perfection. If I forget about the whole getting fired thing. We ate pizza in bed and then alternated between fucking and talking until falling asleep. I've no idea what time it was. I'm deliciously sore, and I stretch beneath the covers, enjoying the way my body remembers every place Zak squeezed, licked, and sucked over the last eighteen hours.

"I didn't mean to wake you." He sits down on the bed and strokes my cheek with the back of his hand. "I was going to run to Grinds and get us some breakfast."

I'm still wearing my watch, and I lift my wrist to find that it's seven thirty. I don't have class until eleven, so I sink back into the pillow with a smile. "That sounds good."

Zak doesn't move, instead staring at me, his fingers running through my hair and a worried expression on his handsome face.

"What's wrong?" I ask.

He sighs and drops his hand. "Please still be here when I get back."

My heart constricts. If I could go back, I wouldn't leave that hotel room. We would have eaten room service in bed and then got nasty in the shower. But I did leave. And now he thinks it's going to happen again.

"I will." I reach up and run my fingers along his jaw, the usually smooth skin rough with stubble. "I promise I'll still be here."

After a second, he nods and stands, grabbing his phone from the desk, but my heart continues to ache long after he's gone. I shouldn't be here, hiding from my life, but it's what I need. Just a minute to take stock and gather myself.

Zak told me last night that I knew what to do. That I was a force to be reckoned with. I'd scoffed, unable to see my way through the shitstorm of the morning's events, but now, in the clear light of day, I know what he meant.

I've always walked through life with confidence. Whether that comes from being born into a family with more money than God, I don't know. But I've always been sure of myself. I'm smart. I'm beautiful. I'm powerful. These affirmations are ingrained in my psyche and make up the very essence of who I am.

I'm not sure when I forgot.

Maybe it's when other people grabbed the steering wheel and pulled my life off track without my permission. I've always known Louis was my future, but everything veered off course so quickly it gave me whiplash.

Now, I need to take back control.

Sitting up, I frown as I remember there's no ensuite. *Fuck.* Well, there's no way I'm going to be sitting here, a mess with morning breath, when Zak comes back. Sliding from the bed, I root around in his closet until I find a navy t-shirt and a pair of black sweats. The t-shirt goes halfway to my knees, and I just stand and laugh at the sweats. There's no point even trying to roll them. I swear, Zak is a freaking giant.

Kicking them off, I dig around in his drawers until I find a pair of shorts and pull them on. Even rolled at the waist, they still fall past my knees, and I'm sure the ensemble makes me look like a child playing dress up. But I don't care. I just need to be decent enough to go to the shared bathroom.

My heart speeds at the thought of running into the Wolves who share his floor, but then I realize they probably heard us going at it all night anyway. My skin heats to nuclear proportions as I grab a towel from Zak's closet, taking a second to breathe before lifting my chin and opening the door.

Fortunately, the hallway is empty as I tiptoe along to the bathroom. Other than the use of gray marble instead of white, it's exactly the same as the one in the Hive. I find some toothpaste and use my finger to clean my teeth before shutting myself in a shower stall and washing. It's not great, but it'll have to do.

Next time, we'll stay in my room and—

I freeze, my chest squeezing. *Next time.* There shouldn't even be *this* time. Panic flutters through my veins as I dry off and pull Zak's baggy clothes back on. What am I doing? I'm literally playing make believe. This is not my life. Zak is not my future.

As much as I chant the words in my head, they don't seem to want to stick.

The hallway is still empty when I leave the bathroom, although I can hear voices downstairs and music coming from more than one of the rooms. I let myself back into Zak's bedroom and drape the damp towel over the door of his closet before reaching for my purse, abandoned beside the bed and pull out my phone. It's almost dead, and I scroll through the notifications expecting something from Louis, but there's nothing. I sigh through my nose. The bastard said he was on *my* side. That he would always put me first. And then he goes behind my back and takes away my career. What's worse is, he hasn't even messaged to explain himself. Couldn't even give me a heads up. The coward.

Frowning, I pull up my family group chat and tap out a message.

> I need to speak to you ASAP. Let me know when's a good time for a video call

I plug into Zak's charger on his desk and then settle back down on his bed, inhaling his scent with a smile. My heart swells at the unwavering faith that man has in me, but I meant what I'd said to him. As much as he says he hasn't put me on a pedestal, it sure feels dizzy as hell up here. Especially when I know I'm going to fall. He said he'd catch me, but who's going to catch him? There's only one way this can end, and it's with Zak's heart in pieces.

Burying my face in his pillow, I inhale, trying to convince myself it's not true. Just as my throat starts to tighten, my eyes burning, Zak springs back into the room, his dimples on full display as he finds me still in his bed.

"You're here," he says, placing two brown paper bags and two take out cups on his desk.

I sit up, pushing my fingers through my hair and forcing a smile. "I promised I would be, didn't I?"

Zak shakes his head and swoops on me, his body pressing me back down onto the bed as he claims my mouth. He tastes of chocolate and peanuts, and I smile against his lips.

"Candy at this time of the morning?" I tease. "When did you sneak that in?"

"I needed energy for the run across campus."

I roll my eyes. "You're addicted."

"There's only one thing I'm addicted to." He grins down at me, wriggling his eyebrows suggestively, and I laugh. His smile fades as his eyes rake over my body, swimming in his clothes. "I like you in my clothes, Kitty Cat."

He grinds his hips against me, punctuating just how much he likes it, and my hands go to his firm ass as I wrap my legs around him, keeping him in place.

"You want to fuck me in your clothes?" I ask, my body waking up at the warmth of him against me.

Zak groans and drops his head to my shoulder. "I really, really do. But I also need food. And coffee. Someone kept me up all night."

I laugh, grinding against him one more time before releasing him. He stands to fetch our food and coffee and I bite my lip at the way his hard cock pushes against the fabric of his sweats.

"I got you a panini and a brownie," he says, handing me one of the paper bags. "And a vanilla oat milk latte. Is that okay?"

I tear open the bag with a grateful groan. "More than okay. Thank you."

He sits down on his desk chair and tears into a sandwich that seems to be more filling than bread, and I smile.

"What?" he asks, wiping his mouth with the back of his hand, his brown eyes dancing with amusement.

I shake my head. "Nothing. I'm just . . . happy."

The word takes me by surprise, but it's true. Right here,

right now, I'm truly happy. And as Zak's smile grows, both dimples in full force, my happiness only increases.

"I've been thinking," I say, putting down my cheese and ham panini and reaching for my latte.

Zak's smile falters as he stares at me. "Oh, yeah?"

"Yeah. About what we talked about on the phone on Saturday." I break off a piece of brownie and pop it in my mouth. When Zak frowns, I clarify, "After college."

"Oh." His frown deepens and he pulls a piece of tomato from his sandwich before popping it in his mouth. "I told you I had it sorted. Porn star, remember?"

I roll my eyes. "Have you thought about staying with lacrosse?"

"No." He shakes his head. "I'm honestly not good enough to go pro and although I love the game, the idea of playing professionally just doesn't do it for me. And that's the fucking problem. Nothing does."

My chest pulls at the frustration in his muttered words. I've known what I wanted for as long as I can remember. I can't imagine not having something that fills me with purpose.

"I didn't mean going pro," I explain. "There are other things you can do, right? Have you thought about coaching?"

Zak's gaze snaps to mine, his eyebrows raising. "What?"

I shrug. "Makes sense to me. You're so good with people, and the way you talk about your nieces, I just know you're good with kids."

The look of wonder that crosses Zak's face has me pressing my lips together to hold in a giggle.

"That's interesting, Kitty Cat," he mutters, placing his nearly demolished sandwich down as he picks up his iced coffee. "Real interesting."

My heart sings at the idea that I might have helped him. After all, he's helped me so much. With that in mind, I'm going to speak to my parents today, no matter what. I'm taking back the wheel, and so help anyone who gets in my way.

Taking another bite of brownie, I glance at where Zak is staring into space as he sips his coffee. Last night, when he promised he'd catch me, he was talking about the mess with my family—with Louis—but I really hope he means it in all ways. Because I can no longer deny what's happening between us. The little shoot I've tried to suppress and keep from growing all these years has taken root and is now a vine, wrapped around my beating heart. I've fallen for Zak Aldridge.

And now I have to decide what I'm going to do with that.

ZAK

Humming to myself, I jog down the stairs. As much as I would have loved to have stayed in bed another day with Jaime, she needs to speak to her parents, and I need to go to class. I already texted one of the brothers who took the class I missed yesterday and got his notes, but I can't afford to fall behind. Even if economics isn't what I want to do with my life.

A fucking lacrosse coach.

It might not even be an option, but it's something I honestly hadn't thought of and . . . I don't hate it. The more I think about it, the more I can see myself helping kids develop their skill, cheering them on. I'm not sure whether I'd want to work at college level or younger, but it's definitely something I'm going to speak to Coach Pearson about after class today.

I'm so lost in my own thoughts, I don't see Alex standing by the kitchen, his arms folded, until I almost smack right into him.

"Hey!" I say, stepping back with a grin. "What's up, man?"

Alex's blue eyes sear into me, his jaw locked. He looks pissed at me. *Fuck.* What have I done?

"I saw Trey this morning," he says. "Said there was a lot of noise coming from your room last night."

My mouth falls open, my skin heating a little as I shrug. "I got laid. And? Let's not pretend that whoever shares a wall with you doesn't have to invest in earplugs. Speaking of which, you should buy shares."

Alex's expression doesn't shift, and I jostle my book bag on my shoulder.

"Who was it?" he asks, although I can tell he already knows the answer.

When I walked Jaime out this morning, we didn't run into anyone, but that doesn't mean shit. There are eyes everywhere with very few secrets amongst Wolves.

"You know who," I say, my own mood shifting. "What's the problem, Alex?"

He glances around, making sure we're alone, but still lowers his voice as he steps closer. "The problem is, Zak, she's fucking using you."

My back stiffens, every muscle in my jaw clenching, as I stare down at him. "What?"

"You're so blinded, you can't see it," he continues, reaching up to put a hand on my shoulder.

I step out of reach and shake my head. "You haven't got a clue what you're talking about."

"Think about it," he says. "She dodged you for years, stringing you along. And now she only comes to you when she needs something. She called you the other night because she was upset, didn't she? Why did she come to you yesterday? Where is she now?"

My jaw works, my fist tightening around the strap of my bag as I stare at my best friend. "Shut your mouth, Rainer."

Alex's face falls. "I'm just worried about you. She runs to you and then pushes you away after she gets what she wants. Is she coming back later? Are you two an item now? Because if you are, I'll be the first to congratulate you."

He pauses and I know he's waiting for me to tell him that we are. That we're together and everything he just said is complete bullshit. But it's not. We're not together. I don't even know when I'll see her next.

"Fuck you, man."

Alex opens his mouth to speak, but I have no desire to hear whatever shit he's about to spew, so I barge past him and head to the front door.

Jaime's speaking to her parents today to try to figure out a way to get her internship back. What we didn't talk about was what that meant for Louis. I kind of assumed after the last twenty-four hours, that she was going to join me in trying to find a way to extract herself from this fucking marriage. Now, I'm not so sure.

If he agrees to let her follow her career, will she still go ahead with it? What does she see for us? Is she just going to ditch me after graduation? Or am I supposed to tag along and be her bit on the side—her dirty little secret while Billionaire Ken is out of town.

The thought knocks me sick, and I suck in deep breaths as I jog down the path toward the common. Even after what we shared last night, and once this morning, it was never on the cards to discuss what we have. I'd kissed Jaime and sent her off toward the Hive with a smile on my face, like a fucking idiot. Scowling at the common in the distance, I kick at the pebbles and decaying leaves, my mood now completely soured.

A ringing in my pocket has my heart skipping, and I fish

out my phone hoping it's Jaime and not Alex trying to apologize for being an epic dick. But it's neither.

"Hey, Mom. What's up?"

"You okay, Zakky baby? You sound blue?"

I huff a laugh. "How could you possibly tell that from four words, Mom?"

"I'm your mother. I know things. And don't try to change the subject. What is it?"

Tilting my head back, I squint at the sky. It's bright blue with not a cloud in sight, although the air is still very much crisp with winter. "Girl problems, Mom. Don't worry about it."

Silence falls between us and I can practically hear all the things she wants to say to me. She doesn't push it, though.

"Did you just call to check up on me?" I ask, when the silence continues. "Was it just your mom spidey senses tingling?"

She laughs softly. "No. I was actually calling to ask if you'd be my date to the Spring Mingle. I got another invite."

My eyebrows shoot up. "Is that normal?"

"I'm not sure," she admits. "A few people mentioned it wasn't their first Mingle, but with two in a row, I can't help but feel it might be positive."

"It's more than positive," I scoff. "Mason Smith is practically giving you a deal."

She lets out a long breath. "I really hope so. You'll come, right?"

My stomach twists. Can I do that again? Be in the same room as her and Billionaire fucking Ken? Can I smile and chat with her parents, knowing they're strong-arming her into giving up everything she wants to farm out heirs?

"Zak?"

I sigh. "When is it?"

"March first."

"Lacrosse season," I mutter. "I'd have to check with Coach, because it would mean taking the whole weekend."

"It's a Friday, if that helps? You could be back Saturday morning?"

And play like shit. "Sure, Mom. Let me look into it."

"Okay. Love you. Bye!"

"Love you, too, Mom."

Slipping my phone back in my pocket, I come to a stop at the bottom of the steps to Emmett Franklin Hall where my class is. As much as the thought of seeing Louis again turns my stomach, I have no idea what things will be like then. It's barely seven weeks away. Will Jaime still be engaged to him by then? What if she's not? What if she chooses me? I can't imagine Mason Smith would be very fucking happy about it. *Shit.* What if he refuses to do business with Mom because of it?

There's so many 'ifs', they make my head spin. And none of them are things I can change. The ball is forever in Jaime Smith's court, hers to pass back to me when she feels the need. Alex's concerned face flashes in my mind and I swallow at the harsh truth of his words.

I don't think Jaime is knowingly using me. She's not that kind of person. I know she's not. But I have to admit it does feel like she is. Sucking in a breath, I start up the steps. It doesn't matter what I think. It only matters what happens. And that's up to Jaime.

If she calls me, comes to the Den, whatever, then maybe we can navigate our way through this minefield together. If she chooses him—if she hides from what we have between us again . . . I honestly don't know what I'll do.

I told her I'd catch her, but what can I do if she won't

jump? How long do I stand here with my arms open, hoping she'll choose me? Swallowing around the lump in my throat, I push open the door to the lecture hall and slump into a seat at the back. I guess I'll just have to wait and find out how long it takes until I break.

BE

As much as I convinced myself I was ready to face my parents, the moment I find myself with my phone in my hand, the dial tone against my ear, my confidence falters.

Mom messaged me to say they would be at home at six their time, and it's been the longest day of my life as I've waited for the time to come around. Even catching up with my notes and going to my lecture didn't manage to stop my mind from wandering.

"Hello, Jaime."

I sit up straight on my bed as my mom's voice comes down the line, my heart leaping to my throat. "Hi, Mom. How are you?"

"Fine," she says, a rustling sounding in the background. "What's wrong?"

I frown at the fact that she's not giving me her full attention. "Where's Dad?"

"His meeting ran over. I'm sure whatever it is, I can help."

My teeth clench together, the frustration that's been

building since I left Zak spilling over. "Mom! Can you please stop whatever it is you're doing and listen to me?"

The rustling pauses and she sniffs. "I *am* listening. Don't raise your voice to me."

I roll my eyes, sighing through my nose. "I was hoping to speak to both of you."

"Yes, well, like I said, your father is busy. You'll have to make do with me or wait until later. Although, he has golf in half an hour. So maybe tomorrow?"

Closing my eyes, I can almost feel Zak's fingers on my back, his calm voice in my ear, telling me I can do this. I can. I'm not scared of my parents. I'm scared of disappointing them. All my life, I've given them reason to be proud. I've been top of all my classes. I've conducted myself with pride. Everything they've asked of me, I've done with a smile.

Except this.

This, I can't do. I can't give up my future—my dreams. I've already given up so much by agreeing to marry Louis, who might as well be a perfect stranger. Especially after the shit he pulled this week.

"Jaime?" Mom pushes. "I've got to go out in twenty minutes, so whatever you have to say, say it now."

Fuck it.

"You know how I always wanted to run a network?" I say in a rush. "Well, I got an internship at KBCX, a station in Portland. I was doing great, and I loved it, but Louis put in a call and got me fired."

The silence that follows my ramble is deafening, and I can barely breathe as I wait for my mother's response.

"Is there a reason he got you fired?" Mom asks, with not an ounce of the indignation I was hoping for.

"A reason? Sure. Louis said he didn't realize I'd want to work, so he took care of it. He wants me to follow him around until I get pregnant, and then I have to stay at home with the baby."

"I'm not sure why you're surprised, honey," Mom says. "If you're both working full time on different continents, there's no way you'll conceive."

I swallow. "Mom. I'm more than an incubator. I'm not even sure I want kids."

"Oh, honey. That's brilliant." The laugh that echoes down the line causes my skin to prickle.

"I'm not joking, Mom."

"Why do you think you're getting married?" Mom asks, her tone suddenly harsh. "This was always the plan, Jaime. Uniting the Smith and Chevalier empires will change everything for both families as well as the business world. Both your father and Claude have been building this shared empire for more than sixteen years based on this deal."

And there it is. I curl into myself, waves of nausea sloshing in my gut. It's not as simple as saying no. I never once said no in the last sixteen years. Sure, as a little kid, I didn't know any better. But I knew at twelve. At fourteen. At sixteen. And I never once said no. I accepted the fate selected for me, trusting my parents to know what was best.

I should have questioned it. I should have said something sooner. I let it get this far with them thinking I was okay with this. I honestly thought I was. Until I wasn't.

"You know," Mom says, her voice softer. "If you just lay low, play the part and give him an heir, he might let you work."

I bark a laugh in disbelief. "He might *let* me work?"

"Yes. Once you've fulfilled your duty, he might soften and become more amenable to the idea."

"I'm sorry," I stumble to my feet and brace myself on my

desk. "I appear to have fallen, hit my head and woken up in sixteen-fucking-oh-five!"

A gasp sounds down the line and I almost laugh at the absurdity of the situation. This is what I couldn't explain to Zak. It's not a simple yes or no. I'm the Joker at the base of a house of cards, and if I fall, everything does. My decision affects so much more than me. I might not have asked for this, but do I have the right to ruin the last sixteen years of my father's dealings? Of Louis and his father?

"Jaime," Mom snaps. "You've always known this was the plan. You're just having cold feet, which is perfectly normal. It might seem scary now, but you just need to open yourself to the idea. Louis is kind, well-mannered and very handsome. You'd be hard-pressed to find someone better."

Guilt flickers over my skin and I close my eyes. "I don't understand why he went behind my back, Mom. Why would he call the station without talking to me first? How am I supposed to trust him?"

"Have you spoken to him about it?"

I still. "No."

"Then how do you know the full story? Maybe the station lied, using him as an excuse."

I frown at my desk before turning and slumping onto my chair. Surely not? If I wasn't doing a good job, they would have told me. Right?

"Speak to Louis," Mom says gently. "Marriage is all about communication."

I nod, even though she can't see me. "Okay."

"Is there anything else you needed to speak to me about?"

"No."

The rustling from earlier resumes. "Okay. I've got to go. I won't mention this to your dad. Love you, honey. Bye!"

The line goes dead, and I step away from my desk, sinking onto my bed and staring at my phone. As much as I'm trying to claw my way out of the pit, I keep sliding back down.

With a weary sigh, I scroll through my contacts and click Louis' name. As I do, it occurs to me that I've never actually called him before. He answers almost immediately, and it takes me by surprise. I guess I figured he'd be in a meeting or something.

"Jaime? Is everything all right?"

"Yes. Sorry." I sit up and force myself to focus. "I wasn't expecting you to answer."

Louis chuckles. "Were you hoping for my voicemail? Sorry to disappoint, but I will always endeavor to pick up for my fiancée."

I almost roll my eyes. His charming act was sweet before he went behind my back and fucked up my career.

"Not at all," I say. "I just know you're busy."

"Well, how can I be of service?"

Taking a breath, I realize I should probably have rehearsed this before dialing. "Erm. I want to know where you get off getting me fired. That internship was incredibly important to me. I know you weren't expecting a career woman as your wife, but you also said you'd always be on my side. Well, your words clearly mean nothing, because you screwed me over the first chance you got."

I come to the end of my tirade, breathing hard, my fingers clenched, Louis' answering silence stretching between us like the Atlantic.

"I'm sorry, love," he says after a long minute. "I'm just trying to process everything you just said. Why do you think I got you fired?"

My mouth opens to argue, but then I falter. "What?"

"Why do you think I got you fired, Jaime?"

"Because I went to KBCX yesterday and they told me I didn't work there anymore." I frown. "I asked them why and they told me . . ."

My words trail off as I recall exactly what they said. They said to speak to my father-in-law. Not my fiancé.

"What, Jaime?" Louis presses. "What did they tell you?"

I let out a slow breath. "They told me to speak to my father-in-law."

Louis hums softly. "I understand why you assumed I had something to do with this after our conversation this weekend, but I'm not going to pretend I'm not hurt that you thought I was capable of doing something like that."

I hold my head in my hands, a new level of nausea cramping my stomach. "How did your father know, Louis?"

"I told him. After our conversation, I spoke to him and said we might need to change our plans because you intended on having a career." He sighs. "When I told you I'm on your side, Jaime. I meant it. I know I was a little surprised this weekend, but I just needed a minute to get my head around it."

Tears brim in my eyes, and I pinch the bridge of my nose. "I'm sorry, Louis."

"It's fine, Jaime. I'll speak to my father and give him what for. I'll be in touch later today or tomorrow at the latest. Hopefully we can get things back on track. Okay?"

"Okay," I murmur. "Thank you."

"No problem, love. I'll speak to you soon."

He ends the call and I collapse in a heap, my tears erupting into sobs. That's not how things were meant to go. Louis is the villain, stealing my future. I was going to stand up to him and walk away, free to choose the ending I want for myself. But instead, Louis remains the prince. Kind, loyal, and too good to be true. Pushing my head into my pillow I scream.

The fact I want someone else isn't enough to risk everything for. Sure, Zak acts like I'm his whole world, but we're here in our Franklin West bubble. What happens after graduation? He doesn't even know what he wants to do. Where will he be? Will he stay here? Go back to Chicago? If I can get my apprenticeship back, I'd hope to be offered a permanent position come July, which would mean staying in Portland. I'm fairly certain I'm going to do an MBA, too.

All the reasons I've laid down in my head for not giving Zak a chance over the past few years are still there. It seems I just forgot about them for a minute. Which hasn't been fair to either of us.

I can't have Zak.

The realization is nothing new. It's the same fact I've lived with since I first laid eyes on him. But this time, it hurts so much more. The pain in my chest is so acute, I curl tighter into a ball, my fist against my heart as it splinters.

There's no way Zak is going to let this go—let *us* go. This thing between us has grown strong. No longer a crush I can flick away with a disdainful look and toss of my hair. It's dangerous now. It's a connection I feel in my bones, earth-shattering orgasms, and a passion I dreamt of finding my entire life. And now I'm going to have to kill it dead. It's the only way. It's time to accept the future that's been laid out for me all along.

ZAK

Seven weeks and three days. That's how long it's been since I spoke to Jaime. The worst thing is, I haven't been able to tell anyone about it. After the argument I had with Alex, there was no way I wanted to tell him he'd been right. He's insufferable enough as it is. And I didn't want to burden Sol with it. He's had enough going on with the shit show between him and Wes. Besides, I don't want to hear bad things about Jaime. There's a reason she's ghosting me. And I'm pretty sure I know exactly what it is.

Things were great between us the day she walked out of the Den, so I can only assume things went to shit after she spoke to her parents. Which means, they must have pulled an epic fucking guilt trip on her ass.

This is something I'm realizing about Jaime Smith. She's a force to be reckoned with, and she'll let you know when she's not happy about something but, beneath it all, she's a people pleaser. She cares. Although our futures are completely different, the fact remains the same: neither of us want to disappoint our parents.

Unfortunately for Jaime, that means marrying Billionaire Ken.

Straightening my bowtie in the mirror, my heart beats erratically beneath the crisp white shirt, and I take a ragged breath. Don't get me wrong. I'm fucking fuming. Ghosting someone is already the shittiest of shitty things to do to someone, but after you've spent twenty-four perfect hours together? No. And I'd tell her just how shitty she's been, if I could find her.

Problem is, she's been laying low. For the first couple of weeks, I waited outside her classes—outside the Hive—with zero luck. It's like she's disappeared. But I know she's around. I've seen her car. The woman should be a fucking ninja.

One thing I do know is that she got her internship back. After a couple of weeks, I got curious, and called KBCX. They wouldn't put me through to her, but it confirmed she was there. Turns out there's secure basement parking at the building, too. Which means I couldn't catch her leaving.

After two weeks, I gave up. I left the ball in her court, and if she doesn't want to see me—if she needs time—then fine. There's been no climbing the Hive and creeping through windows this time. I'm too angry. Too disappointed.

A knock sounds at my hotel room door and I turn away from the mirror to open it. My mom gives a little twirl in the hallway, showing off her gold-satin dress and I force a smile.

"You look beautiful, Mom."

She frowns at me, her mom-spidey-senses no doubt tingling. "Are you feeling okay?"

No. "Yeah. I'm fine. Just a little nervous."

There's even a good chance Jaime won't be there tonight. If she has any idea I'm here, I'm sure she'll find a reason to avoid it.

"This is all to do with Mason's daughter, isn't it?" Mom says, stepping to me and straightening my bowtie.

I shake my head. "Mom—"

"Look." She pins me with a look that has my mouth slamming shut. "I didn't push you last time, but enough is enough. Spill."

My eyebrows shoot up. "There's nothing to spill, Mom."

"Bull. Start talking, Zakary."

I hold her stare for a minute, but I know she's not going to relent. She'll stand here in this room all evening if she has to. With a sigh, I turn and collapse onto the edge of the bed, my head in my hands.

"Fine. I'm in love with Jaime Smith." Mom makes a small squeaking noise, but when I look up, her face is neutral, and she nods thoughtfully. I roll my eyes and continue. "But, as you know, she's engaged to that British guy we met last time."

Mom sits beside me and places a hand on my knee. "You know I'll always take your side, baby, but I'm surprised. If they're engaged—"

"It's not like that," I interrupt. "Look, you can't tell anyone, Mom. Promise?"

She holds her hands up, her eyes creasing with concern. "I promise."

"It's a business arrangement," I mutter, the words alone causing my stomach to roll. "Their parents orchestrated it when Louis and Jaime were kids. It's so they can combine their fucking empires."

When my mom says nothing, I turn my head to look at her. She shakes her head and releases a slow breath. "Are you telling me that they're in an arranged marriage?"

I nod.

"And Jaime doesn't want to marry this Louis guy?"

I shake my head. "Well, she didn't. We've had a back and forth between us since freshman year and this year things finally got started. And then *he* happened. She was going to speak to her parents, but that was in January. I haven't heard from her and . . ."

I trail off with a bitter laugh. I'm the piece on the side. It's a story as old as fucking time. She said she'd leave him for me, but she hasn't. I suppose I should be thankful she's no longer stringing me along.

"Why didn't you tell me last time?" Mom asks.

I pull a hand over my face with a groan. "I didn't even know, Mom. I found out about Louis that weekend. She came to find me that night and we . . . talked. But I didn't want to tell you because I didn't want to risk CHIPnique not getting a deal."

Mom shifts a little on the bed to face me, her eyes narrowed. "Your happiness is worth more than any business deal, Zak. Where are things now? If you haven't heard from her since January."

"I guess she chose Louis." The words are like knives in my gut and my eyes fall closed as I swallow hard. Has she given herself to him properly? The day we'd spent in my room, she confessed they hadn't even kissed properly. Surely, that's changed now. My eyes burn behind my lids.

"You still love her, though." Mom says softly, her hand rubbing soothing circles on my back.

I nod, pressing my fingers to my eyes. "She's the one, Mom. I know it. But she won't . . . She won't choose me. She won't take the chance."

Beside me, Mom sighs. "Then maybe it's time to let her go. If she was really the one, she'd take the chance. You're worth the risk, baby. If she can't see that, it's her loss."

I huff into my hands. It's not just Jaime's loss. It's my

fucking loss, too. And it hurts like hell. Over the past few weeks, I've busied myself with lacrosse, classes, and my friends' love lives. But now, minutes away from potentially seeing Jaime again in the flesh? It's agony.

"Zak," Mom says. "I'll stand by you, whatever you decide. But I also don't want to see you hurt."

I nod and stand, grabbing my jacket from the bed and shrugging it on. "Thanks, Mom."

She smiles, but it doesn't reach her eyes, and I hate that I've tainted tonight. She was so excited when she knocked on my door. Forcing my own smile, I take her arm and we head downstairs to the car.

Either way, I get answers tonight. If she's happy with Louis, I'll walk away. Hell, I might walk away regardless. I swing between fury and misery with such speed it gives me constant whiplash.

We don't speak during the short journey to the Smith mansion, and by the time we join the procession of shiny black cars, I'm seconds away from vomiting. I keep reminding myself, she might not even be here. I have no idea if she comes to all of these events, or if last time was a fluke.

When the door opens and I step into the balmy evening, I suck in a deep breath and help my mom out of the car, aware of the cameras flashing, capturing our every move. It's different this time. Without the distraction of sparkling Christmas trees, the sprawling courtyard is bare, allowing me to take in the enormity of the estate.

"I was thinking of buying a holiday home here," Mom says quietly.

My head snaps to hers, my eyes wide, and she laughs.

"Hilarious." This time my smile is genuine. "You never know. If you get a deal, you might be able to."

Mom squeezes my arm as we move up the steps. "We'll see."

Just as before, a waiter greets us by name, offering us glasses of champagne, and as my mom heads toward the dining room, my footsteps slow.

I'm not sure I can do this. If Jaime's here, how can I spend an entire evening in the same room while she ignores me. Because I doubt she'll speak to me. If she hasn't in the last two months, she won't now. When I swallow, I wince. What if she's happy? What if she's hanging on Billionaire Ken's arm, laughing and smiling.

"You don't have to stay," Mom says, touching my arm. "I'll be fine. Go back to the hotel and order room service."

"No." I lift my chin and straighten my jacket. "I didn't fly across the goddamn country to hide in a hotel room."

Mom's lips press together, but she nods, and together we head toward the open dining room doors. My heart slams against my chest with every step and I can honestly say I've never been so nervous in my entire life.

The room is decorated differently this time. Fresh flowers adorn the tables, and walls, and swathes of sheer materials drape from the ceiling. It's pretty. But I can't appreciate it. Not when my eyes are searching for one thing.

Mason and Melanie Smith are on the far side of the room talking to a small group, their laughter carrying over to where we're standing, my mom checking the seating plan beside me. Jaime isn't with them. Slowly, I scan the room. Louis is here. My jaw clenches as I watch him talking to a glamorous looking couple, all slicked back blond hair and white teeth.

For a second, I'm filled with hope. I can just about stand to be in the same room as Louis if she's not here. I turn, continuing my search, and then my breath catches. She's here.

It takes me a second to process what I'm seeing. It's been so long, I almost believed I wouldn't see her again. That in some way, she wasn't real. But here she is. I can barely breathe as I watch her talking to an elderly woman I don't recognize from last time. She's thinner—noticeably so—and my jaw ticks as I drag my gaze over her flowing pale blue dress, wondering whether it's due to stress. Is it anything to do with me? Does she miss me? How easy was it for her to walk away?

The questions build and build, and despite being vaguely aware of my mom tugging gently at my arm, I can't stop staring. Perhaps sensing my attention, Jaime turns and looks in my direction, her smile immediately fading and her eyes widening.

"Zak," Mom hisses. "Let's go sit down."

Finally dragging my eyes away, I shake my head and follow my mom to our table. All the fury I've felt over the last few weeks has risen to the surface and I don't know how to release it. I want to punch something. Preferably Billionaire Ken's smug face. But it's not his fault. This is all on Jaime.

Yes, I pushed. But she should never have let me in. She should have told me from the get-go that she was engaged, and I would have walked away. Instead, she wove her way into my blood, and now I don't know how to undo it.

Downing my champagne and signaling for another, I let my gaze find hers again. At least she has the decency to look guilty. She should. What she did was cowardly and cruel. And if she thinks I'm going to leave here tonight without telling her exactly what I think of her decision, she's got another thing coming.

BE

I can't eat. What little appetite I had evaporated the second Zak walked into the room. I knew he was coming. I checked the guest list weeks ago and thought I was prepared. It turns out, I wasn't. Because the way he looked at me—the fury and hurt on his face—had sliced through to my core. I've never seen Zak look so angry and I never imagined it would be directed at me.

It's what I deserve. I know that. Cutting him out of my life with no explanation was cowardly to say the least. But I had no choice. Zak makes me weak. If I'd seen him—spoken to him—I would have crumbled. Walking away from him is the hardest decision I've had to make and knowing that he hates me for it makes it all the more painful.

"You should try to eat something," Louis murmurs. "I'm worried about you."

I force a smile and spear a green bean. It tastes like rubber. Everything does.

"You're not pregnant, are you?" Mom hisses from my other side. "Because we'll have to move the wedding forward."

Swallowing the bean with a wince, I shake my head. "I'm not pregnant, Mom."

Louis shifts beside me and my skin heats. I've told him I want to wait until our wedding night, which he was fine with. But I know he's getting frustrated with the fact I haven't let myself be with him in other ways. We kissed a few weeks ago and I hated every second. As soon as I could excuse myself, I hid in a bathroom and cried.

Pushing the rest of my meal around my plate, I flinch as Louis' hand finds my thigh, squeezing gently. I'm going to have to get over it. I chose him. I chose my parents. There's no way I can avoid kissing my fiancé forever.

Tears of frustration prick my eyes, and I reach for my champagne, taking a long sip. I haven't looked up from my plate since it was put in front of me. I can't. If I do, my eyes will find his. And I can't see that hatred again. It'll break me.

As the waiters clear our table, however, my gaze flits to where Zak is sitting with his mom. My exhale is heavy as I find him chatting with the woman he's sitting beside, his attention occupied.

"I'm going to get some air," I announce, quietly pushing back my chair.

Louis pushes back his own chair, but I halt him with a hand on his shoulder and he nods. It's one of the things that makes this so much harder. He's a good man. He deserves a woman who can give him her whole heart. I'm not sure that will ever be me.

Keeping to the back of the room, I make my way to the small single door designated for waiting staff. This way, I don't have to cross the room, and it's my only chance of leaving without being spotted. Although a few of the waiters give me puzzled glances, no one questions as I make my way through into the hallway that leads to the kitchens. With the dining room behind me, I draw in a deep breath. I'll have to go back eventually, but I just need maybe just ten minutes to regroup.

Slipping through another doorway, I make my way out into the gardens, inhaling the sweet scent of my mother's rose garden. It's quiet, with just the sound of the ocean; the distant chatter of the party inside barely audible. Leaning against the wall, I close my eyes.

After several minutes, the sound of footsteps echoes in the distance, and I hold my breath, hoping it's just the gardener or security doing their rounds. Pressing myself against the wall, as though it might hide me, I keep my eyes closed and hope.

"I'm disappointed."

I flinch at Zak's deep tone.

"You're so good at hiding," he continues. "I figured it would be harder to find you."

Reluctantly opening my eyes, I find him standing a little way away on one of the paths winding through the gardens. He must have left through the front door and somehow avoided security to find his way back here. He looks just as gorgeous as always, his hands in the pockets of his tux as he stares at me, waiting for me to speak. But no words come. I have no idea where to even start. Sorry doesn't sound anywhere near enough, and it's not what he wants to hear.

"You made your choice, then," he says, stepping closer.

I press myself harder against the wall willing him to stay back.

"Are you happy with him?" he asks.

As he takes another step closer, I move from the wall, hurrying down the steps to a different path in an attempt to put some distance between us. My heel gets caught between the pebbled gravel and I stagger forward, my foot slipping from my shoe. But I don't stop. Stepping out of my other shoe, I continue down the path, hoping he'll take the hint.

He doesn't.

"Seriously?" His laugh is cold and hard. "You're just going to run away from me? Is that how you want to deal with this?"

Tears sting my eyes, but I keep moving forward, the gravel digging painfully into the soles of my bare feet.

"Jaime," Zak barks. "Stop."

And I do. With my back to him, my breath ragged and my shoulders slumped, I stop. Because I can't run anymore. I deserve every harsh word he has for me.

Zak's footsteps stop just behind me, and he heaves a sigh. "I'm so fucking angry with you, Jaime."

I nod. I'm angry with myself, too.

He moves in front of me and drops into a crouch, causing me to frown. It's then, I realize, he picked up the shoes I left behind. Holding one out, he gestures for me to put it on. My heart twists, a tear breaking free as I step back into my shoes, and he stands.

"You should have had the decency to tell me to my face." Zak shakes his head, staring at the gravel path. "Those first few days, before I realized what a fucking coward you are, I was so worried something had happened."

"I'm sorry." The words slip from my lips before I can stop them.

"I don't want your apology," Zak barks. "I wanted you to treat me like a human fucking being. To show me respect. You *used* me, Jaime. Do you have any idea how fucking shitty that is?"

I nod, tears streaming freely down my face.

Zak groans and turns away, pushing his fingers over his head before looking at me again. "Will you tell me? Will you at least have the decency to tell me why you chose him? I know it's not the fucking money. Is he better in bed? Does he have a better dick?"

A sob tears from my throat, not at his words, but the hurt behind them. Hurt I caused.

"Louis didn't get me fired." I sniff, wiping the tears from my face. "It was his dad."

Zak huffs. "So, that's it? Now Billionaire Ken is on board with your career, he's the right choice?"

I shake my head, trying to find a way to explain that might actually ease his hurt. "Our fathers have been building deals based on our marriage for the last sixteen years. I never said I didn't want this, Zak. I should have said something sooner, but I left it until the last minute. It's too late."

Zak stares at me, his jaw working, and for a second I think he's going to walk away. Then he shakes his head. "Sixteen years is nothing, Jaime. Your marriage to Louis could be the next sixty. Are you seriously willing to sacrifice the next sixty years of your life for sixteen years' worth of business deals?"

He steps closer and my heart skips as I stare up at him. It's painful, being this close to everything I want, but knowing it's not mine to have.

"Tell me you're happy, Jaime," he says, reaching out and tucking my hair behind my ear. "Tell me you're happy and I'll walk away."

He knows. He knows I'm not happy. My tear stained cheeks speak volumes. What he's really asking is for me to lie. I press my lips together and try to muster the strength to give him what he wants.

"I wish I'd been enough for you, Kitty Cat," he says softly. "I think that's what hurts the most. I told you I'd catch you, but you didn't trust me enough to jump. If what you felt for me was anywhere near what I feel for you, the consequences wouldn't have mattered. I'd give up every-thing for you, Jaime. Every-fucking-thing. In a heartbeat. But you would have just let me fall. In fact, you did. I leapt and you stood back and watched me splatter on the goddamn sidewalk."

A groan rumbles in his chest, and he turns and walks away. Even though I know I should let him go, my feet move before I can stop them, words forming on my lips against my control.

"You are enough, Zak," I say. "I'm a coward. I know that. I just . . ."

He stops and turns to face me, the darkness casting his expression in shadow, making it hard to read. "Just, what, Jaime?"

"If I chose you, I'd be hurting so many people. Louis, my parents, his parents, and potentially dozens of busi-nesses tied up in the deals forged because of the marriage."

"So, it was easier to hurt me instead."

"No." I take a breath. "If I chose you, what's to say it would last? You've chased me for years, but what if it's just that? What if you didn't actually like the real me? What if it's just the chase? What if—"

"When did I give you the impression, I was only in it for the fucking chase?" Zak closes the distance between us, gripping my face in his hands, his eyes wild. "When did I ever make you think that you weren't fucking *it* for me, Jaime?"

I tremble in his grasp, fresh tears forming as I try to look away.

"Was that not the real you?" he asks, tipping my face so I'm forced to meet his stare. "When you were in my arms, in my bed, was that fake?"

"No," I whisper.

He lets go and steps back, his hands flying to his head, fingers scrunching his curls. "I love you, Jaime. When have I ever done anything to make you doubt that? I've fought for us since the moment I laid eyes on you. Why would you think that would change now?"

My chest is so tight, I can't breathe. He's right. For almost four years, Zak Aldridge has been a steady constant. He's never once given me reason to doubt him, even when we were nothing more than friends who flirted at parties. It's only then, I realize what he just admitted.

"You love me?" I whisper.

Zak laughs, tugging at his bowtie as though it's attacking him. "Wasn't it obvious?"

My heart somersaults as I take a shallow breath. "You *still* love me?"

He finally pulls his bowtie free and throws it into the bushes, unbuttoning his top two buttons and dragging in a deep breath, his chest heaving with the effort. "Yes, Kitty Cat. I still fucking love you. Even though it makes me the dumbest fuck to ever walk the planet."

My lip trembles and I wrap my arms around myself. Ever since the first day of senior year, I've made one bad choice after another. I've never had this before. Every year of my life has been filled with good choices and happy memories. Sure, there have been hangovers and fall outs, but nothing like this. This year, I've painted myself into a corner, and I wish more than anything I could go back to the start.

If I could, I'd tell my parents I didn't want to marry

Louis. I'd deal with the fallout. It would be awful. Painful. But surely it wouldn't be worse than this. Nothing could be worse than this. Closing my eyes, I whisper the words I've been holding in for as long as I can remember.

"I love you, too."

ZAK

The world fucking stops. I turn to Jaime, blood roaring in my ears as I hear the words I've wanted to hear since freshman year. She looks fragile. Something I never imagined I'd see. Even when she turned up at the Den after being fired, she still exuded an aura of power. The past couple of months have scarred me, but they've decimated Jaime. It hurts to see, but it's also her own damn fault.

"I don't know what you want me to say." I sigh. "Of all the ways I imagined you saying those words to me, this was not one of them."

She swipes at her eyes with the back of her hands and my heart squeezes at the trail of mascara it leaves behind. "I know."

"So, what now?" I ask. "We love each other but you're going to ride off into the fucking sunset with Billionaire Ken."

"Don't call him that."

I bark a laugh. "Sorry. Do you care about his feelings now? Because you certainly didn't when you were in my fucking bed."

My words are harsh and Jaime winces as they fly like bullets from my lips. But I can't help it. Two months of heartache have built inside me, and I can't just make it go away. No one has ever hurt me like Jaime Smith.

"It's not Louis' fault," she says quietly. "Be angry at me, but he's a good guy."

It's too much. Shaking my head, I back away. "I can't do this anymore."

Her eyes widen, but I turn and walk, not knowing where I'm going in this ridiculous Lincoln Park sized garden. I don't care. I just need to be somewhere she's not.

"Zak!"

I don't slow, even when her hurried footsteps chase after me. It's only when her hands grip my arm, that I slow, her feet sliding on the gravel as we come to a stop.

I look away. "What?"

"What if . . ." Her words trail off.

"What if?" I close my eyes, dreading her next words.

"What if I choose you?"

My head hangs. "I don't know, Jaime. It might be too fucking late."

And it's the truth. She cut me so deep, I'm not sure I could ever fully trust her with my heart.

Her hand reaches up, cupping my cheek, and I screw my eyes closed tighter, stiffening at her touch.

"Zak? Please, look at me."

I can't. If I do, I'll crumble. I know it.

"I don't believe you, Kitty Cat," I mutter, moving out of her grasp. "The only time you choose me is when you're upset and need somewhere to hide. I need more than that. I deserve more than that."

"I'm so sorry, Zak." She lays her palms on my chest, and I hate how good it feels. "I thought I'd made the right decision, and if I'd seen you, I would have crumbled. I'm weak for you."

"And that's the problem," I say, finally opening my eyes to look at her. Even with black mascara staining her brown cheeks, her eyes bloodshot from crying, she's still the most beautiful woman on the planet. "What's to stop you changing your mind as soon as you walk away? You say you'd choose me now, but how do I know you're not going to run right back into Louis' arms?"

She winces, her eyes shimmering with fresh tears. "I deserve that."

"Why now?" I ask. "You haven't spoken to me in almost two months. Tell me, what would have happened if I hadn't come here tonight? Would you still have chosen me?"

"Zak, I know the last few weeks have been hard, but believe me when I say they've been hell for me, too. I'm so sorry. But I want to make things right. Please, believe me."

I exhale, the hard truth settling like lead in my gut. "Jaime, you need to make the choice that's right for you. But I can't be a part of it. If you want to marry Louis, then go for it. If you don't want to marry him, don't. I'm removing myself from the equation."

Her eyes widen. "What are you saying?"

"I'm saying." I take a deep breath. "I want you to make your choice for *you*. If you choose not to marry Louis, then maybe we can make a go of things. Do things properly. But I don't want you to leave him for me. I want you to leave him for yourself."

She swallows and I force myself to meet the fear in her eyes. I told her that I would be there to catch her, but she didn't trust me. Now, she's going to have to make the leap alone.

"I was never asking you to choose me, Kitty Cat."

Cupping her face, I drag my thumb over her cheek. "I wanted you to choose what made you happy. I thought I could be part of that happiness, but that's up to you."

Her eyes close and she gives a faint nod, the weight I've been carrying around all year suddenly lighter.

"You were right," I say. "When you told me you didn't need me to rescue you. You've always been capable of rescuing yourself. What you were wrong about was happy endings. Real life has happy endings; you just have to be brave enough to fight for them."

Jaime stares up at me and I smile at the steel in her big brown eyes.

"You were right, too," she whispers. "I'm yours. I always have been."

Still cupping her face, I drop my forehead to hers, breathing in her scent. "Then you'll find your way back to me, Kitty Cat."

We stay like that, my heart thundering beneath her palms, and her cheek beneath my fingers, until music sounds from the house, signaling that dinner has finished.

"We missed dessert," Jaime mutters.

I dip my head, brushing a faint kiss against her lips. "Will that do?"

She smiles, but it doesn't fully reach her eyes, and I know what she's thinking. It's not enough. It's never enough when it comes to us. As much as I'm still angry and hurt, I still want to pick her up and find somewhere quiet where I can kiss her until all the noise in my head is silenced— where I can show her just how much I fucking love her.

But I force myself to drop my hand and step back. We both take a breath and turn to head back to the house, only to find Louis a few feet away, his eyes fixed on us and his jaw set.

JAIME

BE

"What the hell is going on?" Louis strides towards us, his narrowed gaze flitting between me and Zak.

My eyes widen as Zak tenses beside me, clearly sizing him up. "Louis, what are you doing out here?"

"Looking for my fiancée," he grits out. "But apparently I shouldn't have bothered."

My heart sinks. Louis deserves so much better than this. I've been fortunate enough to have two exceptional men in my life and I've hurt them both.

"Can we go inside and talk?" I ask, stepping forward in an attempt to draw his attention away from Zak.

"Is this why you've been pushing me away?" Louis snarls. "Is he your boyfriend? Have you been with him the whole time?"

I shake my head. "It's not like that, Louis."

He finally turns to me, his blue eyes filled with hurt. "What is it like, Jaime? Because I just watched another man kiss the woman wearing my fucking ring."

I wince, reaching for the diamond on my finger. "Please, Louis. Let's take this inside."

Huffing a breath, he shakes his head and storms back up the path. I follow, glancing over my shoulder at Zak, who makes no move to follow. What pains me the most is the uncertainty on his face. He thinks I'm going to cave. That I'm going to convince Louis nothing was going on and walk away from everything we just discussed.

I'm not. Zak was right. All this time, I've been thinking of it as a choice between him and Louis. But it's not. It's a choice between the future I want and the future my parents want for me. It's going to destroy my father when I tell him, but it has to be done. Even if I end up broke and alone, I'll know it was my choice.

It occurs to me that I'll probably lose my internship if I break off the engagement, and I sigh softly. If I'm burning everything to the ground, I may as well go for broke.

Louis heads for the French doors, heaving them open and standing to the side to let me through first. Ever the gentleman. He points at one of the reception rooms, avoiding my eyes. "Wait in there, please."

I open my mouth to speak, but he storms off in the direction of the dining room, and I'm left with no choice but to do as he says. It's a room I haven't been in often, used mostly by my father when he holds meetings at the house. I perch in one of the taupe high-backed chairs and wait.

When the door flies open again, I leap to my feet at the sight of Louis, with my parents just behind, their faces pinched with confusion. My skin heats, my heart thundering as Louis closes the door and stands with his arms folded across his chest.

"What's going on?" my father asks, looking between me and his future son-in-law.

This is it, I realize. I can either tell the truth and free

myself, or I can lie and try to make things right. But things will never be right if I stay on this path. I know that now.

"I'm calling off the engagement," I say, my voice strong despite the way my entire body's trembling.

My father's face turns a fascinating shade of mauve, his mouth opening and closing a few times. "What? Why? What happened?"

"Nothing happened. I never agreed to this wedding. I know I've never spoken out about it before, but that's because it's always been a part of my future. I believed it was normal—that it was the right thing for me—in the same way I believed in the tooth fairy and Santa. I trusted you." I take a deep breath and turn to Louis, who's still standing by the door, because he deserves these words. "I'm sorry, Louis. You are such an incredible man, and I'm lucky to have even been considered as someone you'd want to spend your future with. But you deserve better. My heart has belonged to someone else for a long time, and I've been too scared of walking away from this—of hurting my parents—to realize that marrying you wouldn't be fair to you. You deserve someone who loves you with their whole heart."

"This is ridiculous," my mother snaps. "You can't just end the engagement, Jaime. This has been planned for over a decade. You—"

"You can't force me, Mom," I say, turning to face her. "Cut me off, disown me, whatever you need to do to make yourself feel better. But I'm not marrying Louis."

The relief of saying those words threatens to bring me to my knees, but I stand tall, my chin high, just as I've been taught. I will not show weakness. This is not a negotiation.

My dad sinks onto one of the chairs, rubbing a hand over his face. "I wish you'd come to me sooner, Jaime."

My chest tightens. "I'm sorry, Dad. I tried, but you're never here."

It's a weak excuse and we both know it. If I'd really wanted to speak to my father, I would have found a way, and his sad smile tells me he knows it, too.

"If anyone is wondering where I stand," Louis says, pulling my attention back to him. "I'm also calling off the engagement."

My mother gasps like she's in some sort of bad sit-com, but my dad sighs heavily.

"That's understandable, Louis. I'll arrange a meeting with Claude as soon as possible."

I frown. "What?"

My father looks up at me, his expression pained. "Don't get me wrong, Jaime. This is a mess of epic proportions, but we'll figure it out. Unless you *want* me to disown you?"

A smile pulls at my lips as I shake my head. "I'm so sorry."

Slapping his palms down on his thighs, my father stands and takes my mother's elbow. "Melanie, why don't you go and take a minute then go back to the party?"

She looks at me and shakes her head, her disappointment palpable. But then she turns and leaves, patting Louis' shoulder on the way out.

I turn to my dad, but before I can say anything, he pulls me into a hug. It catches me by surprise and my throat swells with emotion. I can't remember the last time he hugged me.

"I'm sorry you didn't feel you could come to me," he says against my hair. "You're such a strong woman like your mother, I forget that underneath it all, you're still my little girl."

"I'm sorry for ruining everything," I mumble against his

shirt, aware I'm probably staining it with whatever is left of my mascara. "I should have said something sooner."

He sighs, his breath warm against the top of my head. "Yes, well, that would have been better. At least you didn't wait until your wedding day."

I groan and he laughs, pulling back enough to look me in my eyes.

"I love you, Jaime. All I've ever wanted is for you to be happy. I'm going to make more of an effort to make that clear going forward. Okay?"

I smile, my eyes filling with fresh tears. I swear I've never cried so much in my life. Leaning forward, he kisses me on the head and then leaves.

"You know," Louis says, stepping forward until he's in front of me. "There are so many times over the past six years or so, I thought about courting you."

I sniff a laugh. "Courting me?"

He shrugs. "You know what I mean. I thought about coming to the US and taking you on dates. But I was too scared. Every time I made plans to come and spend time with you, I chickened out."

My heart drops as I realize what he's saying.

He reaches out and touches my cheek before letting his hand drop. "That will always be the biggest mistake of my life, Jaime. If I'd made more of an effort . . . If we'd gotten to know each other sooner . . ."

I shake my head. "That's on both of us. I was hiding from this. I could have reached out to you, too."

Silence falls between us, laden with the weight of 'what ifs'. Perhaps we would have fallen in love. Maybe I wouldn't have gone to Franklin West, choosing an East Coast college instead to be closer to Europe. Or maybe I would have gone, but when I met the eye of a cocky lacrosse player from across the room I would have felt nothing more than a flicker of attraction, because my heart belonged to someone else.

I'll never know, and I'm okay with that. As lovely as Louis is, I don't think I want to be part of that world any more than I already am. I don't want to marry my father.

"Be happy, Jaime," Louis says, reaching for my hand and bringing it to his lips. "I'm sure we'll see each other again."

I smile and nod, watching as he closes the door behind him, leaving me alone.

And I finally exhale.

There's a restroom off the reception room, so I take the opportunity to clean myself up. I'm a mess. My make up ruined, my face puffy and swollen. I'm completely numb.

I almost wish my dad had kicked up more of a fuss. The resigned, calm way he dealt with my admission is more painful than if he'd shouted and screamed. He's right. I should have spoken up sooner. I should have trusted him.

But the truth is, I barely know the man. I know he loves me, but I've seen him once or twice a year my entire life. He was never at my award ceremonies, or even my high school graduation. It was the way things always were, so I was never bitter. He can't blame me for not trusting him.

But it's done. Regardless of the fall out.

Readying myself, I step out into the foyer and make my way back to the dining room. My heart skips excitedly at sharing the news with Zak. I'm free. I choose him. I want to be with him.

Every step is filled with purpose as I enter the room, looking at the tables, already cleared, with people standing in small groups mingling and laughing around them. I turn, searching, but there's no sign of Zak or his mom anywhere.

Frowning, I walk over to the head server. "Excuse me. Do you know where the Aldridges are?"

"They left about ten minutes ago, Miss Smith." He offers me a polite smile. "Is there anything else I can help you with?"

I shake my head. "No. Thank you."

As he moves back off into the crowd, I try not to let the disappointment drag me down. What if he thinks I chose Louis? What if he thinks I ran, again?

Turning on my heel, I march upstairs to my bedroom, intent on chasing him to the hotel. I need to tell him. I need to tell him, I chose him.

I tug at the zipper on my dress, desperate to get free of the material, when my phone sounds with a message. Abandoning my struggle, I walk over to my dresser and pick it up.

My heart stutters as I realize it's a voice message from Zak. Sinking down onto my chair, I close my eyes and press play.

"Hey. I'm sorry I left without saying goodbye, but I just couldn't be there. I hope you understand. I hope you made the choice that makes you happy. I'm getting a flight back to Portland tonight. I have a game tomorrow, so it was always the plan to bail early. It's an away game, so maybe I'll see you next week. Maybe I won't. Be happy, Kitty Cat."

I play the message three more times. He's giving me space. Away game or not, he's putting distance between us —giving me a chance to change my mind. But I don't need a chance. I'm not going to change my mind.

Placing down my phone, I rub my temples as my head throbs. A mixture of stress, champagne, dehydration, and heartache. It would be easy enough to find out where his away game is and show up there. Would he want that? I don't know.

Staring at my phone, still lit up in front of me, there's no way I can let three days go by without him knowing. But would he even believe me?

It's not the way I wanted to do this, but fine. I frown, snatching up the device and tapping out my message.

I'm yours

ZAK

Swiping my phone open, I scroll to Jaime's message thread and stare at the last text she sent me until it's freshly burned into my retinas. She says she's mine, but it's been three days since I saw her. Three days since she sent that message and I stared at it the whole flight back to Portland, hoping it was true.

But I wasn't kidding when I said she'd broken my trust. As much as I want to believe it, I'm waiting for the other shoe to drop.

"Seriously, you need to make a decision." Alex groans from where he's sitting with his laptop on his usual chair by the unlit fire. "Either call her or go see her."

I only got back from our away game late Sunday night, and I had a lecture this morning, so I haven't had to face that choice yet.

"No." I shake my head. "I'm not doing that again. If I show up there and she's changed her mind . . ."

Alex's jaw sets and I know he's biting back a thousand comments I don't want to hear. I confessed what had been going on to Sol and Alex on Saturday morning. They were both hurt that I hadn't confided in them sooner, but they understood. Kind of.

Tipping my head back, I toss a red peanut M&M into the air and catch it in my mouth.

"What will you do if she doesn't come to you?" Alex asks.

I sigh, crunching down on the candy and sitting up. "I don't know, man. Drink myself into a stupor? Start an Only-Fans? Fuck knows."

Alex stares at me until I look at him. "Just don't go bottling everything up, okay? Sol and I are here for you. Whatever you need."

"I know." I push to my feet, tossing a yellow candy into my mouth. "I'm going to go do some studying."

Alex grunts in acknowledgement, already refocused on his laptop, and I smile at the fact that my twenty-two-year-old friend has already nailed the demeanor of a grumpy CEO.

Jogging up the stairs, I try to shove aside the worry that ebbs and flows in my gut. I'm the one who pushed Jaime away—told her to leave me out of her decision making. Now, I have to deal with the consequences.

Stepping into my room, I glance at the economics text books on my desk and proceed to collapse onto my bed. There's no way I can concentrate on studying until I know. Closing my eyes with a sigh, I consider asking Alex to find out from Sasha whether Jaime's on campus. Not that the knowledge would help. If she's over in the Hive and hasn't come to see me . . .

Rolling onto my front, I pull my phone from my jeans pocket and pull up my emails. Over the last couple of months, I've been researching lacrosse coaching, and I even visited a couple of schools in Portland to check out some programs. I've decided it's something I'd like to try, and I want to work with middle and high school kids, not college. The idea sparks an excitement in me that I haven't felt with anything else.

Besides Jaime, of course.

A knocking sounds at my window and I roll, sitting up in surprise. My surprise grows as I find Jaime's head peering over the window ledge. *What the actual fuck?*

Jumping to my feet, I motion for her to duck as I open the window outwards. It's then, I see she's got a ladder propped against the side of the Den.

"What the hell is wrong with you?" I laugh. "We have a door."

She frowns up at me. "It's symbolic, you asshole."

Still chuckling, I help her up and into my room, trying not to let my attention linger on the little denim shorts she's wearing.

"Hey," she says, straightening her ponytail and yellow sweatshirt.

I lean against my desk to stop myself from reaching for her. "Hey."

"I messaged you," she says, glancing at where my phone is laying on my bed.

I frown. "When?"

"Three days ago."

"Oh. Yeah. I got it."

Her eyebrows rise. "And you didn't want to reply?"

Scrubbing my fingers through my hair, I let out a breath. "I wanted to, but I was afraid you'd change your mind."

Jaime stares at me for a minute and I wonder whether the truth is too much. But then, she steps forward and places her hands on my chest, her fingers stroking over the material of my black t-shirt.

"I haven't changed my mind, Zak," she says softly. "The wedding is off. And it's staying that way. When I said I'm yours, I meant it."

I nod, swallowing hard. It still feels too good to be true. "So, what now?"

"Now," Jaime says, smoothing her palms over my chest. "It's up to you."

"Up to me?"

"I mean, if you want to start over, we can. Go for coffee. Date. Let me try to build up the trust I broke. I also understand if you want to walk away. I thought that might be why you hadn't replied." She lets her hands drop, but I catch them, gathering her fingers in mine.

"I don't want to walk away," I say, squeezing her hands and smiling as she visibly relaxes at my words. "I didn't reply because I didn't want to push you. This was something you needed to do on your own."

"And you're right. I did."

"Did the world end?" I ask. "How are things with your parents?"

She grimaces. "Mom took it hard, but Dad was surprisingly okay about it all. From what I can tell, he's moving forward with combining with the Chevaliers. He's been working with Louis for years, and he's apparently kind of like the son he never had."

I frown. "How do you feel about that?"

"I honestly don't care. I've never cared about the family business. Maybe that makes me a bad daughter, but I haven't."

Stroking my thumbs over the backs of her hands, I gather her fingers to my chest. "I'm glad things are okay."

"Me, too."

"I also don't want to start over."

Jaime's eyes narrow as she stares up at me. "What do you mean?"

"I mean, I know things are a mess between us, but they always have been. Ever since that kiss freshman year, we've been anything but conventional." Dropping her hands, I cup her face, my eyes dropping to her perfect lips. "Let's pick up where we left off. I'm done wasting time."

Jaime trembles and I dip my head, pressing my lips to hers. She melts against me, and I gather her in my arms, a satisfied moan rumbling in my chest as she opens for me.

All too soon she pulls away, grinning up at me. "It's a good thing I'm not allergic to peanuts, isn't it?"

It takes me a second to figure out what she's talking about, and then I laugh. "Kitty Cat, I'd give up peanut M&Ms for you in a heartbeat."

Her lips twitch as she looks up at me. "Really?"

I shrug. "Sure. Or maybe I'd just brush my teeth twenty times a day and eat them in secret."

She laughs, shoving my chest, and it's the best sound I've heard all year. Sliding my hands down her body, I grip her thighs, pulling her up into my arms. She wraps her legs around my waist and I stand there for a moment, just enjoying her closeness.

"Thank you," she whispers against my lips.

"For what?"

"For fighting for me." She presses a kiss to my cheek. "For not giving up." She presses a kiss to my nose. "For making me rescue myself."

Her lips meet mine and I kiss her softly before pulling back and looking into the depths of her rich brown eyes.

"I'll never stop fighting for you, Kitty Cat. It might have

taken you a minute to realize, but you're in my blood. You're the rhythm my heart beats to. And I have no plans to ever let you go."

"Good." Jaime smiles. "Because I have no plans to leave."

EPILOGUE
SIX YEARS LATER

Sneaking into our dark bedroom, I place my keys down on the dresser and wince at the resulting clatter. The moon leaks in through a slither in the curtains, just enough for me to make out Zak's long body laid on the bed. Tiptoeing over, I open them a little further, allowing more moonlight to filter through, illuminating the room in a silvery-blue glow.

Turning back to the bed, I smile at the sight of his bare torso, the covers low on his hips, as his back rises and falls with sleep. Ever since my promotion to Assistant General Manager at WNC, my hours have been long, meaning I'm usually home after Zak's gone to bed.

There have been a lot of ups and downs over the last six years, but not once have I ever regretted choosing him. He's my biggest cheerleader. My rock. And I thank the universe for putting him in my path every single day.

Chicago, on the other hand, has taken a bit of getting used to. I'd thought Oregon was cold until my first winter here. Weather aside, I love the bustle of the city, and I love Zak's family. Growing up as an only child, with cousins being people I only saw at the occasional wedding, it's been a shock getting used to the busy closeness of the Aldridge clan.

Zak huffs in his sleep, rolling onto his back and causing the covers to slip further revealing the fact that he's not wearing any underwear. I grin.

Quietly shrugging off my jacket, I creep up to the bed, carefully tugging the covers down a little further. His cock is already half hard and I smile, wondering whether it has anything to do with what he's dreaming about.

Tucking my hair over my shoulder, making sure it doesn't fall against his skin, I lean forward and suck the tip of his cock into my mouth. His resulting groan sends a jolt of heat shooting between my thighs, and my eyes flit up to find he's still fast asleep. Smiling to myself, I swirl my tongue around the head before sucking him deeper, fighting a moan at how he immediately thickens in my mouth. His body is sheer perfection. Being a lacrosse coach for our local school district means he's stayed in top physical condition, and I clench my thighs together at the way his abs contract when he hits the back of my throat.

The next time I look up at his face, his eyes are open, hooded and watching me. I pull off, flicking my tongue over his crown. "I'm sorry. Did I wake you?"

He gives me a lazy grin, his dick twitching in my hand. "You can wake me up like that any time, Kitty Cat. Now get up here."

It's not something I need to be asked twice. Climbing up onto the bed, I barely make it level with him before he rolls on top of me, wasting no time licking his way into my mouth and kissing me senseless.

My fingers grip his broad shoulders as his hips flex against mine, and I moan into his mouth. "I need you."

His hands reach down, gripping the hem of my skirt and tugging it up over my hips, but he doesn't bother pulling down my panties, instead pulling them to the side and pushing himself up against my entrance. My head falls back against the pillows as he enters me with a single thrust, filling me in a way I'll never tire of.

"I missed you," he grunts, thrusting into me hard and fast.

My fingers roam his body, pleasure lighting up every inch of me as he fucks into me relentlessly. "Me. Too."

Holding himself up on one arm, he hooks his other under my leg, bending me in half as he pushes even deeper.

I cry out, my moans turning to whimpers as he tears at my blouse, tugging at the material until he frees my bra. His head dips, his teeth tugging at my nipple through the material, and I arch beneath him, needing more. Always needing more.

I reach between us, pulling down the cups of my bra, exposing my breasts to him and he groans, sucking each nipple into his mouth one after the other, teasing me with teeth and tongue until I'm a writhing puddle beneath him.

"Come for me, Kitty Cat," he rumbles against my ear.

Pushing back onto his knees, he presses his thumb against my clit, rubbing circles as he slams his cock into me over and over again, and I cry out loud as my orgasm rips through me. His muscles tense, each beautiful inch of brown skin glistening with the effort of our pleasure as his thrusts slow and he moans through his release.

Gathering me in his arms, Zak rolls us, holding me against his chest. "Love you," he murmurs sleepily against my hair.

He'll fall asleep like this, with me trapped in his arms,

still half dressed in my work clothes. "I love you too," I whisper, pressing a kiss to his chest.

I wouldn't have it any other way.

ABOUT THE AUTHOR

Addison Arrowdell writes spicy, adult romantic fiction. She believes that even the darkest story should have laugh out loud moments and loves writing witty dialogue.

Curious about what's going on between Sol and Wes?

Want to know more about Alex and Sasha?

Interested to know more about Abigail?

Can't wait to find out more about the characters at Franklin West University?

Subscribe for a free FWU novella and all the latest updates and competitions!

www.AddisonArrowdell.com

ALSO BY ADDISON ARROWDELL

Franklin West University:

Stolen (M/F - Enemies to Lovers)

Hidden (M/F - Forbidden Age Gap)

Golden (M/M - Grumpy Sunshine/Sports)

Forbidden (M/M/M/F - Why Choose/Forbidden/Age Gap/Sports)

If you like steamy 'why choose' poly romance, check out:

Road Trip: Extended Edition

If you like witty paranormal romance, check out her Men of Magic Series:

Smoke & Flame (Men of Magic Book One)

Truth & Power (Men of Magic Book Two)

Freedom & Desire (Men of Magic Book Three)

ACKNOWLEDGMENTS

Thank you to YOU for picking up this book and getting to the end! I hope you enjoyed it. If you did, please leave me a review! If you didn't, then I'm sorry my story didn't tickle your pickle or toast your taco.

If you've read the Franklin West books in their suggested order, this is the last one. For now. I'll be taking a little break from our fancy Oregon college, but the next class have new stories to tell in the future...

Thank you to my incredible Romance Crew for reading my words and giving me reason to keep these characters going on their journeys. You ladies are the best!

Until next time . . .

CPSIA information can be obtained
at www.ICGtesting.com
Printed in the USA
BVHW070741020623
665278BV00001B/8